Love's Unfading Light

Eagle Harbor Book 1

Naomi Rawlings

Love's Unfading Light: © Naomi Mason 2015

Cover Design: © Clarissa Yeo 2014

Cover Photographs: Shutterstock.com

Editors: Melissa Jagears; Roseanna M. White

Formatting: Polgarus Studio

To the men and women who served with the United States Lighthouse Service. Thank you for the sacrifices you made to keep vessels at sea safe.

Chapter One

Eagle Harbor, Michigan, June 1880

"I said no." Tressa Danell scowled at Finley McCabe, whose rancid breath wheezed across the bakery counter that stood between them. He wore faded doeskin trousers and a shirt so old and sullied she could only guess what color the fabric had originally been. "But Tessa—"

"Not Tessa, it's Tressa." The mere sound of her first name on his lips—or at least its mispronunciation—nearly made her wince. "I'm Mrs. Danell to you."

Mr. McCabe's lips twitched into a frown beneath his droopy gray mustache. "Now see here, it isn't fitting for your betrothed to be calling you by your surname."

Becoming his betrothed was about as likely as ice forming on the harbor in June.

The door opened, dinging the little bell that sat above the entrance to Tressa's bakery. Good. Maybe Mr. McCabe would leave her alone if she had a customer to attend. She looked over the display of bread, muffins, and cookies toward the front of her shop.

Except it wasn't a customer. Mr. Ranulfson, owner of Eagle

Harbor's one and only bank, stood just inside the doorway.

Her shoulders slumped.

Mr. McCabe moved to the side of the counter and gripped her hand with his dirt-encrusted one, then dropped down on one knee. "Reckon I need to clarify my intentions a bit."

She glanced at Mr. Ranulfson and tried to tug her hand away, but the wizened trapper had a grip as tight as a sprung bear trap. "Mr. McCabe, if you could kindly—"

"Tessa Danell, I'm asking you to be my wife. I promise to love, honor, and cherish you for the rest of my days. Plus I'll leave you my cabin to settle in after I'm gone. And old Nellie. I know my Nellie girl don't look like much, but the nanny goat's good for milking."

Heat started in Tressa's chest and worked its way up her throat. She stared down at the top of Mr. McCabe's head, bald with little flakes of skin waiting to fall off the moment he scratched his scalp.

Behind him, Mr. Ranulfson cleared his throat and took a few steps farther into the bakery, his polished three-piece suit declaring him a regular dandy amid the rough and tumble town of Eagle Harbor, Michigan.

"We could be hitched by tomorrow night." Mr. McCabe spoke as though the other man wasn't in the bakery. "What do you say, Tessa?"

"It's Mrs. Danell. And my answer is the same as it was yesterday." And the day before that, and the day before that, and the day before that. What had she done to make this man think she'd marry him? "No."

"Now see here, a man's only going to ask so many times."

"It doesn't matter how many times you ask; I'm not going to say yes." Which he should well understand considering this was somewhere near the thirtieth time she'd turned him down. She tugged on her hand again, but he still wouldn't release it.

Mr. Ranulfson pretended to examine the crack in the mortar above the window. Why was he acting as if this was a private moment between her and the trapper? Surely he didn't think she should consider the offer.

Or accept it.

"The way I understand things, you don't have much choice." Mr. McCabe drew her hand to his mouth. His chapped lips scraped against her skin as he forced a kiss. "You're needing a man now that Otis is dead. I'll make you a good husband. I promise not to go down to The Rusty Wagon and gamble or head up to Central and visit girls the way yer husband—"

"That's enough." She yanked her hand, finally getting Mr. McCabe to release it. The entire town might know of Otis's indiscretions, but there was a difference between knowing and speaking.

"I'll gladly take the boy in too, might even teach him some trapping." Mr. McCabe's knees popped as he stood.

"No." The word emerged rough and raspy.

"Well then, I'll be seeing you tomorrow."

Tomorrow? She rubbed at her temples, which had started throbbing the moment Mr. McCabe opened the door to her bakery.

He offered her a tight smile and a glimpse of teeth yellow enough to match his tobacco-stained beard—teeth inside a mouth he'd expect her to kiss if they wed.

A shudder ran down her spine.

He squashed his hat atop his head and headed toward the door, the cheery bell tinkling behind him as he left.

She rubbed her temples again and turned to Mr. Ranulfson. "I'm sorry for that…" *Display. Fight. Misunderstanding.* What

3

word to even use?

The banker took a strawberry pie from the shelf. "You should consider his offer, Mrs. Danell."

Why did everyone assume she needed another husband? She'd made the mistake of getting trapped in a marriage once, and she wasn't fool enough to make it again. "I don't need anything Mr. McCabe has to offer."

"Have you recovered your money then? Did Sheriff Jenkins find who stole it?"

A hard lump formed in her throat, and she shook her head. She hadn't even bothered to tell the sheriff about last week's robbery. If the man hadn't lifted a finger to find who had taken her money the first two times, he wasn't going to help with the most recent robbery either. Was it good or bad that she'd only had eight dollars taken this last time? If there was one benefit to having no money, it was that whoever robbed you couldn't steal very much.

Mr. Ranulfson dug around in his pocket for some change and set two dollars' worth of quarters on the counter beside the pie. "Do you have the money to pay your mortgage?"

"I can pay this month's, but I don't have enough to catch up, no." Though the eight dollars that had gone missing last week certainly would have helped.

Mr. Ranulfson sighed so hard he almost ruffled the curtains on the opposite side of the storefront. "I'd like to work with you, Mrs. Danell. Truly I would. I'm not in the habit of turning people out of their homes the moment they fall on hard times, but neither can I ignore your situation forever. Another month has passed, which means you now owe me another ten dollars for June's payment. You haven't paid on your mortgage since February, so that brings you up to fifty dollars even."

"If not for being robbed, I would have been able to pay you."

She wouldn't let tears flood her eyes. She wouldn't.

"But I still need you to make back those payments, and it's time we set a date. Say August first? That gives you two months to get things caught up."

Where was she going to come up with so much? She wrung her hands together, keeping them behind the counter so Mr. Ranulfson couldn't see. "And if I don't have the money by then?"

"I'm sorry, but I'll have to take back your building." His voice was gentle, understanding even. Like he'd done this hundreds of times before. Like he'd perfected just how to deliver such news while keeping the person indebted to him from flying into a panic or rage.

She glanced down at the tips of her boots, peeking out from beneath a faded mourning dress she'd purchased secondhand. If it weren't for her son Colin, she might just let her building go to the bank and start again elsewhere.

Of course, having a little money saved to leave town and buy a bakery somewhere else might be a good idea, too.

"You should know that Byron Sinclair has been spouting off about the fishing boat Otis bought last year." The banker stuck a hand in his pocket and jingled some change as he spoke. "You do know about the boat, don't you?"

She'd kept from getting teary earlier, but she couldn't stop her cringe now. It happened automatically, much like a yawn at bedtime or a deep breath on a crisp autumn day. Yes, she knew of the fishing boat Otis had lost in a game of whist at The Rusty Wagon a week after buying it. She had no money to pay what was owed on that either.

The change jingled again—probably just some spare coins, like the ones he'd used to pay for the pie. Never mind that those very coins could make the difference between her keeping the bakery or losing it.

"I wish I could tell you Sinclair had forgotten all about the boat, but I assume you're better off being warned. He'll try wringing money out of you one way or the other."

"Thank you for the warning." She forced the words over her tongue, though she couldn't think of much to be thankful for at the moment.

Unless the fact that Mr. Ranulfson wasn't turning her out of her home this afternoon counted.

"I best be off then." He picked up the pie and turned for the door.

"Wait." She grabbed the money box beneath the shelf, retrieved eight dollars, and scooped the quarters he'd just given her off the counter. "At least this can cover June's payment."

It was probably better to give him the money before the robber returned. Because after three robberies, there was no point in telling herself that he wouldn't be back or that next time she'd find a hiding spot he wouldn't find for the money.

Mr. Ranulfson held out his hand for the meager pile.

"I'll get more, I promise."

The slightest hint of compassion glinted in his gray eyes, and he sighed again, softer this time. "I hope you do, Mrs. Danell. I'd hate to turn you out of this building, but I don't see any other way."

"I understand." And she did. It was a business decision. Clear and logical. She made them every day when dealing with her bakery. It only made sense that a banker would do the same.

Oh, how had she ever gotten to the point of becoming the poor business decision? The liability rather than the dependable asset?

"Good day." Mr. Ranulfson turned and walked to the door.

"Good day," she mumbled, though there had been little good about it. Or any other day over the past three months since she'd been robbed and Otis had died.

Then again, there hadn't been much good about her days before Otis's death either—except for their son, Colin.

She rubbed her throbbing temples once again. How was she going to come up with forty dollars by August first?

No, it would be fifty dollars by then, because she'd owe the bank for July's mortgage too.

She blinked her tired eyes, eyes she wasn't about to let grow moist with something as useless as tears.

The bell above the door tinkled, and in came Mrs. Fletcher and Mrs. Kainner. She plastered a smile on her face as the women each picked out a muffin and left. If only the two dimes they paid was enough to appease the bank. But if nothing else, they would help purchase more flour.

Wiping her hands on her apron, she headed back into the kitchen. A glance inside the flour sack that had once held fifty pounds told her she only had enough left for two days of baking.

She squeezed the flour in her hand and watched it drift back into the sack. This two-story bakery was supposed to guarantee her a place to sleep and some income. Not a lot, but enough to provide a living for her and Colin since the wages Otis had earned logging disappeared quickly after he returned from the woods every spring.

Now she had little hope of putting a decent meal on the table and giving her son a dry place to sleep come August.

But what was she to do? Stop baking?

She reached for the sourdough rising on the counter, plopped some into a clay mixing bowl, then sifted some flour.

Maybe Mr. Ranulfson was right and she was a fool for turning away Mr. McCabe. The old trapper would be dead in another decade, two decades at most, and that would give her time enough to raise Colin and see him situated.

Unless Mr. McCabe got her with child.

She dropped the sifter into the mixing bowl with a clunk. Even if she had to work twenty-hour days until her fingers were raw and her back ached, she'd find a way to provide for her son that didn't include a yellow-toothed man's bed.

"Is Colin here?" The back door to her bakery sprung open and in bounded Leroy Spritzer, his face streaked with dirt and his dirty blond curls hanging into his eyes.

"Yeah, where's Colin?" Martin Spritzer followed his older brother inside, his bare feet padding across the floor of the bakery.

Tressa wiped her hands on her apron. "I thought he was at the beach with you."

Leroy shook his head, which allowed his bangs to flop enough she could almost make out the green of his eyes beneath. "He never came."

"We stopped by the general store to see if he was sweeping the porch, but he wasn't there neither." Martin blinked up at her, his overgrown bangs were parted to one side and didn't obscure his eyes.

"Perhaps Colin's playing with someone else?"

Leroy shrugged. "I s'pose."

But that didn't make sense. Colin wouldn't go off and find other friends if Leroy and Martin were waiting for him. She walked to the door and peeked into the alley.

No sign of Colin. Where could he be?

"Can you tell him we'll be at the beach when he gets back?" Leroy tromped up behind her.

"Are you certain you didn't see Colin somewhere about town?"

Both boys nodded, their too-thin faces earnest as they watched her.

"All right then." She wiped her suddenly sweaty palms on her apron once more and attempted to focus—on Leroy and Martin, not her missing son. "You said you're going to the beach? You know not to go into the water without an adult there, right?"

"Ma says Cliff's old enough to watch us." Martin scuffed his big toe against the bakery floor. "She don't let us go in the water without him."

Yes, the oldest Spritzer son was nearly an adult now. "That's fine then." Tressa scanned the alley once again before bringing her gaze back to rest on the boys. "Oh, before you go, I've got some extras for you to take."

It'd make more sense to send the food with the boys now rather than walk to the Spritzer house later. If one could even call the weathered shack with quarter inch gaps between some of the wall planks a house.

Leroy spread his fingers and held his hands up. "Ma says she don't want no more of your extras."

Tressa ran her eyes down the boys' thin faces, arms, and legs. Their shirts hung loosely on their shoulders, and if not for the strings tied around the waists of their short pants, both pairs would fall to a puddle on the floor.

Everyone in town knew Ruby Spritzer struggled to keep food in the bellies of her nine children. Or maybe it was ten children? Eleven? The handful of times she'd stopped by the Spritzer house, she'd never gotten a good count. The children popped in and out of everywhere, never still long enough to count. Perhaps lack of food was only part of the reason why the children were all so thin and the other part lay in Ruby not remembering which ones had eaten and which ones hadn't.

But why would she tell her children not to take any more food? "Well, I suppose it's always best to obey your ma."

The boys looked at each other and then nodded slowly, their

eyes as round as dinner plates.

"But I'm wondering if you two are hungry for a snack. Did your ma say anything about eating snacks at the bakery?"

They looked at each other again before Leroy shook his head. "No, ma'am."

"It just so happens that I've got some leftover bread and a little jam."

~.~.~.~.~

She served three customers during the time it took the boys to eat in the kitchen, and in the end, Leroy and Martin left with a loaf and a half of bread, her last jar of jam, and a dozen cookies minus however many they'd scarf down before they made it home. Tressa scanned the back alley once more as they disappeared around the side of the bakery. Still no sign of Colin. Had he found another job to do around town in exchange for a coin or two?

Most likely.

She walked around the back of the bakery, then along the side, before coming out to the front on Center Street. No sign of her auburn-haired boy anywhere. She'd go back inside for a minute, mix up the bread dough and set it to rising, then look for him.

She hastened through the storefront and back to the kitchen. He couldn't have gone far, could he? And in a town the size of Eagle Harbor, someone had certainly seen him.

Unless he'd gone into the woods by himself. Or down to the lakeshore without anyone watching him. The beach stayed busy enough that someone would probably see him, but what if he'd climbed out onto the rocks by the lighthouse? No one would be watching him there, and those rocks could get awful slippery.

But no, Colin knew better than to do either of those things.

Once she knew where her son was, she'd laugh about how worked up she was getting. But at the moment, her hands were so damp they struggled to hold the flour sifter.

She reached for the wooden spoon in a canister with her other utensils and yanked it free.

Crash!

The entire canister toppled onto the counter, sending spoons and whisks flying while the rolling pin clattered to the floor.

Just what she needed. She gathered the spoons and forks and a wire mesh strainer off the counter and shoved them back into the canister, then she stooped to pick up the whisk off the floor.

Where had the rolling pin gotten to? She dumped the dirty utensils into the sink and got down on hands and knees. Traces of flour from that morning's baking dusted the floor along with a glob of muffin batter she must have spilled earlier. The rolling pin had managed to settle against the back wall beneath the counter. She dodged the stickiness and crawled under the countertop before grabbing the pin.

The back door burst open. "Ma!"

Her head came up—*thump!*

"Ouch!"

The mixing bowl teetered precariously on the edge of the counter. She shot out a hand, but—*smash!*

A cloud of fine white flour plumed into the air, the glob of sourdough landed on her lap, and chunks of broken pottery clattered across the floor.

She might as well take the rolling pin and beat herself on the head for good measure. Except her head already throbbed where she'd smacked it against the counter.

"Ma, what happened?" Colin crouched down and peered at her, his hair mussed from running and his forehead drawn into a furrow of little wrinkled lines.

"You're here." The pounding in her chest slowly lessened. "Leroy and Martin said they couldn't find you."

"'Course I'm here. Where else would I be?"

"Is everything all right?" An unfamiliar voice filled the kitchen. Then footsteps thudded against the uneven floorboards and a pair of man's boots appeared beside Colin.

Tressa ran her gaze up, up, up. Past the man's legs and waist and shirt and neck until she stared into a face with a faint golden beard lining its cheeks and chin. Her eyes finally met a pair of light brown ones filled with laughter.

Her cheeks burned. Of all the ways to meet someone.

She scrambled up from her place on the floor, which only sent a fresh plume of flour wafting from her apron and the blob of sourdough tumbling to the floor with a splat.

A booming guffaw filled the small kitchen, followed by her son's tinkling laughter.

"Did you hear that, Ma? It splatted like a mud pie."

Perhaps so, and a ten-year-old boy would probably think that funny, but did the stranger have to laugh? She took a step back from the muck at her feet and bumped into the counter behind her. Her elbow collided with the bag of flour, which slumped toward the edge.

She reached for it, but the stranger grabbed the sack before it fell.

Wedged between a chest that seemed too wide to belong to a living, breathing person and the counter, Tressa looked up at a man tall enough to reach up and touch the ceiling. "Ah… thank you."

He smiled, and faint lines wreathed his eyes—lines that indicated he still wanted to laugh at her. "You're welcome."

A warm puff of breath feathered across her cheek, much different from Mr. McCabe's sour exhalations. Then the man reached across her and placed the bag of flour on the counter against the wall, seemingly unfazed by how his chest pressed into her side.

The small movement gave her room enough to step away from—

Squish.

Another round of laughter filled the kitchen.

She didn't need to look down to know what she'd just stepped in.

Cheeks burning again, she clamped a hand to her hip and glared at the man. "Who are you, and why are you in my kitchen?"

"I, um…" A chortle choked off his words.

"He's Mr. Oakton." Colin spoke through a snicker, one that died quickly when she turned her glare on her son. "The lightkeeper."

"Oh." After living in Eagle Harbor for a year, most of the townsfolk had wandered into her bakery at one time or another, but not this man. She would have remembered, what with the way he towered above them like an oak tree.

"Assistant lightkeeper," Mr. Oakton managed. Then he pressed his lips together as though doing so could somehow hide his urge to start laughing again. "But not for long. Got a shipyard down on Lake Huron my friend and I are buying."

Colin wiped at the flour that had settled onto his face. "He walked me home."

"Walked you home?" She narrowed her gaze and ran it down Colin. Red cheeks, slightly mussed hair, bright eyes, working arms and hands and legs. Why did her ten-year-old boy need someone to walk him home?

"Here, Ma. Remember how I said I'd bring you a quarter for sweeping the porch at the general store? I got two." He held the coins out, his eyes shining. "Maybe we can buy a chicken from the Markhams, or a rabbit from Mr. McCabe next time he comes 'round?"

Something large rose in her throat, and she glanced at Mr. Oakton. What kind of mother did this big, hulking man think she was, sending her ten-year-old son off to work?

But she hadn't sent him. He'd found work on his own.

Because he feels the strain of my debts.

She rubbed at her head, the ache growing worse rather than lessening. What a terrible mother she was turning out to be.

"What's wrong? Should I give the quarters to Mr. Ranulfson instead?" Colin looked at the coins she'd yet to take, then back at her, the joy in his eyes starting to dull. "You can do whatever you want with them, I promise."

"I…" She took the money. The stranger still stood by the counter, his tall form and broad shoulders taking up too much space in a room that had never seemed small before. "I think we best give it to Mr. Ranulfson."

Or maybe use it for flour. Yes, that's what she'd use the money for, flour so that she could keep baking. She simply wouldn't think about how long it had been since she'd tasted chicken, or even a rabbit.

"Did you sell a lot of stuff today?" Colin spun on his heel and dashed into the storefront. "I've been praying you would."

She'd sold some, yes. But not as much as she would have at this time last year, and not enough to pay off what they owed by the beginning of August. Her customers had certainly tapered off this winter after Otis died and news of his numerous debts and swindling attempts had floated around town.

"Well, did you?" Colin called from the other room.

"A handful of people stopped by." She simply wouldn't confess the majority had spent a nickel or dime rather than several dollars.

"Oh. It kind of looks like there's lots of bread and muffins left." And cookies. Plus a pie.

She took a step toward the storefront, only to have the heel of her ankle boot squelch against the floor. How could she have forgotten her shoes were coated in sourdough? She bent and undid the trio of tiny buttons at the top of her worn shoes, feeling Mr. Oakton's gaze on her back all the while.

Oh well. The stranger had already seen her sprawled on the floor and covered with flour. There was little reason to stand on ceremony. She set the shoes aside, leaving the mess of flour, sourdough, and broken pottery to clean up later, and proceeded into the storefront in nothing but her stockings.

If the back of her neck burned a little while he watched her, it was hardly the worst thing that had happened today.

"Sure looks like you've got lots to choose from." Mr. Oakton's boots clunked against the floor behind her. "I was just thinking how we need a couple loaves of bread back at the lighthouse. And maybe some muffins for breakfast in the morning."

Colin turned from where he stood in front of the display counter and sent the lightkeeper a smile that caused his freckles to scrunch up on his cheeks. "Really?"

"That's all right." Tressa twisted her hands together. "You don't need to..."

But the man was already moving to survey her shop's goods.

Had Colin's questions about money given their situation away? She'd worked hard to keep news about them being robbed and owing money to the bank from circulating. The stories about Otis's swindling caused her enough trouble by far. Would people still come to the bakery if they knew she was in danger of losing it?

She stared down at her apron, covered in wasted flour and soiled from the sourdough blob. She'd sunk her every last penny into this bakery. If she didn't make things work, she had nowhere to go and nothing to offer her son...

Except for a blanket on the floor of Mr. McCabe's cabin.

⌐.⌐.⌐.⌐.⌐

Mac plucked his hat off and held it against his chest as he looked around the bakery hewn of rough planked lumber and pitch. Though a few shelves sat empty, baked goods filled a good portion of the storefront, and what he saw looked delicious. Scents radiated from every crack and crevice of the room, a whiff of ginger here, a touch of cinnamon there. And didn't it beat all, the woman had a strawberry pie sitting smack in the center of one of the shelves. His mouth was already watering, and that was before he stepped close enough to see the large grains of sugar sprinkled on top and a fancy curlicue design cut into the flaky dough.

A line of people should be wrapped around this building waiting to purchase that pie alone, not to mention the gingerbread cookies and loaves of fluffy looking bread. So why was no one here? This was strawberry pie, after all.

"Are you really going to buy some bread?" The boy looked between him and the bread uncertainly.

"I said I was, didn't I?"

The doubt didn't leave the boy's eyes.

He'd found Colin crying in the woods. After drying his tears and giving him a quarter to make up for the one a couple bullies stole, plus a second for good measure, couldn't the boy trust him to do as he'd stated?

But then, the child was Otis Danell's son. Having had Otis for a pa, the boy likely had a hard time trusting anyone.

He knew about those kinds of pas far too well—and how their pungent reputations seeped into their innocent son's pores until the entire town thought his little boy stank as bad as his skunk of a father. His own pa had left twelve years ago this summer, and he still couldn't manage to entirely cleanse the stench of his father's deeds off himself, at least not in the eyes of a few townsfolk.

He lumbered toward the loaves of bread stacked neatly onto the far counter. He probably shouldn't spend much, what with how he'd been saving every spare penny for his move to Port Huron. But the woman seemed in need of a customer or two, and he had enough money put by to give himself a good start after he moved.

Three loaves were discounted to half price. He snatched the lot of them plus the two fresh ones. He reckoned Jessalyn Dowrick could use a loaf of bread, what with three little ones to look after and her husband up and gone to the gold fields Out West.

And word around town was the minister's wife had taken a fall and was hobbling about with a turned ankle. Her husband would probably appreciate some bread. Heaven only knew what Finley McCabe ate save for the muskrats and possums he managed to trap. And Ruby Spritzer had so many young'uns running about the place she probably worked twelve hours a day just to keep them fed and clothed.

And there were the Cummingses. Something hard fisted around his chest at the thought of stepping into their cabin now empty of the man who'd taken him in and raised him as a son after his pa ran off, even if he was just to deliver bread. Last he'd heard, Mabel still wasn't faring well and certainly wasn't up to baking.

"That's an awful lot of bread, mister. Are you sure you can eat it all?" Colin's eyes had gone from wary to wide.

So maybe he wouldn't be depositing any extra money in the bank this week. "And the strawberry pie."

"No! I mean…" Mrs. Danell's voice held the softest accent. Not the blunt, forceful sound of the Cornish, nor the rolling lilt of the Irish, but something altogether different. Something so subtle most people wouldn't notice. The woman tucked a falling strand of hair behind her ear and raised eyes as tawny and rich as maple syrup to meet his. He'd seen her around town a time or two, but why hadn't he ever taken notice of Otis Danell's widow before now?

Of course, she hadn't exactly been a widow all that long, and he'd been a mite busy at the lighthouse of late.

Did she realize how much flour was sprinkled through her hair? Or that her forehead was dotted with little white splotches?

"That's too much." Again, the faintest accent tinged her voice. "You can't possibly need five loaves of bread and a pie."

It was little surprise the woman had half a shop full of unsold goods if she went about telling customers not to purchase her food.

"My ma makes the best pie in Keweenaw County." The boy pulled the pie off the display shelf and set it near where his ma stood with the money box.

"Colin, hush now." The woman's cheeks had turned a faint rose color despite the flour dusting them.

"I'm sure she makes a right fine pie." And buying it would be money well spent if for no other reason than keeping the smile on the moppet who beamed at him.

He just might come 'round again tomorrow too. It wouldn't hurt to buy a few cookies to see the boy grin again. Maybe if he was lucky, he'd even get a smile out of his ma.

He might be departing town in two weeks, but there was no harm in leaving a handful of dollar bills and a couple smiling faces behind him.

Chapter Two

Mac reached for the door handle—one he hadn't turned in nearly a month—and let himself into the sprawling log cabin. Coats hung haphazardly on pegs inside the entry room, much as they always had. Boots still warred for top position on the pile in the corner, and mittens, hats, and scarves all lay crammed into the crate beside the boots. But one pair of sturdy mukluks was missing, as was the familiar red and black plaid mackinaw coat Hiram Cummings had worn every spring and fall.

Last time he'd visited, Hiram's things had still been out.

He wasn't sure which was worse.

He stepped inside and jostled the pie and three remaining loaves of bread he'd carried with him from town. Maybe he should have come sooner.

Maybe he shouldn't have come at all.

"Mrs. Cummings, Rebekah, Isaac." He walked into the kitchen. "Is anyone here?"

A creaking sounded from the other side of the large room. Mac set the bread on the table and moved through the open kitchen into the parlor, his boots clunking on the solid maple floorboards.

Mabel sat in her rocker, her graying hair falling about her shoulders as she rocked back and forth, the chair moving in a rhythm as endless as the waves she watched through the series of windows on the north side of the cabin.

Just like she'd done last time he was here, which had been the day after the funeral.

"Mrs. Cummings—Ma?"

"How are you, Mac?" She didn't move her gaze from the window.

He laid a hand on her shoulder.

The rocker slowed, but she still didn't look at him.

"I brought you some bread." He shrugged sheepishly. "Rebekah stopped by the lighthouse the other day and said you still weren't up for much baking." It was mostly true. Rebekah had stopped by the lighthouse, but "not up for much baking" weren't the exact words she'd used. "So I reckoned you might need some bread."

Mabel reached her hand up and rested it atop his, her fingers thinner than they'd been a month ago.

"Why don't I put on some coffee? I've got pie too—strawberry." He'd give half of it to her if she promised to eat something.

Mabel sighed. "Why are you here?"

"To bring bread, like I stated."

"Not to see if I've gone mad yet?"

He swallowed.

"I'm a mess." A sheen of moisture glistened in her eyes. "But I doubt you're any better. We all miss him."

He blinked away the heat forming in his eyes. "Hiram was a good man."

The cabin door banged shut and stomping sounded. "Hardly caught a thing today," a feminine voice hollered from the front entry room. "Borrowing the Foley's dinghy isn't nearly the same as taking the *North Star* out."

Rebekah rounded the corner into the kitchen and set a pile of already-gutted fish in the sink.

"You went fishing?" Mac started toward the kitchen, taking the coffee pot from the hutch and filling it with water and coffee grounds before setting it on the stove. "By yourself?"

Rebekah untangled a strand of long, auburn-colored hair from the button on her collar. Dressed in a too-big pair of men's trousers and a flannel shirt that looked salvaged from the scrap pile, there was nothing polite or dainty about his near-sister's five foot, four inch frame.

"Somebody's got to fish, seeing how Isaac won't so much as look at the water these days." Nothing polite or dainty about her personality either.

"I don't like the idea of you on the lake by yourself." He rubbed a hand over his chin. "Reckon Elijah wouldn't either. I can go out with you some morning, if you need to."

She snorted. "After you've been up all night tending the light? You'd probably go to sleep and fall overboard. I can manage fine."

The mere thought made him yawn. He hadn't been out fishing with Hiram since he'd taken the assistant lightkeeper position three years ago for that very reason, but he wasn't about to let Rebekah fall into the same fate as her father either. "Then where's Isaac? Why isn't he going with you?"

Rebekah jutted her head toward the west side of the house. "In the workshop. Has a fancy notion he can ship those toys he's making off to Chicago or Duluth or some other city and sell them."

He glanced at his adoptive ma, still rocking by the window. He'd seen Isaac around town a time or two in the past month, so he wasn't as bad off as his mother. But toys? From a man who'd been practically born with rigging in his hands? Something was wrong with that.

Something that could only be fixed by Hiram Cummings returning from the grave, he reckoned.

"Any word on when Elijah's coming home?" Rebekah pumped water into the sink and rinsed the fish in a basin. "Maybe he can repair the *North Star*, seeing how Isaac isn't fixing to."

"I got the same telegram as you." *Coming* was all the note had said. "He should be here any day, but he won't stay long. Neither of us will."

"Oh, right."

He didn't have to see her to know she was rolling her eyes.

She wiggled her wet hands. "You've got to skedaddle down to Port Huron and buy up that little shipyard before someone else gets it."

"The shipyard's already ours. We just have to be there by July first when the owner leaves." The deadline hadn't seemed hard to meet when they'd made arrangements this spring, but with Hiram's death and Elijah headed back to Eagle Harbor rather than to Port Huron as originally planned, the date loomed.

Mac moved to the hutch, where he took out a knife and three plates before heading to the pie on the table.

"So you and Elijah are really going to take every penny you've been saving since you were in short pants and leave us?" Rebekah set a skillet on the stove and dropped a heap of lard in, then took out the flour to batter the fish. "Why can't you build boats here?"

Had she forgotten what his father had done twelve years ago? That everyone in town knew he had a scalawag for a Pa? Was it too much to want to live in a place where people assumed he came from honest, hardworking stock rather than a swindler? "You know very well why I can't stay. Elijah too."

Elijah might have his own set of reasons for leaving, but they were good nonetheless.

"That's a bunch of tripe, and you know it. Eagle Harbor could use the both of you."

He clamped his lips together and transferred a piece of pie onto a plate. The woman would argue with him till dawn if he let her.

"Where'd you get that pie from?" Rebekah sniffed the air. "Smells better than one of Ma's."

"Tressa Danell down at the bakery. Had a whole slew of treats in there that looked just as good as this."

Rebekah dropped the fish she was holding into the sink and turned to face him, arms crossed despite the way she had to be getting fish slime on her shirt. "Don't tell me you paid her money for it."

"Why wouldn't I pay her?" Mac thunked the plate onto the table and reached for another.

"Otis owed Pa twenty dollars. Came around last summer claiming his sick wife needed expensive medicine."

"Otis owed everyone money." He kept his movements steady as he dished up another piece of pie. "I gave him ten dollars last summer too, except he claimed his boy was sick, not his wife."

"Saps, the lot of you. I told Pa not to give him money, that Otis was just hankering for a drink and a run at poker. But Pa couldn't stand the thought of some woman staying ill if he refused to lend Otis anything." Rebekah jabbed a finger at the pie. "Mrs. Danell should be making you pies for free until that ten dollars is paid off. I'm not buying anything from her until we've got our money back."

Which was probably why her bakery shelves had been half full rather than completely empty. There'd be enough others like Rebekah in town to do some damage to her business, and given how Colin had been so eager to hand his ma those two quarters,

Mrs. Danell had to be counting her pennies.

Mac planted his hands on the table and leaned forward. "That's so gracious of you, Rebekah Cummings. Right Christ-like too, holding a grudge like that. Otis might be dead, but his widow still has a child to feed and bills to pay. Is she to suffer because of something her husband did, likely without her knowing?"

Rebekah flicked a strand of hair over her shoulder. "Otis Danell has been a lout ever since he was in short pants. I can't help that some woman chose to marry him. If she wanted my sympathy, she should've stayed away from Otis in the first place."

Heat flashed across the back of his neck and tips of his ears. "I'm certainly glad your father didn't judge me by my pa's actions. I suppose you think it's right fine to treat a ten-year-old boy like a criminal if his father is a swindler, huh?"

He picked up the plate with a slice of pie, then turned toward the rocker.

"Mac, no. That's not what I…"

He glared over his shoulder, and Rebekah shut her mouth—for once.

But as he handed Mrs. Cummings the pie and poured her coffee, Rebekah's question lingered, much the way Mrs. Danell's maple-syrup-colored eyes and flour-dusted cheeks still clung to his mind. What kind of woman would marry the likes of Otis?

And why did he care about her reasons for marrying the lying cheat anyway?

᠆.᠆.᠆.᠆.᠆

The sun hung low over the water as Mac rushed down North Street toward the lighthouse, what remained of his pie and bread in hand. By the time he'd coaxed a few bites of the strawberry dessert into Mabel, the fish was ready, so he'd scarfed down three fillets. Isaac had stayed holed up in the workshop, but after he'd finished his fish, he hadn't the time to stop and look in on him.

Not that he was sure he wanted to. What was he supposed to do if he found Isaac like his Ma, staring vacantly at the space where he, Hiram, and Elijah had fashioned the *North Star* and a half dozen other small boats over the years?

But then, would that be worse than finding Isaac making wooden trains and wagons?

The man was meant to sail, and how was he going to—

"Oof!"

Splat!

Thump!

Mac stared down at his strawberry pie, or rather what had been his strawberry pie. It was now strawberry mush, part of which was squished into his shirt while the rest had landed on the ground.

"Mr. Oakton! I'm so sorry."

The softly accented voice drew his gaze away from the mess to the woman responsible—both for the mess and the dessert.

"I was in a rush. I should've looked where I was going." Tressa Danell clamped her hands on her bright red cheeks.

"Ma, splatted again!" Colin pressed a hand to his belly and laughed—the imp. "That's the second time today!"

Yes, the woman had definitely splatted. Right into his chest.

"Here. Let me help y—" Mrs. Danell stopped and looked down where one of her newly-cleaned boots had landed in a pile of strawberry pie slop.

"Oh no." She peered up at him, then down at her boot again.

He should probably cry after paying for a whole pie and only getting one piece at the Cummingses', but he couldn't help himself. He laughed instead.

"It's not that funny." She thumped her boot on the ground, probably to emphasize her point. But seeing how her boot was already sitting in a pile of crumbled pie and her movement sent strawberry bits flying, well, he only laughed harder.

"Here, at least let me help." She took her apron—her none too clean apron since it had a giant sourdough stain on it—and began wiping at the strawberry clumps on his stomach.

He couldn't begin to guess how, precisely, that was helpful since she was only spreading the mess from his shirt to her apron. But he wasn't going to complain about standing this close to a woman with maple-syrup eyes.

Or one with creamy, slender hands that rubbed small circles on his chest and stomach. Did she know flour still clung to her hair? Oh, she'd brushed most of it out, but being this close, he could see a smattering of white specks amidst her light brown locks.

The circles on his stomach slowed, and she looked up at him, her apron stained beyond help and her fingers now covered in pie filling.

"Oh. I probably shouldn't be... that is, I suppose this isn't... I mean..." She moved her hands to her cheeks, much like she had when she first smacked into him. Except this time—

"Ugh!" She jerked her hands away, but too late. Strawberry already smeared her face.

"Look, Ma," Colin choked out between spurts of laughter. "You're as messy as Mr. Oakton now."

"Colin, it's not polite to laugh at others' misfortunes."

The boy only giggled harder.

Mac smiled and ran a finger through some of the mush still clinging to his shirt. "Colin, you're looking a bit too clean." He swiped the side of the boy's cheek.

Colin laughed again, doubling over at the middle. "I'm still not as messy as you and Ma!"

No, but a little more mess wouldn't hurt. He took a step toward the boy, who turned to run, but Mac was faster, snaking out an arm to catch him. He'd meant to splat some filling on Colin's nose, but somehow he ended up with the boy smashed against his sticky stomach.

"Not his shirt!" Mrs. Danell wailed.

It was too late. His back was smeared with red goo.

The boy turned in his arms, grinning devilishly as he scraped at the remaining mush on Mac's stomach and reached up.

Mac jerked away, but not before Colin managed to smear strawberries across his neck.

"You didn't," he growled.

Colin shrieked—the high, happy sound of a boy having fun—whirled, and ran across the street, where he darted behind the general store.

Mrs. Danell took a step forward. "I'm so sorry, Mr. Oakton. I don't know what came over him. That was rude and inconsiderate and—"

"Fine. It was just fine. I'm the one that went after him first. Just understand one thing." He stooped to swipe his hand through some of the strawberry slop left on the ground.

"What's that?"

"Your boy's going to need a thorough scrubbing before bed tonight." He jogged across the road toward the back of the general store, leaving Mrs. Danell alone with the rest of the strawberry pie.

When he rounded the building, a single strawberry hit him in the shoulder, leaving a large red stain before it dropped to the ground. Colin stood grinning from several feet away—until his gaze dropped to Mac's hand full of fresh strawberry ammunition.

"No! I didn't mean it!"

Mac took a step closer. "You didn't mean to throw a strawberry at me just now?"

The boy's face flamed beneath his strawberry-covered cheeks. "Well, maybe…" He attempted to dart past Mac and out into the street, but he underestimated how far Mac could reach.

In the ensuing scuffle, half of Mac's pie filling ended up on his neck and in his ear, but he managed to smear strawberry mush on Colin from hair to elbow. The boy's every muscle worked to keep Mac's strawberry covered hands from rubbing his face.

"Stop! Stop!" He breathed between happy giggles.

"What have you two done to each other?" Mrs. Danell stood at the side of the building.

At her frown, Mac straightened and glanced down at a strawberry-covered Colin. Maybe he'd been a little too intent on revenge.

"We need to get Ma!" Colin swiped the filling from Mac's hand and wiggled away from his grip.

"Ah, Mrs. Danell." Mac started after Colin. "Watch—

But Colin grabbed onto her sleeve, smashing strawberry into the dark fabric of her mourning dress.

She squealed and tried to pull away, but Colin kept a good latch on her and she started to giggle as he reached up for her face. "No. No. Don't you dare!"

And, oh, could that woman smile. She might be clothed in a dreary, too-large mourning gown and have worry lines etching the sides of her mouth, but a smile transformed her from the skittish, weary widow he'd met in the bakery into someone outright beautiful.

Colin grabbed her wrists. "Hurry, Mr. Oakton. She's going to get away!"

And he realized in that moment, he didn't want her to get

away, to go back to her bakery where she'd scrub down her son and then work into the night.

He wanted her to smile and laugh for just a bit longer.

He reached her in three quick strides, messy hands poised to attack.

"Wait! Don't help him. I'll bake you another pie if you leave me alone." Her words came out breathless as she struggled through another giggle while Colin pinned her wrists at her sides.

His lips tipped into an irrepressible smile. "Are you bribing me, Mrs. Danell?"

"Get her face!"

She squirmed in her son's grasp. "Two pies. I'll bake you two."

He didn't move. "Two pies, you say?"

She nodded, a touch of concern beginning to mix with the smile on her face. "Two. I promise. Whenever you want them. One for the pie that…er, got smashed. And another for leaving me alone."

It was something to consider. She was still smiling, after all, and she was certainly dirty enough. And if the single piece of pie he'd had earlier was any indication, her pies were a pure delicacy in a northwoods town like Eagle Harbor.

"Colin, let your ma go."

The boy frowned but released his grip, and Mac took a step back, giving her room to move around him.

Triumph gleamed in her eyes.

And that did it right there, her womanly gloat. Before she could protest or Colin could grab her wrists again, he rubbed both his hands down the sides of her face. "Mrs. Danell, what rosy cheeks you have."

Chapter Three

He'd smeared her face! Intentionally reached up and put sticky, strawberry pie filling all over her cheeks! She fought back the urge to smile as she tromped down the street towards Jessalyn's house. After all, she shouldn't be happy about having to deliver bread with strawberry residue stuck to her skin.

But he'd made Colin laugh. Didn't that count for something? The boy was far too serious these days. And seeing both Mr. Oakton and her son covered in strawberry mush had been rather entertaining—even if she was going to have to scrub Colin down for an hour and soak his clothes once they returned home.

But if Mr. Oakton ever walked into her bakery and asked for another strawberry pie, she was charging him five dollars. Two dollars for the pie, and a three dollar early cleaning fee in case he decided to use the pie for fighting rather than eating.

"Ma, slow down. You're walking too fast."

"I don't want to be any later." But she paused for a moment while Colin rushed to catch up. She needed to drop the bread off at the Dowrick house before dinner, and she'd already been running late after cleaning up her first mess at the bakery.

"You're walking too fast again." Colin called as she approached the small, single-story dwelling.

She climbed the steps slowly and knocked on the door.

"Coming," a feminine voice called from inside.

Colin joined her on the stoop and peered up with a loaf of bread tucked safely under his arm, the only thing to escape the strawberry battle unscathed. "You still have red stuff stuck to your neck."

Did she? Her entire face felt sticky, though she'd tried to wipe the mess off her skin with the shoulder of her dress. Now she raised her sleeve to her neck and rubbed.

The door popped open just then, and Jessalyn Dowrick stood with six-month-old Megan propped on her hip and two-year-old Claire peeking out from behind her skirts.

"Tressa, hi…" Any remaining words died on her lips, and her eyes widened as they tracked down Tressa and then moved to Colin. "What happened to you two?"

Tressa sighed and rubbed at the stickiness on her neck once more. Unfortunately there was only one way to answer that question—Mr. Oakton had happened. "Just a little accident with a pie on the way over."

~.~.~.~.~

Mac hurried up the path to the lighthouse that overlooked the harbor. If he'd been late walking from the Cummingses' home before, he was doubly so now.

Pie slop. He glanced down at his belly. What had convinced him to smear Mrs. Danell's face with it? He probably shouldn't have. No, he *knew* he shouldn't have, and not just because he'd given up a chance at two free pies.

What gentleman went around chasing ladies with pie slop?

Mrs. Danell would probably never again sell him another

strawberry pie, but he fully intended to try buying one anyway. Or maybe he should walk into her bakery and ask for a replacement. She'd ruined his first pie by rushing around the corner of the telegraph office and running smack into him.

Oh yes, he could just imagine the look on her face when he walked into the bakery tomorrow and claimed she owed him another pie.

A flash of light glinted at the top of the lighthouse tower.

He raised his eyes to the glass panels. Was Grover up there already? It wasn't yet time to light the lamp.

Tucking what was left of his bread under his arm, Mac hastened over the well-worn path and pulled open the door of the red brick lighthouse.

"Grover?" He plopped the bread on the table and headed for the circular stairway at the front of the lighthouse. "You here?"

A voice mumbled from somewhere above him, and he groaned. How many times had he told Grover to let him light the lamp?

Then again, the man probably wasn't lucid enough to remember a one of the dozen conversations.

Mac sprinted up the three flight of stairs. "Wait a minute and I'll…"

He slammed to a halt as he reached the top of the iron stairs and the round platform that held the fourth order Fresnel lens.

Grover's wrinkled hand shook as the old lightkeeper held a burning match to one of two lamps sitting on the table that extended from the base of the lens.

"Grover…"

"Hush up now. I don't need your help."

No help. Sure.

The light failed to take—likely due to the way Grover couldn't keep his hands from trembling. All that kerosene in the bottom of the lamp, only inches away from the match. If Grover bumped one of the lamps off the table…

Mac took a step forward. "Let me."

The old man stomped his foot, causing the iron floor to shake. "It's my night to light the lamp." He reached for another match. "I can start a deuced fire."

Exactly. "I don't mind helping, honest."

Grover struck the match once, twice before it ignited. The flame danced as he held the matchstick to the lamp, but this time the wick took. Mac moved around the lens that dominated most of the tower floor space and reached for the lamp. "At least let me put it inside the—"

"I said leave me alone." Grover stomped his foot again, the thud causing the iron platform to vibrate harder beneath their feet.

Did the lightkeeper not notice? Could he not envision the lighthouse going up in flames if one of those lamps fell?

There wasn't much flammable in the tower. Actually, there wasn't anything flammable in the tower except for the lamp itself. The base upon which the lens sat was iron, as was the triangular little table that extended from the lens base. The walls of the tower were either glass for the windows or brick on the outside and iron on the inside with a concrete core in the middle. The only thing that could catch flame was the kerosene itself. But still, fires claimed lighthouses along the Great Lakes every year.

"I've been starting this here light since you were in short pants," Grover straightened his shoulders. "I don't need you interfering none."

Mac clamped his teeth down on his tongue. Why had he let himself linger so long at the Cummingses'? Or get distracted by a strawberry pie fight? He'd been beating Grover to the tower every evening to light the lamp. Some days he'd shown up as much as an hour early—and then endured a nice lecture about how he was wasting kerosene by starting the lamp two hours before dark rather than one. But a lecture was better than watching a man who couldn't keep his hands from shaking play with matches and kerosene.

Grover hobbled nearer to the Fresnel lens, his limp more pronounced than usual. He carefully opened the brass door, then turned back for the burning lamp.

The image of him dropping his coffee cup at breakfast flashed through Mac's mind. He held his breath.

Grover somehow managed to place the small kerosene lamp inside the hulking lens. The bowed shape and slatted glass of the lens would then diffuse the lamp's tiny flame until its light could be seen fifteen miles or more out to sea.

Grover closed the lens door, and Mac relaxed. Maybe Grover was right. Maybe years of keeping the Eagle Harbor Lighthouse made the ailing man somehow more capable in this area than in others.

Maybe. But tomorrow, he'd be sure to be here two hours early.

Grover shuffled to the stool sitting against the far wall of the tower and plopped down. Then his gaze narrowed, as though seeing Mac for the first time that night. "Why is your shirt covered in...? What *is* that?"

"I need to wash up." Mac turned and headed down the stairs. It was easier than explaining.

~.~.~.~.~

"Have more people dropped off mending?" Tressa stepped over a collection of dolls and rounded a little wooden wagon as she and Colin followed Jessalyn through the parlor of the Dowrick house.

"Yes. Sorry about the mess." Jess waved her free hand absently at the men's trousers and shirts piled on the couch, heading to the kitchen with a lightness of step that belied the two children clinging to her.

Fish sizzled and popped on the kitchen cook stove. The room might not be large, but Jess had done her best to make it homey with calico curtains and a pitcher of wild flowers sitting on the table. Against the far wall, Jessalyn's oldest daughter, Olivia, set out forks and spoons though she was barely tall enough to reach the table.

Tressa nudged Colin. "Go help."

He scowled but set the bread on the hutch, scampered over to the table, and began setting plates.

"I almost fell over today when a couple more shanty boys stopped by with shirts and trousers." Jess flipped the fish with one hand while holding Megan against her hip. Claire still gripped the bottom of her mother's skirt and had popped her thumb into her mouth at some point. "I haven't done any advertising, but I'm in no position to turn away work."

No, Jessalyn Dowrick certainly wasn't. "But you're having fish tonight. Does that mean Thomas...?"

Jess hardened her jaw, her sky blue eyes losing their brightness. "No. Still no word from my husband." She said the last word as though it were a scourge.

Tressa understood the feeling.

"I'm not sure whether to hope he strikes it rich in those gold fields and sends money back or pray he dies without a cent for leaving us the way he did."

Tressa glanced at the children. The babe was oblivious, of course; little Claire pulled her thumb out of her mouth, studied it a moment, and then popped it back in; but Olivia over at the table bit the side of her lip and stared at her feet.

Tressa cleared her throat. "I shouldn't have mentioned it."

"No. It's fine. Not like Thomas's doings are any secret in a town the size of Eagle Harbor." Jess stirred the greens in the frying pan.

That didn't mean the children needed to hear their mother wish their father dead, no matter how angry Jessalyn was.

"Here, give me Megan while you cook. I'd hate to see her get burned." Tressa reached for the babe and settled her on the side of her dress not coated with strawberry residue. She would've taken Claire as well, but the toddler's hand had tightened on her mother's skirt when she'd taken Megan. "If you didn't get money from Thomas, how'd you come by the fish?"

"Rebekah Cummings stopped in today. Said she didn't catch enough this morning to bother icing, so she was giving away what they couldn't eat. Right sweet of her to think of us, wasn't it? And then wouldn't you know, Mac Oakton dropped by with a loaf of your bread."

"Mac Oakton?" Tressa nearly choked on the name.

Jess flipped the fish fillets. "He's a good man, that Mac Oakton."

Was he? Mr. Oakton had seemed decent enough earlier, but seeing how she'd been fool enough to marry Otis, she hardly trusted herself to be good judge.

Still, she couldn't help but be a little curious about the man who'd slathered her face with strawberry filling. Now if only she had a way to ask Jessalyn about him without appearing overly interested.

"We have plenty for dinner." Jess bent and moved Claire from the front of her skirt to the back where there was little chance of the child getting burned. "You should eat with us."

Tressa patted little Megan's back and bounced her gently on her hip. "I just wanted to drop off bread. I'm not going to take your food."

"The Lord has been good to us today, and there's no reason not to share His blessings." Jess gave her a firm look, which somehow managed to be intimidating despite her flaxen hair and light eyes. She didn't need to speak for Tressa to hear her lecture. *You need a meal of fish and beet greens just as much as we do.*

"I don't think—"

"Aw, Ma, the fish smells good." Colin piped up from where he set napkins around the table. "Please, can we stay? Pleeeeease. I can even run back to the bakery and get those gingerbread cookies nobody bought."

Tressa looked down at the babe in her arms, her fuzzy head nestled against her shoulder. "I suppose."

"Good." Jess gave a brisk nod and transferred fish from the stovetop onto a platter. "But since the meat is ready now, Colin can fetch the cookies after dinner."

"So what do you want to do with this bread?" Tressa gestured toward the loaf Colin had set on the hutch.

"We'll have some with jam for breakfast." Jess carried the platter of fish and greens to the table. Plucking Claire from her skirt, she set the angelically blond child on the seat beside her.

Across the table, Colin and Olivia climbed onto a wooden bench, which left the chair on Jess's right open for Tressa.

"Here. I can take Megan." Jess held out her arms.

Tressa ran a finger absently down the little bundle's back. "I don't mind. Besides, a mother should be allowed one meal a week without jostling a babe on her lap." Tressa slid into her chair, scooting it back ever so slightly to make room for the sleepy child.

"Let's say grace." Jess bowed her head and led them in a

prayer—one that thanked God for the fish, beet greens, bread, and coming cookies, but made no mention of the absent Mr. Dowrick.

"I'm hungry." Colin placed a piece of bread on Olivia's plate and then took one for his own. "Ma, do you think Mr. Oakton gave away all the bread he bought?"

"*All* the bread?" Jess stopped chewing. "How much did he buy?"

Tressa bit the inside of her cheek. "I think it was a mistake."

"Five loaves, and it wasn't no mistake." Colin spoke around a mouthful of bread. "He even bought a pie."

The pie, yes. The stickiness on her face turned suddenly warm.

"Well, I certainly appreciate him stopping by our house. Mistake or not." Jessalyn reached for a piece of bread.

"It was very thoughtful." She could barely move the polite words over her thick tongue. How could Mr. Oakton afford to give away all that bread on an assistant lightkeeper's salary, even if some loaves were half price? She eyed the bread under discussion—one of the fresh loaves rather than one of the three-day-old ones he'd bought. Something in his mind must be addled for him to have given away the best.

Jess broke a filet of fish into pieces for Claire and slipped a bite into the girl's mouth. "That's a right pretty picture you make with a babe in your arms, Tressa."

"I miss it sometimes." She tilted her head to the side, nuzzling her cheek against Megan's fuzzy head. She'd never quite forgotten how perfectly a babe seemed to fit in her arms.

Jess smiled. "You should think about having another one."

"Uh…"

"Yeah, Ma. I want a little sister like Megan. Or Olivia. Just not one like Claire." Colin scowled at the shy toddler, who merely stuffed a handful of broken bread in her mouth. "She's no fun."

Tressa kissed the top of Megan's head and drew in her sweet baby scent. There'd been a time when she'd wanted a passel of little ones. But she was a mere girl back then and had no notion of what was involved in creating children—or being married to Otis Danell.

These days she could barely manage to care for herself and Colin. How much more heartache would she have had with a batch of young'uns?

No. Even in her current situation, more children wouldn't have meant heartache. It would have meant extra arms to hug her. More squirming bodies piled on her lap when she read stories before bed, more giggles when she took them to the beach, more—

"Tressa?" Jess asked softly. "Are you all right?"

Tressa cleared her throat. "Yes, of course. But, ah… as lovely as babies are, we both know I'm never marrying again."

"I understand." Compassion flickered in Jess's eyes.

It was an odd decision to make when there were a slew of bachelors drifting around the northwoods wilderness of Copper Country. But she'd married for protection once, and that had increased her problems. How many more would she gain if she married a second time?

Maybe that was part of why she and Jess were such good friends. Any other woman would advise her to marry, but Jess understood why she'd never do so again.

"You mean you won't get hitched to Mr. McCabe?" Colin asked a little too hopefully.

Tressa jerked upright in her chair, causing Megan to stir. "Why would you… think… we'd…?"

The boy rolled his eyes. "Because you send me outside whenever he comes into the bakery, and he never buys anything. And I might have listened through the window a time or two."

So much for trying to keep the trapper's intentions secret. "No. I'm not going to marry Mr. McCabe."

"Good." Colin gave a pronounced nod. "If you need more money for Mr. Ranulfson, I can go to Central and get work."

"No." The word flew from her mouth, sharp and definitive.

"I think you're a bit young yet to work underground." Jessalyn's calm, reasonable voice floated over the table.

"Heard they hired an eleven-year-old last week. His pa died and his ma needed money. Did you know they pay their drill boys fifteen dollars a month?" Colin puffed out his chest, an action that made him look ridiculously boyish rather than manly. "That would be enough to make Mr. Ranulfson happy, wouldn't it?"

"I don't care whether it would be enough or not, I won't send you five miles away or commit you to working twelve-hour days underground." Where had Colin even gotten the notion he could work as a drill boy? "Do you understand how dangerous mines are?"

They'd taken her father's life, and she wasn't about to give those dark, crumbling tunnels filled with copper her son's life too. Not now when he was ten years old—and not in six years either, when most men started working underground.

Colin's chin came up determinedly. "But what happens if we lose the bakery? Are we going to go back to living in the woods? I'd rather work in the mine." He stuck a bite of fish in his mouth only to pause his chewing. "You won't have to work as a cook in a lumber camp again, will you? Especially not without Pa there."

The mere thought caused her face to turn cold. Otis might not have been much by way of a husband, but he was big and surly enough to keep other men from bothering her, even at a lumber camp where she'd been the only woman amidst a horde of bachelors.

"Of course we won't go back to the lumber camps." Though in

truth, she couldn't promise much of anything. If she lost the bakery, they had nowhere but the woods to go. "You shouldn't worry, Colin. I won't lose the bakery."

Please, God, don't let me lose the bakery. She forced an overly bright smile to her face.

"Oh! I know what you can do if Mr. Ranulfson kicks us out." Colin smacked the table, a sudden grin lighting his face. "You could marry Mr. Oakton. He'd make a better pa than Mr. McCabe."

Marry Mr. Oakton? Her stomach churned and her face got that cold feeling again. Perhaps the man had been kind today, even played with Colin and teased her a bit with the pie, but that hardly warranted agreeing to spend the rest of her life under his thumb. "I just said I'm not marrying—"

"It might be a little soon to ask such a thing of your ma, Colin." Jessalyn smiled at the boy, her expression a touch too serene to be trusted. "But I am curious as to why he stopped by the bakery and bought up five loaves of bread and a pie."

Tressa reached up and touched the still-sticky side of her face.

"Oh, he didn't just buy stuff," Colin volunteered. "He smeared pie mush all over Ma's face."

Jessalyn's gaze jerked back to her, eyes narrowed. "*That* was the accident you had with a pie?"

Tressa swallowed. "It started out as an accident, but it may have gotten a little more involved at the end."

"He was standing so close, I thought he was going to kiss her." Colin scrunched up his nose and made a disgusted face. "But then he smeared pie on her face instead."

"I see," Jessalyn said.

Tressa slid down a little in her chair. Her friend was seeing something that wasn't there—she'd told Colin the truth, she wasn't marrying again, teasing man or not.

Chapter Four

Mac yawned as he headed down Center Street toward the bakery. The day was sunny, the sky a clear blue, the lake a curious combination of calm and wavy. Gulls circled overhead, and just beyond the edge of town an eagle lighted off a tree branch. It was a good day. A perfect day. The kind of day that made a man want to grab a fishing pole and play hooky from work.

Work. Mac yawned again and rubbed at his eyes. That was the problem. He couldn't take off from work, not ever. According to lighthouse service regulations, he and Grover were both supposed to work four hours on, four hours off, throughout the night. The service didn't want keepers getting sleepy and letting the lamps flicker out or the flame get too big and flare, causing the pressure inside the lamp to crack the glass and possibly even the Fresnel lens itself.

But how was he supposed to go downstairs, curl up in his bed, and sleep when Grover was in the tower watching the light with his shaky hands and uneven gait?

Surely Grover didn't think he could go on keeping the Eagle Harbor Light forever.

Or maybe he did. If Mac hadn't written to the lighthouse service inspector this spring, how would the inspector down in

Detroit ever have known there was a problem with Grover?

Not that the letter had done much good, seeing how the inspector still hadn't arrived with a replacement.

Maybe he needed to wire the man—except that would cause more problems. The widow Hendricks at the telegraph office might be as sweet as a summer rose, but one wire to Detroit, and the entire town would know of Grover's condition.

Mac blinked his eyes, still a little blurry from last night's lack of sleep, and paused outside the bakery door. At least he'd come up with a solution to one of his problems—the lighthouse grounds. The United States Lighthouse Service expected them to be kept immaculate. With Grover's inability to walk and his own inability to sleep, the yard was getting away from them. Hopefully Mrs. Danell would allow her son to help. If Colin cleaned the yard, maybe Mac could squeeze in a nap.

He let himself into the bakery, the little bell above the door setting off a wave of tinkles. He stopped when his gaze landed on Mrs. Danell, standing tall and proud to the side of her counter despite the flour smudged on her cheek.

But she wasn't alone. Oh, no. Finley McCabe knelt before her, her hand clasped in his, though she was trying to tug it away.

"As I said, Tessa," McCabe yammered. "We should get ourselves hitched." Had the man not heard the bell? "I got myself a real nice cabin out back of town, and—"

"It's Mrs. Danell," she growled. "And my answer hasn't changed since yesterday."

Finley McCabe had taken to proposing to Mrs. Danell? The old trapper would make just as poor a father as Otis had, probably as poor of a husband too.

Mrs. Danell glanced toward him, a soft flush stealing across her cheeks despite their dusting of flour.

Had she dropped another bowl of flour on herself, or did working in the kitchen mean she was always spattered with food of some sort?

The wiry old trapper sprang to his feet. "Now see here, Tessa. Folks are talkin' about how you're gonna lose this bakery as soon as the bank runs out of patience. You need a husband, and I'm offering for you and your young'un. The words coming out of your mouth should be 'Thank you, let's call for a minister.'"

"Lose the bakery?" Mac mumbled. Was her situation that dire? Yesterday he'd figured the woman was a bit low on funds, but getting kicked out of her home was another matter entirely.

Mrs. Danell's back straightened and her chin took on a determined angle. "No, Mr. McCabe. You won't ever hear those words from me. Now if you'll excuse me, I have a customer waiting. The next time I see you in my shop, it had better be to buy something rather than waste my time."

The top of Finley's head turned beet red, and he waved his scrawny little finger in her face. "You're going to regret this. Just see if you—"

"That's enough." Mac stepped forward. "You heard the woman. Either buy something or get out."

McCabe spun and stalked toward Mac, causing the scent of stale body odor and something sour to war with the aromas of sugar and flour saturating the bakery. "Oh, and aren't you a fancy one to be talking. Clive Oakton's son defending the likes of Otis Danell's widow. Maybe the two of you should get hitched. A fine pair of thieving, lying, cheating tricksters you'd make."

Mac's right hand clenched into a fist. McCabe didn't even reach his shoulder. One punch was all it would take. Just one.

And the story about how Mac Oakton was following in his father's drunken, brawling footsteps by clobbering a smelly but upstanding citizen would be around town within the hour.

"I'm here for a pie." He kept his voice even.

The trapper chortled, flooding Mac's face with a rush of rancid breath. "Sure you are." Then he turned and stormed out of the building.

"I'm sorry." Mrs. Danell rushed toward him, her hands twisted together in front of her skirt. "Do forgive me. I shouldn't have spoken to him like that with you in the store. Now he's embarrassed and angry."

"You did right giving McCabe a comeuppance. It wasn't your fault he got huffy."

"Yes, but he insulted you, and he—"

"Nothing I haven't heard before." And it wasn't, though he'd prefer to keep a pretty thing like Tressa Danell from hearing such tales. Had she been in town long enough to hear about his father? It wasn't the first thing people talked about anymore—not like after it had first happened—so maybe she didn't know.

If she did, she wouldn't be so apologetic over such an insignificant slight. Especially considering what he'd done to her last night. Mac rubbed the back of his neck. "Ah, about yesterday, I probably shouldn't have—"

"That's correct." She crossed her arms. "You most assuredly shouldn't have."

He tried to nod agreeably. Tried to look contrite. Would have managed if not for the memory of her face smeared with strawberry slop. A smile pushed up one corner of his mouth. "But you looked so becoming with red cheeks."

She huffed. "I had to wash our clothing twice to get everything out, thank you very much."

"Admit it, you had fun. And you can hardly complain about me smearing food on your face when you manage the same amount of damage on your own." He swiped at the splotch of flour on her cheek with his thumb, covering it with a fine white dust. "See there?"

She blushed again, her skin turning redder than the strawberry slop from last night.

"Nothing is ever clean for long in a bakery." Her words were quiet, too quiet, and laced with that faint accent he still couldn't place.

Then she swallowed, and he glanced at her neck, at the very place the pie filling had dripped along her throat last night, right below the curve of her jaw, where her collarbone met her neck.

"Mr. Oakton?" Another whisper, this one slightly breathless.

He brought his gaze back to her face, though he should probably look away entirely. A man could get lost far too easily in those sweet maple-syrup eyes with soft gold flecks sprinkled throughout the darker tan.

But instead of glancing elsewhere, he stood like a fly enticed by syrup, staring down at a fine porcelain face—a face he had no business noticing since he was leaving town in a couple weeks.

He took a step away from her and cleared his throat. "Do you have another strawberry pie?"

She took her own step back and raised an eyebrow. "Even if I'd baked a strawberry pie this morning—which I didn't—I certainly wouldn't be selling it to you."

"Of course not. You'd be giving it to me. You're the one who ran into me last night and ruined the one I'd already paid for."

"And you're the one who forfeited any future pie when you smeared my face with strawberry filling."

He couldn't help his grin. "And as I already said, you look lovely with rosy cheeks."

"Yes, well, I'm glad you think so. Now, can I interest you in other goods? I have muffins. Cookies."

"If I come back tomorrow, will you have a strawberry pie?"

"If I have another strawberry pie, I'm charging you five dollars. Two dollars for the pie, and a three dollar early cleaning fee in case you decide to use the pie to stain our clothes again."

He made a tsking sound and shook his head at her. "Such contempt towards me when you were the one who started the fight."

"What I did was an accident! Everything you did was on purpose."

And so it was. What a sight the three of them must have made standing in the alley behind the general store last night. "How'd you get the stains out?"

She dropped her arms to her side and her shoulders lost their tautness. "I couldn't, not even after two washings. There's still a light mark on Colin's shirt. Were you able to clean yours?"

He shrugged. "Didn't even bother trying. That was a mighty expensive accident you caused me, considering the cost of my shirt, the pie, and the price you want to charge me for another."

"I truly am sorry." Her gaze dropped to her toes. Again.

Did she look away so often when talking to other people or just him? "I didn't come to the bakery to drag another apology from you." Though he certainly wouldn't complain if she decided to ease her guilt by replacing his pie. "I'll take some of those sugar cookies today though, maybe a dozen? And a strawberry pie for tomorrow."

She moved behind the counter and smiled serenely. Too serenely. "That will be five dollars and fifty cents, paying for the pie in advance."

He choked back a laugh and held up his hands in surrender. "You win, Mrs. Danell. No pie for me until the price drops back down. But I will take those cookies."

"Fifty cents then."

She filled a small paper sack with the scrumptious looking treats while he fumbled around in his pocket for coins.

"Is Colin around? I've got a job for him to do at the lighthouse. If he's interested in earning a couple quarters, that is."

"I'm sure he'd like that." She folded the top of the bag. "But he's fishing with the Spritzer boys right now. Do you know Leroy and Martin?"

"Sure do. Didn't realize your boy was friends with them though." In fact, he hadn't realized Colin had friends at all given the way he'd found the boy crying in the woods yesterday. A couple of friends could do a boy right good, especially one who'd just lost his pa.

"I can send Colin to the lighthouse when he gets back."

"Appreciate it." Mac gave a little nod of his head and reached for the cookies.

She kept her grip on the bag and met his eyes. "You don't have to do this."

"Do what?"

"Give Colin work. Buy things from here. Be ni—"

The word stilled on her lips, but he could guess its meaning well enough. "You've got yourself a good boy, Mrs. Danell. I have a hunch he's not just out fishing for fun, but to put food on the table. We can use a lad like him around the lighthouse. That's not being nice. I'd rather hire someone who knows how to work than a hooligan."

"It's only that... that..." Her hands were doing that fidgeting business where she kept twisting them together. "Sometimes I worry if I'm raising him right. His father wasn't the most upstanding of men."

Just because the boy's father was worthless doesn't mean your son will turn out that way. Mac was a living testament to that, but he kept his mouth shut. "I'll take good care of him at the lighthouse."

He took a couple steps toward the door, then stopped and looked back over his shoulder. What a picture she made in a faded mourning dress too big for her slender frame. She had a white apron tied about her neck and waist, but not even the extra cloth could hide how ill the dress fit. Her hair was falling from its sloppy updo to frame her face, and a splotch of flour he hadn't noticed earlier clung to her jaw.

"For what it's worth, Mrs. Danell. You did the right thing turning McCabe away. Eagle Harbor is crawling with single men, and there's got to be a decent one or two who'll offer for you. Best to wait for one of them to come around."

Her cheeks turned pale and her shoulders stiffened. "I'm not waiting on someone better, for I shall never marry again."

He blinked. Had he misunderstood what McCabe had said about her losing the bakery? "Then what are you going to do?"

"Precisely what I'm doing now—earn a living for me and my son."

"What if your plan doesn't work?"

Her chin came up the slightest bit. "Then I'll try harder."

Did she really think a few months of hard work would solve all her problems? He only hoped a good man was waiting for her and Colin when she realized she couldn't do everything herself.

‾.‾.‾.‾.‾

What are you going to do if you don't marry? Tressa rolled her eyes as the door closed behind Mr. Oakton's towering frame.

Why was she allowed to live on the income she took in from

the bakery while she had a husband, but as soon as he died, she was suddenly unable to care for herself?

Tressa stomped back into the kitchen and took up a broom, sweeping the floor with hard, quick strokes. Mr. Oakton had looked at her like she was daft for wanting to provide for herself. Well, she wasn't daft. She was smart and every bit as capable of taking care of them as Otis had been.

More capable, even.

After nine years of living in a company house with her father at the Central Mine and ten years of living in the woods, following Otis around to various logging camps where she often worked as a cook, she finally had someplace that belonged to her. Whenever she'd moved to a town with Otis, they'd settle in for a month or two before he decided it was time to up and leave. They'd spent time up near Copper Harbor, then down by Calumet, and over by Lac La Belle, before finally coming back to his hometown of Eagle Harbor. But when she'd moved here with him last spring, she'd found this bakery for sale, taken some of the funds Otis had earned during his winter of logging, and made a down payment.

Colin had made friends instantly, and for the first time in his life, he belonged somewhere. She wasn't going to give up everything she'd worked for just because someone had robbed her. And that was the only reason she was in this situation in the first place. Business had dropped during the winter months when things slowed and the harbor closed due to the ice that formed on Lake Superior, but that was to be expected, and she'd saved during the busy months so that she'd be able to stay ahead during the slow winter.

She hadn't expected to be robbed and have her husband die within a week of each other though. How could she have prepared herself for that?

But she'd fallen on hard times before, and she'd always come out stronger in the end. Her debt to the bank was no different. She was going to stay. She was going to fight. She was going to make a living—and she wasn't going to send Colin into the copper mines to accomplish it.

Maybe she needed to expand. If certain townsfolk were no longer coming to her for bread, then she'd go to them. She'd bet some of the shanty boys and Cousin Jacks who went to Jessalyn for mending would buy bread. And it shouldn't be too hard to get the general store to carry her baked goods. Maybe she could even supply a few loaves to the boardinghouse.

Yes, that was the perfect solution. No reason to stay inside waiting for a steady stream of customers when she could go find them.

And she would find them. She had to.

Tressa leaned the broom against the counter and strode through the kitchen with a briskness that scattered the pile of flour and dust she'd just swept. Heading into the storefront and straight for the money box beneath the counter, she removed the four dollars and twenty-five cents she'd acquired since paying Mr. Ranulfson yesterday—never mind that all but seventy-five cents of it had come from Mac Oakton. She then stuffed the funds in her pocket, yanked off her apron, and smiled politely as the bell jangled and a group of sailors stepped inside.

By the time she headed for the front door, she had five dollars and twenty-five cents in her pocket. Though she didn't need all of it to purchase ten pounds of flour, she took it with her lest her unwelcome visitor return during the few minutes she was gone.

Afternoon sunshine greeted her as she stepped outside, though the cool breeze from the lake muted its warmth. She shielded her eyes against the light and tromped down Center Street, dodging the occasional patch of mud left from the spring thaw. Turning left onto First Street, she headed up the road until it intersected with North Street near the Foley Smith General Store.

The mixed scents of leather, flour, and tobacco surrounded her as she marched inside and steered herself toward the baking supplies. She had enough lard and sugar to get her through to next week, but the sugar cookies she'd mixed up this morning had taken all her flour.

Last summer she'd purchased flour by the barrel, which was cheaper in the long run but cost more up front. When business had started to falter over the winter, she'd taken to purchasing fifty-pound sacks, but she didn't have enough money for that today. So she hefted a ten pound sack into her arms and turned toward the proprietor at the back of the store.

"Excuse me." Mrs. Ranulfson, the banker's wife, brushed past her with barely a glance, her fancy hat bobbing in the air as she headed to where Mrs. Foley and Mrs. Kainner stood by the bolts of fabric and ribbons.

Tressa carried her sack to the counter and set it down.

"Good afternoon." Mr. Foley blinked at her from behind his spectacles, then smiled blandly.

She smiled back and reached for the bills lying in her pocket. "I was wondering—"

"Mrs. Danell." The click of shoes sounded on the floor behind her. "Just the woman I needed to see."

Tressa's fingers tensed around the bills in her hand.

Byron Sinclair sauntered toward her, taking his time though a man with a box of cigars waited for Mr. Foley's attention behind her. Mr. Sinclair's three-piece suit lay in sharp, crisp lines without a hint of a wrinkle or blemish. Mr. Ranulfson might wear similar clothing, but she'd wager Mr. Sinclair's outfit cost three times that of the banker's—and this was probably one of Mr. Sinclair's cheaper suits.

"Buying flour are you?" he asked.

The ladies near the fabric stopped talking amongst themselves and turned to look at them, as did the shanty boy perusing the center aisle.

"I'm out," she answered simply.

"Perhaps you're not aware, but your husband purchased a small fishing craft from me last spring."

She was aware, very aware. Otis had claimed buying the craft would enable him to sell his catch during the summer months, creating more money for them when he wasn't logging.

Of course, Otis had only taken the boat out a handful of times on the mornings he wasn't ill from drinking the night before.

"We'd worked out a payment schedule for the boat," Mr. Sinclair announced—and *announced* was the correct word for what he was doing, because he made certain every person in the store could hear him. "But your husband only ever made one."

"And you want money." Never mind that Otis had gambled away his boat within a couple weeks. "Perhaps we could discuss this somewhere else?" Like outside, away from all the ears. "Just let me pay for my flour first."

The owner of Great Northern Shipping placed his hand on top of the flour sack and curved his lips into a smile devoid of sympathy. "I'm afraid that's the problem, Mrs. Danell. If you have money to be purchasing flour, then you have money to be paying me."

The flimsy bills weighed heavily in her hand. "This is for my business."

"That's hardly my problem, wouldn't you agree, Mr. Foley?" Mr. Sinclair held out his hand for the money and looked to the proprietor.

The other man cleared his throat. "Well... you see..."

"Didn't I hear you mention Mr. Danell left an unpaid account here at the store?" Mr. Sinclair added.

"That's not true." She narrowed her eyes at Mr. Sinclair. "I've always paid our account."

"I'm not referring to the account you and your husband shared." Mr. Sinclair offered her another tight smile.

Tressa looked to Mr. Foley, whose face turned decidedly pale. "What's he talking about?"

The man rubbed his nose beneath his spectacles. "Ah, you've always been very good at paying your balance, Mrs. Danell, but your husband had a separate account."

She tried to swallow, but her throat had trouble carrying out the simple action.

Mr. Sinclair leaned against the counter, completely relaxed despite the scene he was creating. "Mr. Foley, was that account paid in full upon Otis Danell's death?"

"That's not any of your business," Tressa snapped.

Mr. Sinclair merely quirked an eyebrow at her, as though her objection didn't deserve a response.

Mr. Foley coughed ever so slightly. "No, the account wasn't paid."

"How much," she whispered.

"Eleven dollars and four cents."

It wasn't a terribly large sum, but under the circumstances...

"Are you in the habit of letting patrons who fail to pay their debts continue shopping at your store?" Mr. Sinclair tapped his fingers on the counter.

"Usually we refuse to sell anything more on credit." Mr. Foley pushed his spectacles higher up on his nose. "But if they have money when they make their purchases, then—"

"The woman before you has quite the debt, wouldn't you say? She doesn't just owe the store, but other individuals around town as well."

Mr. Foley slanted a glance her direction. "I suppose."

Heat bloomed in her cheeks as she looked between the two men, then around the store that had seemed to have doubled its customers since this wretched conversation started.

The group of women by the fabric were all scowling at Mr. Sinclair, but Mrs. Kainner, the owner of the town's only respectable boardinghouse, stepped forward. "Seeing how this is Mr. Foley's establishment, I think he should run it however he wants, without any interference from you, Byron Sinclair. After all, I'm sure you don't consult him when it comes to the affairs of Great Northern Shipping."

"Yeah, you might own Great Northern Shipping, but that don't mean you own the entire town." The man standing behind them with the cigars muttered.

The iron band clamped around her chest loosened just the slightest bit. She owed Mrs. Kainner and the stranger a batch of cookies, to be sure.

Mr. Sinclair, his smile still in place, turned back to Mr. Foley as though Mrs. Kainner and the other man's objections didn't matter in the least. And they probably didn't, at least not to business owners like the Ranulfsons and Foleys. Mr. Sinclair was powerful enough to snuff the life from the mercantile and bank if he wanted.

"I'm sure you don't want word spreading that customers can skimp on paying their accounts," he said to Mr. Foley. "Think of all the money you'd lose. Dockworkers, shanty boys, miners—"

"That's enough." Tressa glanced at Mrs. Kainner and then back at Mr. Foley. They'd caused enough of a scene already, and Mr.

Sinclair wasn't about to let her win, not with so many people watching. She slapped her bills on the counter beside Mr. Sinclair's hand. "Here. I hope you're satisfied."

"That's not even enough to cover a payment."

She turned and fled down the aisle, bursting through the door into the bright sunshine.

How would she ever make enough money to keep her home if she couldn't even buy flour?

˜.˜.˜.˜.˜

Mac found Colin and the Spritzer boys sitting on the lighthouse rocks, their fishing poles dangling in the water, and their bucket empty of fish.

"Shouldn't you have a catch by now?" Mac walked across a large, flat rock above the boys and then hopped down to where they sat just above the water, the boulder's surface slightly damp from an occasional tall wave.

"We had three of them." Leroy spoke flatly as he turned, his dark blond hair hanging over his eyes. "Martin got one that ran from his fingers clear to his elbow. But them boys took it."

"Someone took your fish?"

The younger Spritzer boy—Martin, was it?—nodded.

Colin merely sniffled.

Mac surveyed Colin a little closer, his shirt and short pants noticeably damp and his hair laying in wet little curls against his scalp. Perhaps the water on the rock wasn't from waves then. "What happened, Colin?"

The boy swiped at his cheek and stared down at where his fishing line disappeared into the ebbing and swelling water. "We had three whole whitefish, enough for dinner today and tomorrow, and they..." His voice cracked and he wiped his cheek again. "Then they took the bucket and dumped it on me. Said I already stank like rotten fish to begin with. More fish water wouldn't hurt."

Mac settled his hand on the boy's shoulder, probably a mistake considering the undeniable fish-like aroma wafting from his wet clothes. He'd had his own share of stolen fish and unwanted swims after his pa had left with half the townsfolk's money. "Could you take a break from fishing? I need someone to pick up the lighthouse grounds for me. I'll pay you a quarter."

Colin shook his head vehemently. "No, I promised Ma I'd bring back dinner, and Mrs. Spritzer needs fish too. We had enough for everybody." Colin looked over at his dry-clothed friends. "Then Erik Ranulfson came along with his friends and...and..."

Mac sat down on the other side of the fish bucket. "Guess I'll stay here until you three get yourself some dinner then."

"You're staying with us?" Colin asked.

Mac glanced at the Spritzer boys, Martin watching him with large, dark eyes and Leroy blinking from beneath the hair hanging in his face. "Wouldn't want that Ranulfson scamp getting any ideas about coming back, would we?"

"N-n-no." Colin's lip trembled.

"After you get your fish, I'll teach you three something a very special man taught me a few years back."

The bleakness in Colin's eyes faded to curiosity. "What?"

"It's called how to throw a punch."

Chapter Five

Home. Elijah Cummings stared out over the small inlet rimmed with sand, the treacherous rocks that lined the shore surrounding the harbor, the tree-covered hills rolling over the land beyond. Beneath his feet, the schooner cut through the choppy open waters of the world's largest freshwater lake toward the natural bay where he'd grown up.

He curled his fist around the paper in his pocket, the one he'd gotten from the telegraph office in Boston. Though it had only been in his pocket for ten days, the telegraph was worn and faded to the point it was nearly illegible.

That's how long it had taken him to travel from Boston, Massachusetts to Eagle Harbor, Michigan. The telegram had sat in Boston for two weeks before that, awaiting his return from a jaunt across the Atlantic.

He looked out over the blue waters of Lake Superior. No matter how many times he sailed into Eagle Harbor, whether on his pa's little mackinaw fishing boat or a big schooner like this, he never tired of the view.

He leaned on the gunwale and looked out over the lake that could turn ferocious in an instant. It could steal life from the best of them, as though men's lives were no more significant than leaves fallen to the ground in autumn.

Elijah squeezed the note in his hand, only four short words. *PA DROWNED. COME HOME.*

It had to be wrong. Pa knew this lake, had been sailing it for years.

The message was probably a ploy sent on Pa's behalf to get him to come home rather than go to Port Huron where he and Mac had already made their first payment on a small shipyard.

Yes, certainly that was it—a cruel, badly thought out ruse. His father couldn't drown. He was a strong swimmer, a smart sailor. Sure, this lake could be a threat. But it was, after all, only a lake, and his pa was skilled enough not to drown in it.

Behind him, mariners shouted to one another, taking in the sails so the vessel slowed as it headed between the two wooden platforms marking safe passage into Eagle Harbor.

In a few minutes, he'd leave the boat and walk down the pier, down North Street, and down the path to the rambling cabin that sat along forty acres on Lake Superior. He'd walk in the door and see Pa sitting at the kitchen table while Ma fried up some fish. Rebekah would put on coffee that would be as black as coal and as thick as the liquid copper they poured into ingots at the smelters. Isaac, Rebekah's twin, would be sitting at the table, talking about a new plan he had for a boat, something that would cut through the water faster than the *North Star*, hold more fish, have bigger sails. There was always a newer, better boat design for Isaac to try.

Elijah rubbed a hand over the scruffy beard Ma would demand he shave as soon as he stepped into the house. Yes, that's exactly what he would find. He wouldn't believe anything else, because Pa couldn't be dead. He'd know if his pa was gone; his heart would possess a sick sense of impending doom rather than a swirl of bewilderment.

The schooner's stern cleared the dock, and a shout rang out from the captain. The sails dropped while the boat slowed and turned, then drifted smoothly against the dock as the wind buffeted her. The dockworkers alongside the schooner tied off the ropes while sailors attached the gangplank. In under a minute, crates were being hauled up from the bowels of the ship and carted down to the dock. Byron Sinclair stood on the pier in the center of it all, proud and polished, looking not only as if he owned the ship on which Elijah stood, but the very air the town breathed.

If he never again laid eyes on Sinclair for the rest of his life, it wouldn't be soon enough. Elijah grabbed the valise lying at his feet, walked down the planking with long strides, and bumped Sinclair's shoulder. Hard.

Sinclair tipped his hat as though the slight hadn't occurred. "Sorry about your father's passing, Elijah."

Passing? Elijah stopped to stare at Sinclair, the man's smile cold beneath his shiny hat and perfectly tailored suit.

Every hope, every wish, every dream crashed and splintered into tiny shards against the dock.

A worker patted him on the shoulder, the man's face familiar. "Yeah, I'm sorry too. A right shame."

Something foreign burned behind Elijah's eyes, and his jaw clenched so tightly his teeth began to ache.

Pa can't be dead. He can't! He wanted to scream it, but his throat was too constricted to work, so the words echoed in his head, over and over, while the dockworkers and Sinclair looked on.

"Elijah." A masculine voice rang out. An understanding one.

He turned toward shore and glimpsed his friend making his way up the pier, his head and shoulders rising above the rest of the crowd. "Mac."

Mac slapped a hand on his back and kept it there, turning it into something like an embrace despite them standing in front of several dozen people. "It's good to have you back, Eli."

He crushed the telegram in his pocket. If only he could say it was good to return. But it wasn't.

~.~.~.~.~

Crash!

Mac jolted from where he sat in the lighthouse parlor with the logbook spread before him. Setting down his pen, he pushed away from the writing desk and strode into the kitchen.

Another clattering sound rang through the lighthouse.

"Grover. What are you doing?"

The man looked up, his gray hair sticking up in fuzzy little tufts. "I was j-just scraping my p-plate."

Pottery shards lay at his feet along with chunks of sausage and eggs. The man's chin trembled and his hands shook as he gripped the edge of the sink, likely unable to let go without falling.

"How many times have I told you to let me clear the table?"

Grover's head came up a notch, even if it trembled slightly with the movement. "I'm the head keeper. It's my job to see that this place stays orderly, just look in the handbook."

Never mind that Grover shouldn't be the head keeper anymore. Mac took in the stubborn set to Grover's chin, the way the man squared his shoulders though he still gripped the edge of the sink to keep himself upright.

The man didn't understand how ill he was, plain and simple. "You need to wire Detroit, Grover. You need to tell the inspector about your shaking."

And his trouble walking, the way he failed to remember whose night it was to light the lamp, and how he couldn't seem to stand up straight anymore.

"I don't need to tell that inspector anything. I'm hearty as a horse."

Mac cast a quick glance out the window, revealing another sunny day of blue waves and bluer sky. Why hadn't the inspector written him back yet?

God, please send that inspector. Today.

"Now get on with you." Grover made a shooing motion with his hand. "I can clean up my own mess."

The table still held leftover eggs, coffee, and a smattering of dishes. He could demand Grover go lie down while he cleaned up the mess himself, but that would only get him a more crotchety and obstinate boss. The only thing Grover could hurt at the moment was more dishes.

That sure seemed better than having a lighthouse engulfed in flame. He'd save his next confrontation for over who got to light the lamp.

Turning, he headed back into the parlor and plopped down at the writing desk, taking up his pen to finish recording yesterday's events. Not much had happened. Blue skies, blue seas, wind out of the northwest...

Elijah's ship had docked.

He made painstaking strokes against the thick paper, trying to match his own overlarge handwriting to Grover's squat penmanship from a year ago. This was one area in which Grover had gladly conceded his duties, probably because the man knew his shaky writing would permanently record the severity of his condition—whatever it was.

The door to the lighthouse banged open, and Mac's pen jolted across the page, leaving a streak through the words in the line above.

"What happened here?" Elijah's unmistakable voice resonated from the kitchen.

"Nothing that concerns you," Grover snapped. "Ain't you ever heard of knocking?"

Mac pushed to his feet and walked to the doorway that separated the kitchen from the parlor.

"Do you need help?" Elijah bent to retrieve pottery shards.

"I said it wasn't none of your concern!" Grover clamped a hand around the back of a kitchen chair. Could Elijah see how badly it shook? How Grover's knuckles turned white under the strain of keeping himself upright?

Elijah dumped the broken pieces into a pile on the table and brushed his hands off on his trousers. "Reckon I'll find Mac then."

"I'm here."

Elijah's eyes came up to meet his, but no look of relief or brotherly understanding crossed his gray irises. Instead, his eyes darkened into an impending storm.

"Why didn't you write to tell me?" He stalked past Mac into the parlor.

"Tell you what?"

"That my mother's on her way to becoming mad with grief. Don't you think that's a rather large omission on your part?"

Mac heaved out a breath. "What good would it have done? You were already coming home. You'd see for yourself. Besides, it's not like I could get a letter to you while you were traveling."

Elijah moved to the window and stared out over the open lake to the west. "They're a mess. As though Pa dying wasn't bad enough, it's like my entire family died with him."

Was Mac in a better place than any of the Cummingses? If not for the lighthouse and his plans to go to Port Huron, he might have struck out into the woods by himself after Hiram's death and stayed there. "It was a bad storm. Came up quick and brutal-like. We barely got the lamp lit before the rain came gushing. Isaac and Rebekah were in town. They ran here looking for your dad's mackinaw. And they saw… saw…"

Mac pressed his eyes closed, but that didn't stop the vision from filling his mind. The wind whipping across the lake, the waves froth-tipped and vicious, and the *North Star* caught in the uncontrollable swells. She'd only been several yards from port when the wind caught the sails, dashing the boat upon the rocks before it capsized.

"Someone should have rescued him." Elijah's firm voice resounded through the small parlor.

Mac's eyes sprang open. "What?"

"It only would have taken a rowboat and a man or two. They do it all the time on the Atlantic."

"They have trained lifesavers on the Atlantic, and you sound as crazy as your sister. She wanted to go out to where the boat capsized. If Isaac and I hadn't held her back, you'd have two graves to visit at the cemetery rather than one."

Elijah turned from the window, his jaw working back and forth. "What am I going to do? We've got to leave in two weeks, but Ma…"

Mac clasped a hand on Elijah's shoulder. "You're allowed to grieve a bit before you start worrying about anything else."

"If Pa were still here, I know what he'd do, what he'd say. There's that verse he always quoted…" Moisture gathered in Elijah's eyes, and he blinked. "That one about God's ways being better than our ways, about God's plan being above ours."

"From Isaiah 55. 'For my thoughts are not your thoughts, neither are your ways my ways, saith the LORD. For as the heavens are higher than the earth, so are my ways higher than your ways, and my thoughts than your thoughts,'" Mac quoted. Hiram had often made his family recite verses over the dinner table.

"Yeah, that one. He'd say this was all part of God's master plan."

"He would." And sometimes that made keeping his own faith harder, knowing what Hiram would have thought. Maintaining his faith despite setbacks had never seemed difficult for Hiram. Mac looked down at his feet. "I'm having a hard time sensing any divine plan at the moment."

"Me too."

"Have you been to the cemetery yet? I can walk up with you. Isaac did a right nice job carving the tombstone."

Elijah shook his head. "I was thinking of going this morning, but…"

Mac thumped him on the back. "I'll go with you. Not doing much of anything this morning besides frustrating Grover anyhow. Then we'll organize a shindig at the beach tonight. Cook some fish over the fire, get Emmett Jakkobsin to play his fiddle, so you can see everyone in town. You've been gone two years. Things have changed."

"Change?" Elijah snorted. "In Eagle Harbor?"

So maybe not much had changed.

Elijah straightened and stared at the south-facing wall, as though he could see through the flowery wallpaper into the town. "I don't suppose Victoria's here? That we could invite her?"

Mac pushed all the air out of his lungs in a giant sigh. "She hasn't been back since you left. Heard a rumor that the entire family is staying in Milwaukee for the summer and not even her pa will be up."

Elijah's shoulders fell. "Can't say I expected much different."

No, but for some reason, the man had hoped. Mariners like

Elijah didn't up and marry the daughters of shipping barons. Everybody seemed to understand that—except Elijah.

"Let's go visit Pa's grave."

"You're a good brother." Elijah slung his arm over Mac's shoulder. "I probably don't tell you as often as I should."

Brother. Mac's throat tightened as he steered Elijah through the kitchen and out of the lighthouse. The Cummings family had done so much for him over the years.

If only it had been enough to erase the scourge of his father's past actions from his own reputation. But not even having Hiram Cummings take him under his wing had accomplished such a feat.

Chapter Six

Tressa slid two more loaves of bread into the oven then took a step back, fanning the heat from her face and neck. The soles of her feet throbbed and her shoulders ached, which was to be expected considering she'd baked ten loaves of bread between last night and this morning.

Ten.

She'd gone to the boardinghouse yesterday afternoon, and Mrs. Kainner had decided that yes, she'd buy bread from Tressa, at least for the next month or so. Mrs. Kainner had heard a rumor that Mr. Ranulfson from the bank had been to visit, and the widow apparently didn't cotton to the idea of another widow and her son being kicked out of their home.

Then Jessalyn had agreed to sell bread to her clients and refused to take a percentage of the sales off the top, regardless of how hard Tressa had insisted. Jessalyn then turned around and promptly sold Tressa's last two loaves to the shanty boys who'd stopped by for their mending.

With the money from Jessalyn, Tressa had gone back to the Foley Smith General Store just before closing to purchase flour. When she spoke with Mr. Foley privately, he agreed to stock her bread and any other baked goods she provided as long as the store could take a thirty percent commission. And the dear man hadn't balked at selling her flour since Byron Sinclair was nowhere in sight, but he said that if she could work out a way to pay off Otis's account, he'd be grateful.

Perhaps Eagle Harbor contained a few good souls despite Byron Sinclair and all the rough bachelors employed in the various Copper Country industries.

Which meant she now needed to bake pies, and perhaps some cookies and muffins if she could manage them before collapsing from exhaustion.

She moved toward the counter at the back of the kitchen and sifted flour into a mixing bowl for a couple pie crusts.

She might not be making as much money as she would have if more people came directly to the bakery, but she wasn't about to complain. Maybe if she worked hard enough for the next two months, she could scrounge up the funds she'd need to pay down her mortgage.

If Mr. Sinclair didn't find a way to get his hands on her money first.

And if the robber didn't return.

She tossed a few dashes of sugar into the pie crust and reached for her canister of lard.

"Mrs. Danell."

She cringed at the sound of the sharp male voice coming from the front of her shop.

"Mrs. Danell!"

Brushing her hands off on her apron, she scurried out of the kitchen.

"Mr. Ranulfson." She smiled brightly. Surely he'd be happy to hear of her expected growth in revenue. "What brings you by on this fine—"

"Do you know where your son is?" he demanded.

"He's at the lighthouse doing chores for Mr. Oakton." The smile dropped from her face. "Why? Is something wrong? Did something happen to him?"

"Nothing happened *to* him." Mr. Ranulfson stalked back and forth across the small confines of her bakery. "It's what happened *because* of him."

"Because of him?" She twisted her hands in her apron.

"He punched my son in the nose. Dr. Greely says it's broken."

"I… ah… there must be some mistake. Colin doesn't go around punching other children." He didn't know how to fight; that was one thing she'd made certain his father never taught him.

Mr. Ranulfson stopped pacing and planted his hands on the counter, leaning over the rough wooden planks to stare straight into her eyes. "Oh, your son punched him all right. My Erik wouldn't make up such a story, nor could he feign a broken nose. Rowley Gleason and Jedidiah Fletcher were there as well. All three of them blame your boy."

Her hands wrung tighter in the fabric of her apron. "I-I don't know what to say. I'm sorry. I had no idea. I'll bring Colin home immediately, and I'll… I'll pay for the bill from Dr. Greely."

And she would, no matter how big a sum.

"Yes, Mrs. Danell. You absolutely will." Mr. Ranulfson straightened and repositioned the hat on his head before turning sharply and shoving through the door.

Tressa looked down at her hands, now shaking. She'd never allow Colin to do such a thing again, even if she had to lock him in his room for the entire summer—after he found a way to pay Dr. Greely's bill, that was.

She stomped back into the kitchen, checking the still-baking bread before darting out the back door to Jessalyn's. Hopefully the other woman would be able to spare half an hour to watch the store while she confronted Colin.

Ten minutes later, she tromped her way down Center Street toward the harbor, while Jessalyn was tucked into the bakery's kitchen with her three flaxen-haired girls. Turning onto Front Street, crowded with townsfolk hurrying to and fro, Tressa dodged an elderly man, then darted through a pack of younger children, only to run smack into a man's chest.

He wore a three-piece suit, but unlike Mr. Ranulfson's and Mr. Sinclair's attire, this suit smelled of tobacco smoke and cheap perfume.

She drew her gaze up and held back the disgust itching to crawl onto her face. "What are you doing here?"

Reed Herod stared down at her with eyes that were blue enough to belong to an angel, but had somehow been given to a fiend, a face smooth enough to belie the decade or more he'd been in the brothel business, and lips charming enough to hoodwink men and women alike. The years had been kind to him, kinder than they should have been given the den of iniquity he ran at Central.

"I'm here on business." He spoke easily, his voice filled with the smoothness he likely used to lure in brothel girls.

A shiver skittered up her spine. "I doubt Eagle Harbor wants anything to do with your kind of business."

He chuckled at that, long and low. "Ah, little Tressa Prynne, how long has it been? A decade? And you're still as innocent as I remember."

"Danell. It's Tressa Danell now." And he, of all people, should remember that.

His lips flattened into a firm line, and he ran his eyes down her body. His gaze wasn't lustful, but cold, calculating—which was almost worse.

Almost.

"Do you ever regret it, Tressa? You could've saved yourself a decade of hard living working for me."

"No."

"Certainly you're aware none of my girls dress in discarded rags such as that atrocity you're wearing."

She crossed her arms over her chest, as much to shield the patched spot just above her waist as to defy him. Could he see the way her hands trembled? Did her eyes show her fear? Either way, she needed to get away from him. "If you'll excuse me, I have an errand to run."

She took a step around him, but he reached out to snake a hand about her upper arm. "Not so quickly, I'm afraid. I was on my way to your bakery to speak with you."

"M-me? I don't have any business to conduct with you." That possibility had ended the day she married Otis.

"I think this is a conversation we best have in private." He attempted to pull her off the road and toward the shadows between the warehouse and shipping offices.

Because that was just where she needed to be found, standing in an alley alone with a brothel owner. She dug her heels into the dirt and jerked her arm away. "Anything you have to say to me can be said out here."

His charming blue eyes scanned the street, ever busy with wagons and passersby. Several sailors on the other side of the road watched them, as did the farmer with the vegetable-laden cart rolling down the road.

"Fine." Mr. Herod pulled a piece of paper from his pocket. "You're aware, I'm sure, that your husband's logging camp this winter was only two miles from Central. During that time, he totaled up a bill of sixty-two dollars and forty-three cents at The Dark Stallion, which was to be garnished from his wages come spring. Seeing how your husband was killed just before the spring thaw, this, Mrs. Danell, is for you." He handed her the paper. "I don't suppose you have enough funds to pay me in full?"

She scanned the sheet with its frightfully neat handwriting. "It's too much."

"Everything's written out clearly." He tapped the long column of expenses.

"But you have bills for... for..." Her throat closed off.

"Women?" Mr. Herod chuckled. "Don't tell me you assumed your louse of a husband was faithful. You might be innocent, but you've never been daft."

Heat bubbled through her veins, and she shoved the paper against in his chest. "I'm not paying a cent. How dare you ask me to compensate you for my late husband's indiscretions."

He took the paper back from her and slipped it into his pocket. "I assure you, Mrs. Danell, this is a perfectly legitimate bill. If needed, I can bring you before the magistrate. It won't be the first time I've had to force payment."

Tressa cringed at the thought of standing before the magistrate up in Central and putting Otis's habits on public display for the entire mining town. And the magistrate probably wouldn't care that she was being asked to pay for her husband's trysts, not when he likely visited Mr. Herod's establishment himself. "Fine, then. I'll pay you in bread."

"Bread?"

She licked her suddenly dry lips. "I'll bake it for you to serve at your saloon and your profit will work down Otis's debt."

He ran his gaze down her again, and this time there was nothing calculating about it. "There's a quicker way for you to pay off that debt, if you're so inclined."

She met his eyes despite the leer shining overly bright in them. "Not just bread, but pies, muffins, and cookies. I'll only trade baked goods for my debt."

"I'm afraid that will take too long for me to recover my losses. Though if you come work for me..."

"Never."

"Fine. I'm a reasonable man, Tressa, so I'll accept payments of fifteen dollars a month. In fact, I'll give you until August to start paying. You'll be settled up before Christmas that way. But if I don't receive a payment, the next time I see you, it will be before the magistrate." He straightened his waistcoat and took a step past her, looking back over his shoulder as he spoke. "You could take that boy of yours to the mine to earn the extra money for you. However you need to get it, I want what you owe."

He sauntered down the road, turning onto Center Street as though he hadn't a care in the world. And she supposed he didn't. After all, he wasn't the one with a collection of debts that grew larger each day. Why, he could probably wipe away Otis's entire tab without feeling a pinch in his finances.

He could, but he wouldn't. Because he was just as set on making money as Mr. Sinclair was.

Never mind that her dream of providing a good home for Colin and a decent living for herself slipped farther from her fingers.

"Mrs. Danell."

She turned at the sound of her name to find a towering oak tree of a man moving toward her.

"I figured you'd be at the bakery."

"I, ah..." She looked up at him. Mr. Oakton was bigger than Otis had been—which was saying something given her late, logger husband's burly muscles. But rather than wear a perpetual scowl like Otis had, the corners of his lips always seemed to twitch up into a half grin, and his eyes always carried a hint of merriment.

Though those cheerful eyes flickered with concern just now. "Are you unwell? You look pale."

She pressed a hand to her cheeks. Was she pale? How could she not be after Mr. Reed's dastardly proposal and the suggestion Colin work at Central?

"Were you headed somewhere?" He looked up and down the street before offering his arm. "I'll walk you."

"Actually, I was going to find Colin." Whom she suddenly wanted to crush in a very big, very tight hug... about two seconds before she lectured him for breaking Erik Ranulfson's nose.

"I was coming to talk to you."

"You were?" She wiped a strand of hair out of her face. Why did his seeking her out make her feel so... so...?

What? It shouldn't make her feel anything.

"Yep. I was wondering if I could take Colin to Sunday school tomorrow."

"Absolutely not." That boy was going to spend every spare second he had working to pay off the bill for Erik Ranulfson's nose.

His forehead drew down into a perplexed expression. "Sorry. Didn't realize you had such an aversion to church."

"Church? Oh, no. I don't have anything against church." Tressa glanced down Front Street to where the white clapboard building stood with its steeple. The building didn't look intimidating, not with its four-paned windows, clean siding, and small bell tower. In fact, it didn't look much different from the chapel at Central that had readily invited her and the other miners' children to Sunday school when she'd been younger. "Colin's just never seemed interested in going before."

"It's only for a couple hours. You can get some baking done while we're gone."

"Or you could go with them." A stranger wearing a dusty hat, who'd evidently stopped beside them on the street, decided to interject himself into their private conversation. "We'd love to have you both."

She stiffened and glared at him.

Mac sent the man a look as well, though she wasn't able to interpret the message hidden inside it.

She squinted at the stranger, who looked pretty well planted to the road. Maybe he hadn't stopped beside them at all. Had he been there the entire time and she just now noticed?

No. Of course she would have noticed the tall man with kind gray eyes sooner. Being around Mr. Oakton didn't make her oblivious to everything.

"I'm Elijah Cummings, by the way." He tipped his hat to her, revealing a wealth of caramel colored hair beneath it.

Elijah Cummings. She'd never met him, but she'd heard of him before—a person couldn't be in Eagle Harbor a week without hearing of the Cummings family. Elijah was the oldest Cummings son, the one who'd been away when their pa had died last month.

"And you are?" Mr. Cummings looked at her expectantly.

"I'm sorry for not making introductions," Mr. Oakton stated. "Elijah, this is Tressa Danell, owner of Eagle Harbor's one and only bakery. Mrs. Danell, this is Elijah Cummings, Hiram and Mabel Cummings's oldest son."

The skin around the other man's eyes crinkled in question. "Danell, as in related to Otis Danell?"

A faint warmth stole across her cheeks. "He was my husband, yes."

Hopefully that information didn't make him think she and her late husband were cut from the same cloth.

And why did she let such things bother her? Mr. Cummings was nothing but a stranger.

A stranger who was friends with Mac Oakton.

Not that Mr. Oakton's opinion of her mattered a whit either. She certainly didn't need his approval to sell bread.

Mr. Oakton cleared his throat. "Otis passed away this spring. Logging accident."

"I'm sorry for your loss." Mr. Cummings tipped his hat toward her again.

"Thank you."

"I suppose you'd like to collect Colin?" Mr. Oakton glanced down the road toward the lighthouse. "I left him picking up rocks and sticks on the lawn. After he finishes with that, he's going to—"

"Talk to me. The boy is about to receive one rather long lecture." She'd make him finish his work for Mr. Oakton and then walk him by every shop in Eagle Harbor until he scrounged up enough spare jobs he could pay for Dr. Greely's services. And if that wasn't enough punishment, she'd think of something else. But one thing was certain, her son would never, ever break a person's nose again.

She started toward the lighthouse. She'd already wasted too much time today. Jessalyn shouldn't have to spend her entire morning at the bakery.

A strong hand clamped down on her shoulder, swinging her back around. "You're going to lecture him for picking up rocks?"

She blew out a breath that ruffled the strands of hair falling into her face. "No, for punching Erik Ranulfson. Now, if you men will excuse me."

She tore away from them and moved down the street at a brisk pace. The lighthouse stood tall and proud atop the rocks at the end of the road, just beyond the pier where a three-masted ship was docked and workers scrambled to unload the cargo. She barely glanced at the men she passed before starting up the rocky path to the lighthouse.

Colin stood on the grass near the kerosene shed, bending and straightening as he retrieved debris from the yard and put it into the tin pail he carried.

"Colin William Danell, you've got some explaining to do."

Colin dropped his pail and rushed to meet her. "Ma, you won't believe what happened! Erik Ranulfson—"

"Yes, Erik Ranulfson. You broke his nose. His father said you punched him."

The grin on Colin's face faded. "I broke it?"

"You most certainly did. Punching another boy in the face, Colin. Truly?"

Colin peered behind her, likely at Mr. Oakton and Mr. Cummings, whom she assumed had followed. "I was just doing like Mr. Oakton said."

"Mr. Oakton?" The man who'd just asked to take her son to Sunday school?

"And it worked, Ma. It really worked!" Colin's eyes shone with hope and the grin inched back onto his face.

A grin. Over breaking another child's nose. She'd never taught him to be happy over hurting anyone or anything, but someone else clearly had.

She planted her hands on her hips and turned to glare at Mr. Oakton.

⌐.⌐.⌐.⌐.⌐

The second Mrs. Danell's hands landed on her slim hips, Mac swallowed. Then he stuck a finger in his collar and tugged.

Unfortunately the action did little to loosen the suddenly constricting material.

She took a step toward him and tilted her nose in the air, never mind she didn't even reach his chin. "Did you tell my child to break Erik Ranulfson's nose?"

Colin had broken the ruffian's nose? He must not have been close enough to hear that part of the conversation. Hang it all, the boy was a quick study.

"Probably deserved it," Elijah muttered beside him.

Mrs. Danell turned blazing eyes on Elijah. "I beg your pardon?"

Mac glanced at Colin, whose little shoulders had started to droop. "I didn't tell him to break noses. I taught him to defend himself."

"Defend himself?" The more agitated she became, the more pronounced her accent grew. Maybe it was Cornish after all, though subtle enough not to sound rough or harsh. "So you told him fighting was all right?"

Elijah chuckled, then gave him a thump on the back. "Why do I feel as though I've been in this conversation a hundred times already?"

Elijah had certainly had this conversation before, though he used to fight with Gilbert Sinclair rather than one of the Ranulfson boys. Mac resisted the urge to smile at the memories. There had always been less shrieking and more bellowing, seeing how Hiram Cummings was usually the one lecturing. And the chiding usually ended with Elijah's backside getting tanned.

"Do you think this is amusing, Mr. Oakton?" Mrs. Danell stepped near enough the tips of her shoes touched his own. She glared up at him.

The disapproval in her eyes might have been effective—had she not stood a half-foot shorter than him.

"I sent my son up here assuming you were having him work, not teaching him to be a hooligan."

"But Erik was trying to take my money," Colin wailed. "He said he was going to take my quarters before I could give them to you because you were a... a..." His cheeks burst into little flames, and he glanced at his mother. "I can't say it, Ma, because it's not true."

Her jaw opened and closed once, twice before she clamped her mouth shut.

Mac crouched down and looked Colin straight in the eye. "Did you tell your Ma what Erik and his friends did yesterday?"

Colin shook his head.

"Yesterday?" Her voice was whisper soft this time. "There was trouble yesterday?"

"And the day before that." Mac stood and rested a hand on the boy's shoulder. "Go on. Tell your ma."

"I... uh..." Colin dug the toe of his worn shoe into the dirt. "Ever since Pa died, Erik Ranulfson's taken a disliking to me. First, he started snitching my lunch at school, and now that school's out, he tries to take whatever I've got, like the quarter I earned for sweeping the porch at the general store. That's why Mr. Oakton walked me home two days ago. He found me and offered me two quarters just to be nice. Then yesterday when I was fishing, Erik stole our fish. We had three of them, Ma." He looked up hopefully at his mother. "Mr. Oakton saw what Erik and his friends had done to me and said he'd teach me to fight. He said I should learn to defend what's mine. There's nothing wrong with wanting to keep my fish or my quarters, is there?"

She pressed a hand to her lips and blinked once, twice, before her voice emerged soft and shaky. "Why didn't you tell me?"

"You were busy with the bakery." Colin went into his mother's arms and spoke with his head pressed against her chest. "I didn't want to be a bother."

"I wish you'd told me sooner." Tenderness wreathed her face, and she planted a gentle kiss atop Colin's head. "And you're never a bother."

A lump lodged in Mac's throat, though he couldn't precisely say why. He'd never doubted Mrs. Danell's love for her boy, and yet, seeing her hug him and tend to him caused a wealth of long-forgotten emotions to rise in his chest. Had his mother ever treated him in such a manner? He reckoned so, before she'd disappeared.

Mrs. Danell brushed hair back from Colin's face. "Had I known, I wouldn't have agreed to pay Erik's doctor's bill when Mr. Ranulfson came by the bakery."

The boy pushed away from her. "You have to give Mr. Ranulfson more money?"

"We'll see about that. First, we're going to make a list of all the things Erik has taken from you, starting with that very first lunch. Then we'll go to the bank and compare the bill from Dr. Greely to the one for Erik's theft and see who owes whom money."

Colin gave a nod. "Sounds right good, Ma. Right good."

"Come. Let's make that list and stop by the bank. Then you can come back here and work some more."

Colin grabbed her hand.

"Mr. Oakton, do you mind if my son takes a break?" She turned to look at him.

"Not at all," he croaked.

Hand in hand, Mrs. Danell and her son started for town, but she paused for a moment and cast a glance over her shoulder.

"Thank you." She didn't speak the words so much as mouth them, then she smiled softly.

The same smile that had taken over her face when she'd

watched him and Colin smear each other with strawberry pie. The gentle curve of her lips softened her entire face and made her appear innocent, trusting, little more than a girl herself rather than a woman who'd spent too many years married to the likes of Otis Danell.

"Mac ole' boy," Elijah slung an arm around his shoulder. "You should've told me you'd snagged yourself a sweetheart."

A sweetheart? Mac rubbed the back of his neck, which suddenly seemed to burn hot. "But I haven't."

"Could've fooled me."

"It's not like that. She's just…" *determined, smart, spunky, adorable when her shoes were covered in dough, flour smudged her cheeks, and strawberry pie filling dripped down her neck.* "…someone who needs a friend. And I know what that can be like in Eagle Harbor."

"Friend, huh?" Elijah's eyes twinkled. "You should invite her to the beach tonight."

Would she dance with him if she came? Give him another glimpse of that gentle smile? "I'll have to leave at dusk. Lighthouse to tend and all that."

"I still think she'd come." Elijah watched as she and Colin made their way down Front Street. "If the right person asked."

Chapter Seven

His belly full from lunch at the lighthouse, Elijah paused on his walk down Front Street and glanced over his shoulder. Sure enough, Mac's towering form tromped down the side of the hill the lighthouse sat upon, heading in the opposite direction. Elijah whistled, pretending as though he didn't know exactly where Mac was headed or what he intended to ask Mrs. Tressa Danell once he reached the bakery.

His giant of a friend had found a woman. Good. It was more than he could say about himself.

Or rather, he supposed he'd found a woman as well—just not one he could marry.

He straightened and stared at the two towering mansions that sat side by side near the intersection of Front and Center Street. Belonging to the Sinclair and Donnelly families, they presided over the town much the way European castles of old must have towered over a village of peasants. They stood two stories taller than the clapboard and log-hewn structures that comprised the rest of Eagle Harbor, and that was about how the shipping tycoon families thought of themselves—two levels above everybody else.

But not Victoria.

Had she married by now? She'd certainly been away long

enough to find a husband, likely one who'd set her up in a house ten times more lovely than the mansion on Center Street.

A house a hundred times fancier than the rambling cabin his family owned on Lake Superior.

Maybe Mac had the right of it. He needed to find a woman who lived in his world of rigging and fish guts rather than one who lived in a world of silk and gold.

"Elijah! Elijah Cummings!" Elijah paused and searched the street that ran along the harbor's beach. A horse and buggy tromped by and a group of Cousin Jacks sauntered along the far side of the street, their Cornish heritage evident by the rough lilt in their speech. To his left, workers loaded a ship that had come in that morning, hauling scores upon scores of copper ingots up the ramp onto the deck before the copper was taken deep inside the vessel.

"Elijah!"

He turned fully around to find Mrs. Kainner rushing towards him.

"Thank goodness I found you. It's terrible. Just terrible." She waved her hand wildly toward the dock. "We have to do something."

He blinked and glanced at the dock again. Everything looked to be in order. "What's the problem?"

"The rose bushes! Byron Sinclair wants to pull them out. I told him no, but does he listen? Of course not! Claims they get in his workers' way."

The row of rose bushes growing in the rocky soil on the far side of the dock had been around for as long as he could remember, a large, overgrown type of division between the lighthouse grounds and town pier.

Mrs. Kainner's body shook, causing her tightly coiled gray hair to bounce. "Do you know how many hours the Eagle Harbor Beautification Society spends pruning those bushes every year?"

Not many, by the look of it. Maybe if the beautification society spent more time working and less time gossiping, the bushes wouldn't—

"You can't let Mr. Sinclair tear those roses out. It's town property. He's got no authority to do so!"

"That's true." But it was the sort of thing Byron Sinclair would do whether he had authority or not.

Which was precisely why he'd left Eagle Harbor. Shouldn't all men be held to the same laws and standards regardless of how much money they had? "What, exactly, do you expect me to do, Mrs. Kainner?"

The older woman gave an exasperated huff. "Why, say something at the next town council meeting. Make sure Byron Sinclair is ordered to leave those bushes alone."

"I'm not on the town council. That was my father." And he didn't even know when the next meeting was.

She blinked and tilted her head up at him, her bony little nose pointing into the air. "You're not going to take Hiram's place?"

"No." The word came out harsh, and Mrs. Kainner blinked again. "That is, I won't be staying in town long."

"But your father…" The widow's lips puckered into a pathetic little frown.

His father. Yes. His father was great. His father was perfect. His father could do anything and everything under the sun according to half the town, even walk on water.

No, not water. Pa had been able to do everything but walk on water. He glanced to the south where the cemetery rose on the hill overlooking the town. The wound in his heart, cauterized after spending a morning with Mac, opened anew.

"My father can't be replaced, Mrs. Kainner. Least of all by me." His voice held a rawness he didn't dare contemplate.

"So you're not going to save the roses?" Her jaw trembled, and Elijah had a sick feeling the shaking was due to a budding sob rather than her previous indignation.

"Mrs. Kainner, I really—"

"What if Mr. Sinclair takes your father's position on the town council?" Mrs. Kainner eyes grew round and moisture glinted in them. "Will we do something then?"

If Byron Sinclair took his father's seat on the council, the town would have much bigger problems to worry about than roses. "I believe council members have to be full-time residents of Eagle Harbor. Byron Sinclair only lives in Eagle Harbor for the summer."

But who would take his father's position on the council? Would the town vote, or did the other council members appoint someone until the next election was held?

Why was he even pondering the matter? He was only staying in town long enough to see to Ma and his siblings.

And now that he was thinking about siblings, was that Rebekah down on the beach?

In men's britches and one of Pa's old shirts?

"If you'll excuse me, Mrs. Kainner." He stepped away from her and strode toward his sister bent over an unfamiliar dingy.

"Don't forget about the roses!" she called after him.

Roses. He had a ma who sat in a rocking chair all day, a sister who dressed like a man, and a shipyard that would slip away from him if he wasn't in Port Huron shortly. Why not add roses to his list of concerns?

He tromped down the incline that led from the road to the beach and across the wide swath of sand that rimmed the inside of the harbor. Sure enough, his sister stood at the side of a little rowboat he vaguely remembered one of the townsfolk owning.

"What are you doing?"

She quirked an eyebrow at him and continued piling fish into crates. "You grew up with the same pa I did. Do you really need to ask what happens to fish once I haul them to shore?"

"Where's Isaac?"

Rebekah snorted. "Back home in the workshop. Did you think he'd be anywhere else?"

"You mean you went out on the lake alone?" He thundered the words so loud some of the dockworkers turned toward them.

Rebekah tossed a fish into the crate and straightened, arms crossed and chin high. "Yes. I went out alone. The fish won't catch themselves. I can't get Isaac near the water, and you've been sailing the Atlantic for two years. Somebody has to earn money." She reached for a crate and hefted it over the side of the dinghy.

"Perhaps so, but that person isn't you. What if a storm came up? What if you couldn't row back to shore quickly enough to escape it?" He clamped a hand on the back of his neck, unwilling to let his mind wander to what exactly would have happened had a storm blown in. "Go home where you belong, put on a skirt, and stop traipsing around town like a man."

Rebekah set the crate back in the boat and jabbed a finger at him. "Don't tell me what I can and can't do. You weren't here. You don't know. I watched Pa die. *I watched him!*" Her eyes, which had been flashing with green fire, suddenly filled with tears. "A dinghy was sitting on the beach. I should've taken it. Oh, why didn't I take it? I might have saved him."

She covered her eyes with her hands—hands that were far from clean after handling the fish.

"You're not a life-saver." He walked around the side of the boat and reached for her, but she pulled away.

"So that means I had to watch Pa die?" Tears streaked down her dirty cheeks and fell to the sand. "Never again, Elijah. Do you hear me? Never again will I stand helplessly by. I'll buy the Foley's dinghy and work like a man until I'm old and gray if that's what it takes to care for my family. But I refuse to watch my mother starve while my brothers go off and do whatever they please." She sniffled as more tears ran down her face. "Now if you'll excuse me, I've got fish to ice."

She hefted a crate and stalked up the beach to the fish house.

He reached for a crate to follow, but then dropped his arms helplessly to his side and turned toward the mouth of the harbor. She was right. He didn't have the foggiest notion how it would have felt to watch Pa's ship go down. But of one thing he was certain: Had he been Rebekah, Mac and Isaac wouldn't have been able to keep him away from the dinghy.

Instead, he'd been clear across the ocean when Pa had drowned.

Mac had said this morning that God had a plan in all of this. Did He? And if so, where was it? He couldn't see any plan at all, just a deep, confusing mess.

And a shipyard waiting in Port Huron.

Chapter Eight

"Come on, Ma. Walk faster." Colin stopped several yards ahead of her on the street and then ran back to tug on Tressa's hand.

Fiddle music played from the waterfront, where waves lapped gently against the sand and a crowd had gathered on the beach. A mosquito buzzed near her ear and frogs sang out in a chorus that fought against the lively tune. The sun had begun its westward descent, but didn't yet hang low over the water, leaving them another couple hours of daylight.

All in all, it was a rather perfect evening for a stroll.

"You're barely moving." Colin gave her hand another tug.

"I'm enjoying the evening." Or trying to, given the unsettled sensation in her stomach and the damp, clammy feel of her hands. Mr. Oakton might have invited them, but how was she supposed to set aside her worries for a few hours and have fun when she might be kicked out of her home before the end of summer?

She should have declined the invitation and stayed home to bake pies for the mercantile, never mind Colin's round eyes pleading for her to accept Mr. Oakton's offer. Then again, maybe Mr. Oakton had made it a point to ask in front of Colin so she couldn't say no.

"Ma," Colin groaned. "I won't have any time to play if you

keep walking so slow."

"Run along without me, and I'll be there in a few minutes."

He bolted toward the beach like a horse broken free from a boulder-laden wagon.

She continued at her own pace. Maybe tonight wouldn't be so bad. Colin was clearly excited, and perhaps she'd meet another shop owner willing to sell her bread. Between Colin and the bakery, she didn't get out much and visit, not like some of the women in town did. It probably wasn't neighborly of her, but though Eagle Harbor was a fairly small town, she'd only gotten to know a handful of people in the year she'd been living here.

Voices grew louder along with the strains of fiddle music. Tressa stepped off Front Street onto the sandy beach. A fire blazed in the center of a small crowd, and a few couples danced off to the left. Children were building sand castles along the shore for what looked to be some sort of competition, and Colin hunched over one of the castles with two other boys.

Mr. Oakton must not have arrived yet. Head and shoulders taller than most, he should've been easy to spot.

Tressa scanned the crowd for someone familiar. A flash of flaxen hair caught her eye. Jessalyn. If nothing else, she could hold little Megan for a few hours and let Jessalyn talk, dance, and eat without a babe pinned to her hip.

"Tressa, you came." Jessalyn wove through the crowd. Claire clung to the bottom of her mother's skirt, casting frightened, wide-eyed glances at the adults towering above her, while Megan pressed against Jessalyn's shoulder, her little face scrunched up as though she was about to cry. "Have you eaten yet? The fish is superb."

"No, but let me take Megan."

"If you can. She won't go to anyone tonight."

Likely not with the commotion. Tressa held out her arms.

Megan's face contorted more, and Tressa rubbed her hand over the soft hair atop the babe's head. "Easy now. There's a lot of people out and about tonight, but you still love your auntie Tressa, don't you?"

Megan's face relaxed and she reached for Tressa with a soft coo before nestling her downy head in the crook of Tressa's shoulder.

"That's it, love." She stroked a hand down Megan's little spine. "You've got a soft spot for me, don't you?"

Jessalyn grinned. "As I said the other night, you look good with a babe in your arms."

"Mrs. Dowrick, there you are." Clifford, the oldest of Ruby Spritzer's ever-expanding brood, came up behind them, a wide grin playing across his face.

Jessalyn glanced toward the shoreline. "It looks like you escaped the sand castle competition for a few minutes."

"I told Leroy and Martin I'd play for about a half hour before I went off to find some food. Suzanna and Grace are there too, but the girls don't have a habit of running off the way the boys do." Clifford shrugged. "The young'uns stayed home with Ellie and Ma, so I don't have too many to watch."

What would it be like to keep an eye on four children somewhere like this, especially when Clifford wasn't quite an adult himself? Tressa glanced toward the growing collection of sand castles. Having Colin at the beach away from her with so many others here was enough to make her nervous.

"Cliffy!" Claire cried as she released her mother's skirt and clapped her hands.

"Hey there, Claire girl." Clifford hunched down to Claire's level. "Feeling a little shy tonight?"

Rather than bury herself into her mother's skirt again, Claire simply nodded and popped a thumb in her mouth.

"You feel like a horsey ride?"

Tressa nearly laughed. As though there was any way shy little Claire Dowrick would leave her mother's side in such a crowd.

But the girl nodded her head and reached for Clifford. "Me like horsey rides."

Clifford swung her onto his shoulders. "Hold on tight." He planted Claire's pudgy little hands against each of his cheeks and stood.

With the way Clifford's narrow, lanky form already loomed above everybody else's, Claire towered over the crowd.

Tressa narrowed her eyes at the child. Since when did Claire go to anyone besides her mother?

The child's face bunched up into a brilliant smile, and she pointed. "Water pretty."

"Oops. Keep a hold of me, baby doll. You don't want to fall, do you?"

She shook her head vigorously.

A tender smile wreathed Jessalyn's face as she watched her delighted child. "Have fun on your horsey ride, Claire."

"Go, horsey, go!" Claire bounced on his shoulders.

"We'll go in a minute." Clifford turned to Jessalyn. "So I talked to Jake Ranulfson, and he said we can use his pa's boat on Tuesday if the young'uns want to go sailing."

Jessalyn glanced at the harbor and then back at Clifford. "Are you sure it's all right?"

"You know how Leroy can be. Once he gets an idea in his head, he won't let it go. I've been promising to take him and some of the others sailing for half the summer, and Claire's always been fascinated with the sailboats." His eyes sought Tressa's. "Colin's invited too, Mrs. Danell."

Claire giggled and pointed again. "Sailboat. Sailboat."

"I suppose they can go, but I'd like to come as well," Jessalyn said.

Clifford shrugged despite the joyful little weight on his shoulders. "That should be fine."

"Go, horsey. Go, horsey." Claire bounced on his shoulders.

"Colin might be working at the lighthouse, but if not, he can go," Tressa added.

"I'll let you know what time." Clifford repositioned his grip on Claire's legs and turned toward the water. "Want to go look at the sandcastle your sister's building?"

"Sandcrastle. Sandcrastle," Claire echoed, and they started off through the crowd.

"At least she's easy to spot up on his shoulders." Jessalyn smiled after them.

"I'm amazed she'll go to him when she refuses everybody else." Tressa repositioned Megan against her chest. The babe yawned and snuggled in.

"You remember how Thomas left when Claire was still a babe?" Jessalyn's cheeks flushed and she stared down at her hands. "Around the same time, Clifford's ma had a pregnancy that went bad. He took a liking to Claire right off."

"He's a good boy, always looking after his brothers and the like."

"Ruby was worried he'd turn out like his pa, but he's nothing like Merrick, though I don't know what Ruby will do when Clifford goes off to find work. She has so many little ones running about she can hardly watch them all."

"Ellie's old enough to help these days. And I'm sure Ruby can use the money Clifford could make." Though in truth, she was surprised Clifford wasn't working already. He was certainly old enough to get a job in the mine at Central or even on one of Byron

Sinclair's ships. But Jessalyn was right. Ruby would struggle even more with her brood without Clifford to help.

"But if Merrick takes whatever money Clifford makes..." Jessalyn shrugged. "Maybe that's why he's still at home."

Tressa swallowed. She'd not thought of that. Her late husband might have swindled half the town, but thankfully he'd always found extra money on his own, letting her keep the little she put by for necessities.

"Come now. You've yet to eat." Jessalyn pulled her toward the fire at the center of the crowd, which turned out to be two fires—a large one where people congregated, and a small one with a rack set above it for roasting fish and potatoes. "Have you ever tasted Rebekah Cummings's fish? It's the best on the Keweenaw Peninsula."

Two youths handed out baskets of cooled fish and potatoes, and a woman in trousers turned the food over the fire.

"Here you go, ma'am." One of the young men thrust a basket into her free hand.

"Thank you."

The woman at the fire narrowed her eyes at Tressa.

She took a step back. She'd seen Rebekah Cummings around town a time or two, though the other woman had never come into the bakery. She was beautiful, if one looked past the men's garb to her unblemished skin, softly pointed chin, intense eyes, and the rich, thick hair that was only half pulled up, the rest falling in heavy waves about her shoulders.

But the rigid way she held herself bore little resemblance to Elijah Cummings's easy manner, and their hair certainly wasn't alike. If she hadn't known they were siblings already, she never would have guessed they were related.

"Excuse me, ladies." Sheriff Jenkins stopped beside her and

reached for his own basket of fish—probably not his first of the night given the way the man's stomach protruded above the waist of his trousers.

"Oh, Sheriff. I've been needing to talk to you." Tressa handed the baby back to Jessalyn. "Have you gotten any further with—"

"I haven't found your money, Mrs. Danell." He shoved a bite of potato in his mouth. "And like I told you last time, I don't expect to recover it. Now if you'll excuse me."

He moved past her, his food in hand.

"Have you made any inquires?" She trailed behind him, squeezing her way through the people that seemed intent on swallowing him in the crowd. "Surely you must be a little closer to finding who took it."

"I told ya, it was likely someone Otis owed. And seeing how he owed a good many people…" Sheriff Jenkins broke through the crowd and headed down Front Street, eating as he walked.

She scrambled after him as he headed toward The Rusty Wagon.

"But have you asked around? I mean, if he owed that many people, maybe someone bragged about finding a way to get money from him. Maybe that's the person who's been robbing me."

"You're not gonna listen, are you?" He stopped just short of the saloon steps.

Tinny music punctuated by ribald laughter poured out the open windows and into the evening. A group of men brushed past, loggers by the look of their flannel shirts and boots.

The sheriff ran his eyes down her once, and shook his head. "I've been sheriff in these parts for nigh on twenty years now. The money's gone. I ain't gonna be able to get it back. That's the way it goes with these types of things. You seem like the honorable type, the hard working sort of woman, which makes me wonder how you ever got yourself hitched to a man like Otis, but if someone stole from you to get back at your husband, they'd have spent the money on cards and women before the week was out. It ain't gonna still be lying around somewhere."

"But…" She hadn't planned to say anything seeing how so little had been stolen the first two times, but it seemed like the robber didn't have any intention of stopping. "The thief came back last week. I'd hidden the money box in the kitchen behind the sack of flour, and he still found it."

The sheriff sighed. "How much?"

"Everything." Her eyes burned. "You have to stop him, because I can't afford to keep losing money like this. He took almost an entire mortgage payment."

"I'll try to keep an eye out around your place. See if I can spot someone sneaking in the back." He tugged up the trousers that sagged below his protruding stomach despite the suspenders he wore. "That's your best hope, to catch him in the act."

She blinked. Somehow she couldn't imagine the large man before her catching anyone, ever.

His trousers stayed up for a second or two before slipping right back down beneath his girth. "Does he come at a certain time? Day or night?"

"Always in the evening, after the shop is closed." The first time the back door had been unlocked, but she'd been locking it tight whenever she left ever since, yet he still seemed to find a way inside.

"Even if he's caught, you'll not be getting back any of what he already took. Do you under—"

"Well I'll be. If it isn't Otis Danell's pretty wife." A man came up behind her.

"What are you doing here, sweetheart?" Another man stepped

to her side, a mariner, if his hat was any indication. "Come to give us our money back?"

"Leave her alone." The sheriff hitched up his trousers again. "This doesn't concern you."

"If you're figuring out a way for her to pay you back what Otis owed, then it concerns us."

"Yeah, we want our money back too." This from one man in a trio that stopped beside the sheriff.

"Is that Otis Danell's wife?" One of the men that had been standing on the porch with a cigar straightened. "Otis owes me five dollars from last fall. I fronted him money for a game of poker, and he took off for logging camp before paying me."

Tressa swallowed. "I'm sorry my husband owed you money, but I can't repay you."

"I find that rather hard to believe."

She froze at the sound of the cultured voice coming from the porch. Reed Herod must have come out when he'd heard the commotion.

She sucked in a breath of air that was suddenly so hot and heavy it burned her lungs, and forced herself to meet his gaze. "It's true, unless you want to be paid in bread."

"Paid in bread? What's she talking about?"

"I want my money."

"If she don't got money, I can think of another way for her to pay us."

A brief smile flickered across Mr. Herod's lips, there and then gone before anyone but her would notice.

Someone gripped her arm. She tried to tug away, but his hold only tightened.

"Yeah, I say she pays us. Now."

"She ain't one of Herod's girls, Bugsy." The sheriff's voice boomed over the group. "Any of you touch her again, and you'll find yourself in a jail cell for the night."

"I don't want to touch her. I just want my money," a man's voice wheezed.

"I say we make up a list of all the people Otis owed, and she can work her way through paying us all back."

Shouts of agreement rang through the air.

"Otis owed money to everybody." This from the sheriff again. "If you expected to see it again, you shouldn't have lent it or gambled with him in the first place."

At least the sheriff defended her, but in a group of ruffians such as this, he'd likely be the only one. She glanced at the porch again, where Reed Herod still stood, watching with an impassive face. Her stomach churned, and she couldn't stay and listen to them anymore without bursting into tears.

"I… I think I best be going." She spun and darted through the cluster of people, breaking free before anyone could stop her.

"Run if ya' want, but we'll have a list of what you owe waiting for ya' tomorrow," a man called after her.

Tressa wrapped her arms about her middle and fled down North Street toward the beach. She'd get Colin and then head home. Why had she even left the bakery tonight? As the sheriff had pointed out, this was the exact time the robber liked to come, and she'd been gone for long enough he could have already searched the entire shop.

A catcall sounded from the direction of the saloon, followed by a bout of raucous laughter. How had her husband kept company with that lot?

Because he was one of them.

If she had the chance to go back to the day she married Otis, she'd—

Smack!

She stopped short, her face pressed against the towering wall of a man.

Large hands landed on her shoulders and pushed her back a step. "Do you make a habit of running into all men, Mrs. Danell? Or just me?"

Her face warmed. She'd smacked into Reed Herod earlier that day. And Otis had certainly gotten frustrated at her habit of running into him before. "I guess I should do a better job of watching where I'm going."

Mr. Oakton chuckled, warm and deep and nothing like the mean laughter that had floated from the men outside the saloon. "At least I wasn't carrying a strawberry pie this time. Now what's wrong?"

Where to start?

But no, she wasn't going to start, because as nice as Mr. Oakton was, her problems weren't his concern.

"Sorry I was late." His voice rumbled deep in his chest. "There was trouble at the lighthouse. Grover was... well... I'm just plain sorry, I suppose."

Was that a tear slithering down her cheek? She wiped it away with her palm and looked around. They were standing at the edge of the beach, closer to the pier and lighthouse than the party. "What are you doing here?"

"Looking for you."

"Why?" She took a step back from him. "Did Otis owe you money too? Is that why you're being so nice? You thought being kind would get me to give you your money first?"

His forehead drew down. "Jessalyn was concerned when she couldn't find you after you'd walked off with the sheriff. That's why I went searching for you."

"So Otis didn't owe you anything when he died?" She swiped another tear from her cheek. That seemed unlikely. Mr. Oakton was just the type of man Otis would target. Honest and hardworking and compassionate.

"Not so much as a nickel."

She narrowed her eyes, running them over a body tall enough to stand out on the rocks and hold the lamp himself as he guided ships to harbor. His eyes darted away from her, much like Otis's always had when he'd been lying, and the tips of his ears had turned red enough she couldn't miss the change despite the golden rays of twilight. "Has anyone ever told you that the tips of your ears turn red when you lie?"

His ears turned redder yet, and a faint flush stole along the side of his neck, but his eyes came back to meet hers. "So maybe he asked for a few dollars last summer, but I never expected to see the money again."

"You're not going to ask me to repay it?"

"No."

She pressed her eyes shut. Why did his answer make her want to cry?

"Walk with me for a bit." Mr. Oakton grabbed her hand, nestling it snugly in his, and started toward the edge of the water. "We won't go too far. I need to head back to the lighthouse soon anyway. But I wanted to apologize for inviting you when I couldn't be at the gathering."

She looked over her shoulder at the cluster of people gathered around the fires. "But Colin—"

"He'll be fine. Jessalyn's there, as are Elijah and Clifford."

"Otis probably owed them money too, but they're too nice to tell me."

"Tressa." He stopped walking and planted both hands on her

shoulders, leaning down so she was forced to look him in the eye. "Your husband's gambling, squandering, and debt wasn't your fault."

"I didn't know what he was like when I married him. I promise I didn't. It's not like a man volunteers he's a wastrel when he offers for a girl nobody wants. I think about that day sometimes and wonder if I should've done something different. If I should've..." Her words trailed off, because really, what else could she have done? Reed Herod had been her only other choice.

"What day?" Mac's gentle voice could barely be heard over the lap of the waves, distant fiddle music, and muted chorus of toads and crickets.

"The day they buried Pa and I married Otis. The mine wanted their house back, and—"

"The Central Mine?"

She nodded. "We came over from Cornwall after Ma died. Pa was a big man, not unlike you, and he got a job straightaway mining copper."

"Ah, so you're a Cousin Jenny after all. That explains the lilt to your speech. Not quite Cornish, and yet not quite Midwestern either."

"You could have asked when we met. My heritage is no secret."

He swiped a strand of hair away from her face, tucking it behind her ear and causing her skin to warm with the contact. "But that would've taken away some of the mystery, and I enjoyed guessing."

Mystery? There was nothing mysterious about her. She was a plain, ordinary immigrant with an unimaginable heap of debt.

"So what happened with your father?" He kept his fingers at the spot just behind her ear, until his touch turned from a soft warmth to a steady burn.

"An explosion killed him and two others. Then the mine needed their house back, and nobody knew what to do with me."

"How old were you?"

"Six when we left Cornwall, fifteen when Pa died." She blinked back the moisture building in her eyes. She wasn't going to cry, not about the debt she owed, not about Otis's friends demanding payment, and certainly not about an event that had happened eleven years ago.

But when she looked up into Mr. Oakton's eyes, golden and gentle and caring, a lump lodged in her throat and tears burned anew.

~.~.~.~.~

Fifteen. Mac dropped his hand from her face and clenched it at his side. Now he knew what kind of woman married the likes of Otis Danell.

Not a woman at all, but a girl with nowhere to go.

He understood well enough how the mines in Copper Country operated. Companies were happy to have immigrant workers come, especially ones with mining experience from places such as Cornwall. Half the Cornish seemed to be related in one way or another, and they were always asking for jobs for their cousins and brothers and uncles back in Cornwall—most of which happened to be named Jack. So the Cousin Jacks and Cousin Jennys came and the mines rolled out company houses, one right after another. The mines then rented the houses to workers for a pittance while setting up other necessities such as stores and schools and doctors' offices. The work was hard and dirty, but if a person could stand setting off explosions underground or hauling rock for twelve hours a day, the mine took care of everything the workers needed.

But mining was hardly safe, and when immigrant workers died, their families were left with little support and oftentimes had no way to return to their homeland.

Mac ran his gaze over Mrs. Danell—Tressa. Had she had all those rich, wavy tresses at fifteen? Those eyes like maple syrup? No decent, unmarried woman north of the Portage Waterway would've considered getting hitched to Otis Danell. The man must have been thrilled when he happened upon the chance to marry Tressa, even as young as she was.

It probably wasn't even legal for her to marry so young, but the mine wouldn't have cared as long as her marriage freed the company house for a new worker's family.

"So you accepted Otis's offer because you had no other choice." His voice sounded rough, like rock being ground into sand.

She wrapped her arms around herself and shivered despite how summer's warmth tinged the breeze off the harbor. "There was another choice. Otis just looked like the better one."

Otis Danell was the better choice? "What else...?"

The stricken look on her face gave it away. Of course. A certain line of work was always available to women, especially pretty ones, and Reed Herod owned a rather big brothel over by Central.

"I would've chosen Otis too." He barely managed to get the words out before his throat dried up.

She rubbed her arms and stared out over the harbor, its calm waters a blunt contrast to the storm of emotions playing across her face. "No one told me he was a swindler. It's as I said, a man doesn't volunteer that kind of information when he offers for you."

Mac couldn't blame the man. He'd tell a couple dozen lies himself if doing so would protect Tressa in some way.

He took a step closer, the hem of her skirt brushing his trousers. A subtle warmth emanated from her, and along with it, the faint scent of sugar and baked flour. "I'm sorry, Tressa."

"For what? You haven't done anything." She stared up at him, and the waning sun kissed her skin with its golden hue.

He wanted to kiss her too, right on the tip of her nose. And then maybe he'd kiss her forehead, her jaw. He glanced at her lips and swallowed.

"Mr. Oakton?"

He exhaled, and his breath ruffled the strands of hair hanging by her cheek—the very ones he'd anchored behind her ear not five minutes ago. "Mac, you can call me Mac. And I'm sorry for your sake, not mine. I'm sorry for how you lost your pa and for the life you've had to live since."

Her gaze flitted up to his before scanning his cheeks and jaw and then skittering back up to meet his eyes again.

Had her life been that hard? Did she have so few friends she didn't know what to do with another person's sympathy?

"I, um…" Her tongue darted out to lick her lips.

And he leaned down to kiss her. Just a brief touch of his lips to hers, one that lasted only as long as the jump of a fish in the harbor, yet long enough to leave his body humming with energy.

Tressa blinked up at him, her cheeks suddenly more red than gold in spite of the sun's dying rays. "I'm to blame. It's not your fault."

"Of course it's my fault." His hands tightened on her shoulders—her shoulders? Since when was he holding her shoulders? "I'm the one who kissed you, not the other way around."

Her cheeks turned a deeper shade of red. "I-I meant about Pa dying and me marrying Otis. That's what you apologized for, isn't it?"

She was thinking about something he'd said before he'd kissed her? He released her shoulders and took a step back. He must be going about this whole kissing business wrong if her thoughts were clear and his all a jumble.

Or maybe a simple kiss didn't mean as much to her as to him. She was a widow with a child, after all. A brush of the lips probably didn't send her blood to racing seeing how she'd shared a marriage bed for over a decade.

She took a few steps away from him, which was probably good. She'd been through a lot, losing her pa, marrying Otis, facing the ill will of some townsfolk. The last thing she needed was Clive Oakton's son sullying her reputation with a kiss.

"I should head back to the lighthouse now and check on Grover, see to the lamp." And he needed to get away. Fast. Before he lost part of his heart to the woman.

Chapter Nine

What was taking so long? Tressa glanced at the clock hanging on the wall. Was it broken? Surely it had been longer than two minutes from the last time she checked.

She dug her hands into the mixture of flour, water, and lard that would soon become crust for four pies. She'd done nothing but bake since she'd gotten more places to sell her baked goods.

Well, except going to the beach last night.

And kissing Mr. Oakton—or rather, Mac.

Which brought her back to why he'd not yet returned with Colin. He'd said Sunday school and the following church service wouldn't take more than two hours. So where were they? Had something gone wrong?

She finished pressing the dough into pie plates and wiped her hands on her apron. Perhaps she should walk over to the church and check on Colin before she filled the crusts with strawberries and set them to baking.

She glanced at the clock. Three more minutes had passed. There was nothing for it. She simply had to go check on her son. She'd get nothing done until he was—

The back door to the kitchen burst open and Colin bounded inside.

"Thanks for letting me go to Sunday school, Ma! It was great!" He pranced over and wrapped her waist in a hug, burying his face in her side for an instant before he released her.

"I'm glad." She glanced toward the door Colin had left open. No broad, masculine body the size of a mountain filled the space. Was Mr. Oakton not coming?

She refused to think about the pinch of sadness that lodged in her chest. After their kiss last night, perhaps it was good he hadn't seen Colin home.

What would she do if he wanted to talk about it?

Or kiss her again?

She fanned her suddenly warm face.

"Did you know there's a story in the Bible about a man who was swallowed by a giant fish?" Colin sauntered over to the counter and plucked a cooling muffin from the baking tin.

"Yes, I've heard it." Perhaps she'd even read it once or twice before Otis had used her Bible for kindling.

"How come you never told me?"

She reached for a large spoon. "I don't know."

She'd taught him a few Bible stories—Abraham and Moses, King David, and Jesus's life, death, and resurrection. Had she somehow neglected to teach him the story of Jonah?

Probably so—God had rescued Jonah from the belly of a whale after only three days. She'd moldered for eleven years in a marriage to Otis, and now she still wasn't free from her husband, given all his debts.

What was she supposed to tell her son? *God saved Jonah but he won't save us?*

She spooned the mixture of strawberries, sugar, and flour.

"You should've come with us."

She turned to half face her son, who was happily shoving a

106

second muffin into his mouth, and plopped the strawberries into the pie. "I had a lot of baking to do."

"You could've come anyway."

At the sound of the deep voice resonating from the back door, she dropped her spoon. It hit the edge of the counter and bounced to the floor, sending strawberries across her kitchen.

"Making messes with strawberry pies again?" Mac's overlarge frame filled the doorway. "I figured you learned your lesson about that last time."

Why was her throat suddenly dry? Her face hot?

"One of those pies is for me, right? To pay me back for the one you ruined?" He came closer by two or three steps, but it seemed as though he took ten. Seemed as though he stood close enough for his arm to graze hers as it had last night, right before he'd bent down and brushed her lips with his own.

Not unless you intend to pay me five dollars for it. She willed herself to speak the words, but when she glanced up at him, still standing across the kitchen, her tongue stuck to the roof of her mouth. Was he thinking of last night too?

He shifted his feet and looked around, seemingly just as uncomfortable as she.

Did that mean he regretted the kiss?

That would be a good thing. Yes, yes, it would. If he regretted it, then there was no chance he'd do it again, and kissing a man was the last thing she wanted to be doing.

Wasn't it?

"The pies are to sell at the general store, not here. And thank you for bringing Colin back. I've been able to get a lot of baking done, though I've plenty more to do." She turned back to the pie crusts waiting on the counter and reached for another spoon.

Boots thumped behind her, and her dirty spoon clinked in the sink a moment later.

Why must he be so kind, first buying goods from her, now cleaning up her mess? She pressed her eyes shut, but doing so only brought back memories of the warm puff of his breath on her face before he kissed her, the soft feel of his lips, the tender look in his eyes afterward.

Had Otis ever kissed her like that?

Did Mac's peck even count as a kiss?

It had been simple, just a soft brush of the lips. Steeped in comfort and assurances rather than full of demands she'd never quite been able to meet.

No, Otis had never kissed her that way. Not once.

She pressed the back of her hand to her lips, now burning with the memory of that brief touch, and glanced over her shoulder at Mac.

Was she to have these memories every time she saw him? A kiss was just a kiss. Nothing special, nothing fancy, especially not when it lasted a mere second.

So why did she want another?

No, she didn't want another one. She couldn't. She had no business kissing a man she never intended to marry. And since she didn't intend to ever marry again, that pretty much took care of dreaming about more kisses.

Mac pumped water into the sink, then used a rag to wipe up the strawberry residue left on the floor. "So Colin tells me that Erik Ranulfson owes you a dollar and fifty-five cents."

"Yes, when Mr. Ranulfson found out what had been happening, he called Erik into the office at the bank and had both boys write down a list of what was taken. The lists matched fairly well, and Mr. Ranulfson insisted on paying every penny Colin claimed." At least the banker had been fair with her rather than shoving off her claims. He'd been rather furious with his son, however. "I think Colin's seen the last of Erik Ranulfson."

"Until school starts."

She turned to look at Mac, who still seemed to be standing too close even though he'd moved back to the sink. "I hadn't thought of that, but there shouldn't be a problem."

He offered up a smile. "I imagine the school at Central was a bit bigger than the one here in Eagle Harbor. Hard to ignore someone your age when you're shoved into the same one-room school house together."

"You speak as though you've had a lot of experience in the matter."

He laughed outright at that. "It's a small town, Tressa. A small town with a long memory."

She cocked her head. "Who did you use to fight with? Anyone who's still around?"

"Ma, what did the sheriff say last night?" Colin's voice sounded from the front of the bakery. "Did he find who's been stealing our money?"

"Someone's been stealing from you?" Mac thundered, his smile replaced with firm lips and a hard jaw.

"Ah…"

"Three times." Colin came back into the kitchen, a ginger cookie in his hand and a scowl on his face. "The sheriff hasn't caught him yet."

Mac didn't glance at Colin, but kept his gaze riveted to her. "Why didn't you tell me?"

Because it wasn't his concern? Something told her that answer would only get her into deeper trouble with him. Though why she was in trouble at all, she didn't know.

"I didn't want word to get out." If the sheriff was right and one of Otis's creditors was the thief, what prevented the other people Otis had owed from trying the same thing? So far she'd done a pretty good job of keeping things quiet, but with each robbery that happened, the chances of word spreading grew larger.

"Is there truth to the rumor that you're in trouble with the bank too?"

And the chances grew of that story spreading.

"And what about the rumor that there's a list of creditors at The Rusty Wagon?"

And that one. Though heaven knew she wasn't planning to tromp down to the saloon and ask for the list. She wasn't legally obligated to pay those people, was she?

"What's a creditor?" Colin popped the last bit of cookie in his mouth. "And Erik says lots of people owe money to the bank, and they're not in trouble. So how come we're in trouble for it?"

She sent Mac a furious look, though the look he sent back was just as dark, then she stomped into the storefront. The last thing she needed was for Colin to worry about losing his home more than he already did. Soon he'd be trying to convince her to let him work as a drill boy again.

"Ma?" Colin followed behind her. "You always talk about paying back Mr. Ranulfson. Why are we in trouble when nobody else is?"

She wiped off a shelf that didn't have a speck of dust on it, but at least it gave her hands something to do and kept her face away from her son. "I didn't have money to buy the bakery outright last summer, but banks will lend money for something big, like a building, and let you pay a little of the money back every month. Which is what I did for the bakery. I saved up money because I knew our winter months might be slow, but when we were robbed, well…"

Her fingers strangled the fabric of the cloth she held. "Lately, I haven't had enough to pay Mr. Ranulfson each month."

"Because someone keeps robbing us."

"Correct." She squeezed the word through her scratchy throat.

"So is that why Mr. Ranulfson might take our home?"

"Uh…"

"If you can't pay enough times, the building will go back to the bank, yes, and you'll have to leave." Mac spoke the words easily, as though he were discussing the cold spring they'd had and not that she might be homeless in a couple more months. But his gaze was intense enough to slice through her like a knife through one of her flaky pies.

Colin glanced between the two of them. "So Erik's pa can really kick us out if he wants to, and there's nothing we can do about it?"

"Yes." She forced herself to meet her son's eyes, but the heat of Mac's gaze still singed her.

"Why don't you head into the kitchen, son." Mac jutted his head toward the doorway. "Check on those muffins your ma has in the oven."

Son. Despite her ire, she drew in a soft breath at the word. Mac didn't mean it like that. He probably called every boy in town "son." And yet the word offered a glimpse of quiet nights sitting on a back porch and snowy days tucked beside a parlor fire. Of time spent fishing together and Sundays spent attending church as a family. If only…

If only nothing. It didn't matter how charming or caring or compassionate a man seemed; marriage wasn't for her.

Besides, Mac was leaving Eagle Harbor in another week or so.

"How long until Ranulfson turns you out?"

Or maybe he needed to leave town right now. Then she wouldn't have to answer questions he had no business asking.

"Tressa?" He kept his voice low, likely so Colin wouldn't hear, and came around the counter into the storefront where she stood.

She stared at the rag in her hand, more gray than white, and nearly worn through in places. There was no point in keeping it a secret. Word was already out about her being behind with the bank, and if she got kicked out come the first of August, the entire town would know before the end of that day.

"Two months. August first."

"And how much do you owe?" He was standing too close again, so close he wouldn't miss the tremble in her jaw or the way her hands shook as she twisted the rag.

"I wouldn't owe anything if I hadn't been robbed. I worked for that money. I saved it up. I had enough to pay everything with extra on top."

"How much?"

"Fifty dollars to the bank, and seventy-two dollars and thirty-six cents gone in the robberies. The robber empties my money box each time."

His hand settled on her shoulder, or maybe not precisely her shoulder, but at the curve where her shoulder met her neck. She raised her gaze to his and found compassion so rich and thick that she could nigh cloak herself in it come winter.

Would he kiss her again? She took the slightest step closer, his hand still warm on her neck.

But rather than move nearer, he spoke. "So not only do you have to earn the money, but you have to find a way to keep the robber from coming back."

She pulled away. Clearly his nearness was making her go daft, which meant she needed to be on the other side of the room if she wanted to keep her wits about her. She turned and headed toward the opposite side of the shop and another dustless shelf. "I've hidden it better this time. Maybe he won't find it."

"Or maybe he'll pull a knife or a gun out and threaten you until you tell him where it is." He followed right behind her, and if the tone of his voice was any indication, he wasn't feeling overly compassionate anymore. "A robber, Tressa? Truly? And you just thought this problem would go away if you didn't tell anyone about it?"

"More like I was hoping it wouldn't get any worse if I kept it quiet." She busied herself with cleaning the shelf. "I've been talking to the sheriff. What else am I supposed to do?"

"Evidently something more since the thief keeps coming back."

"Sheriff Jenkins thinks it's someone Otis owed. Someone who wants to get his money back bad enough that he'd steal from me. So given the list of people he owed..." She rubbed the shelf harder. What were the chances a stain that had been there since she'd bought the place would come out if she scrubbed hard enough with a dry rag?

"What has the sheriff done to find him?"

"Ma, where'd this come from?" Colin appeared in the doorway to the kitchen holding a package wrapped in brown paper and held together by two strings tied at the top.

She tucked the rag into the waist of her apron and headed to him. "I don't know. Where'd you find it?"

"By the back door." He plopped it onto the counter.

A five dollar bill was tucked beneath the string that tied the package together. She glanced through the doorway to her kitchen. "You said it was by the door?"

Colin nodded. "I went up to my room after I took the muffins out, and when I came back down, it was sitting right there on the counter."

She looked to Mac. "Did you do this?"

He held up empty hands. "If I'm going to give a person something, I'm the type that hands it to them. Wouldn't occur to me to be sneaky about it."

"Can we open it, Ma? Please?" Colin bounced up and down on the balls of his feet.

She untied the string and folded back the paper to find a freshly plucked chicken and a dozen carrots.

"A whole chicken?" Colin's eyes grew round. "We can eat on that for an entire week!"

She nodded absently and set the package on the bakery counter, then she walked through the kitchen and opened the back door. Not so much as a shadow moved in the empty alley.

It was too much. She couldn't take this gift from... from... well, she didn't know who. But how was she supposed to return it when she hadn't the faintest notion of where it had come from? "Who would leave this?"

She felt rather than heard Mac's presence behind her, the warmth of his solid body as he looked over her shoulder into the alley. He clasped both her shoulders in his large, bear-like hands. "I don't know, Tressa, but if it's that easy to get in and out of the back of your bakery without you knowing, then that robber is going to keep returning."

She pulled away and ducked beneath his arms and back into the kitchen. "I've been locking the doors as soon as I close for the evening. It's not as though I'm hanging a sign in the window that says, 'Door is open. Come rob me.'"

"Then maybe you need to keep this back door locked all the time."

"But it was locked the last two times we got robbed." Colin scratched the back of his head, then snagged one of the muffins he'd take out of the oven.

"Then you need a new lock." Mac stepped out the door and into the alley. "I'll be back with one shortly."

"Can I come with you?" Colin shoved a bite of muffin in his mouth and darted outside.

Tressa scowled. "I don't need—"

"Sure, son." Mac settled a hand on Colin's shoulder, similar to how he'd touched her in the storefront, but somehow different too. "You can help me pick out the lock."

Colin blinked up at him, his eyes round and sincere. "We need a good strong one to keep Ma safe."

Mac nodded gravely as they started down the alley together. "That's exactly what I was thinking."

Tressa sunk her teeth into her tongue and swallowed the objections on its tip. He couldn't just up and buy her a lock. It was too much. But if a new lock was all she needed to keep from being robbed again, she could pay him back later—after she caught up her debt to the bank.

If the thief actually had a key, he'd had full access to her and Colin and the bakery for months. Thankfully, he must only be after money since that was all that had gone missing.

Unfortunately it was also the thing she needed more than anything else at the moment.

Or almost more than anything else. Because it was almost worth being robbed again to see Colin beaming up at Mac, and Mac resting a hand on his shoulder and calling him son.

Chapter Ten

Mac rolled his head from side to side, stretching the cramp in his neck from sitting hunched on the lighthouse stool for the past four hours.

"Isaac won't even go near the water." Elijah stalked around the platform at the top of the tower. He marched the eight steps from Mac's stool to the table attached to the lens base then pivoted to retrace his steps.

Never mind that it was barely six in the morning and Elijah had been pacing long enough for Mac to count his steps. "Did he say why he wouldn't?"

Elijah paused and stared out at the entrance to the harbor, his gaze likely skimming the spot where his father's boat had capsized. "He claims he wants nothing more to do with the lake that killed Pa."

"Give him more time." His voice came out as a rasp, and he swallowed.

Elijah turned. "Have you been to the workshop? Have you seen the rows and rows of toys Isaac's making?"

"No." He didn't cotton to the notion of Isaac listlessly hanging about the workshop the way his ma listlessly sat in the rocker and stared at the waves. Though to hear Elijah speak of it, there was nothing listless about Isaac's toy making.

Was that better or worse? Mac rubbed the back of his neck and stood. He opened the Fresnel lens door and reached inside. Warmth from the little flame that had burned for the past twelve hours engulfed his hands. He took the lamp by its base and set it on the inflammable iron table that protruded from the base of the lens.

"And then this morning, while I'm in the deuced workshop trying to convince Isaac to come fishing, Rebekah leaves without me." Elijah stomped his foot, causing the iron platform to tremble.

Mac blew down the lamp chimney to extinguish the flame. "Can you wait until I have the fire out before you shake the floor?"

"Sorry." Elijah blew out a breath. "We're supposed to leave for Port Huron in a week and a half, but my family…" His voice grew tight, and he moved his gaze back to the windows. "What should I do?"

"Get some coffee."

Elijah glared, but if he was going to bound up the lighthouse steps at dawn and start listing everything wrong with their lives, he should have at least brought something to keep them awake.

"We'll get to Port Huron on time." Mac rubbed the back of his neck. "Even if one of us needs to leave before the other."

"Sure, we can split up. I hadn't thought of that. As long as one of us is there by July first, that would meet our sales agreement."

Mac looked away. Probably not the best time to tell Elijah he couldn't leave the lighthouse until a replacement for either Grover or himself arrived—preferably both.

"I still don't know what I'm going to do with Rebekah. She was storming around the house in trousers yesterday, muttering you'd gone daft and never should have invited your Mrs. Danell to the beach since Otis owed Pa money."

"She's not my Mrs. Danell." A kiss that spanned half a second didn't make a woman his, did it?

Elijah raised an eyebrow at him. "I'd argue with you about that if I wasn't so frustrated with Rebekah. She knows better than to hold a grudge over ten dollars. And prance about town in trousers."

Mac fiddled with the wick knob on the side of the darkened lamp. Elijah was right. Rebekah might be hurting over her father's death, but that didn't mean she should belittle Tressa behind her back.

"And speaking of your Mrs. Danell, does she owe the bank? I heard rumor to that end."

"She does, though some of that trouble is no fault of her own. But she's a strong woman. I think in the end... well, she might... I don't know." She'd looked so lonely standing on the beach two nights ago, so certain no one cared for her as she told him the story of her father's death and nearly-forced marriage to Otis. "She keeps telling me her trouble isn't my concern. Even after I kissed her, she wasn't any more forthcoming with her situation."

If not for Colin, he'd not even know she'd been robbed.

"You kissed her?" Elijah surveyed him. "You kissed a widow of three months when you're leaving in a week and a half?"

Mac twisted his lips together. Why had he told Elijah? It wasn't as though Tressa had been excited about that kiss, wasn't as though he was going to be in town long enough to see whether something beyond that lay in store for them. Except kissing her hadn't seemed so bad when he was on the beach with her. "Maybe."

"What happened afterward?"

"I... kissed her, and then... I didn't."

"That's it?"

He scowled. "At least I don't wait thirteen years to kiss the woman I'm pining after." Wait. Was he pining after Tressa?

"Who says I haven't kissed Victoria?"

Mac straightened. "You kissed her and never told me?"

"We were sixteen and thirteen, and she left for boarding school the next day."

"So that's why you didn't brag about it. You kiss so badly you drive women away."

Any other time, Elijah would've laughed, but this morning his friend remained silent.

Mac rubbed his eyes and walked around the lens toward him. "I'm sorry. I'm tired and mulish. The words just tumbled out."

Elijah looked toward the back of the lighthouse where iron panels rather than glass comprised the wall. If there'd been a window, he'd be staring straight at the Donnelly family mansion. "Nothing would've come of it. She's likely married and settled, perhaps even in the family way by now." Elijah moved his gaze back to the glass to watch the workers loading copper onto a steamship.

Mac rested a hand on his shoulder. "God has a woman for you somewhere, just not that one. It's been three years since you've seen her, no use pining—"

"More like three seconds." Elijah straightened, his eyes glued to a point beyond the glass.

"What?"

Elijah jabbed a finger toward the dock. "She just disappeared behind that stack of barrels." He whirled and darted down the stairs as though... well, as though the love of his life was waiting at the bottom.

The trouble was, Victoria Donnelly wasn't waiting for him. She never had been, and she never would be.

Mac scanned the dock, but saw no sign of Victoria. What a pair the two of them made, Elijah loved a woman he could never have, and he was knotted up over a woman he had to leave.

~.~.~.~.~

Elijah took the stairs two at a time, his boots pounding against the vibrating iron staircase as he raced down three stories of steps. He pushed out the door and darted down the rocky path toward the beach. It might've been someone else standing on the dock with her dark brown hair pulled into an updo, wearing a fancy yellow dress and hat while she watched the ship being loaded.

But it wasn't. The moment he stepped onto the dock, his suspicion was confirmed. Her height, the chestnut-brown shade of her hair, the proper way she held her shoulders...

"Victoria." He didn't speak loud enough for her to hear, and yet she turned anyway, her gaze searching until it landed on him.

He stood there, half expecting her to turn back as if she didn't recognize him after so long, but a smile lit her face. She gave instructions to one of the dockworkers carrying a small crate, then started toward him.

He should move forward. A running leap might not be appropriate, but standing as still as one of the boulders along the shoreline probably wasn't the brightest of ideas. Yet his feet wouldn't move.

She stopped in front of him. Dark shadows smudged the skin beneath her eyes. Her soft hazel irises didn't shine with the glow of a wife newly in love. Had she been married for a long time? Betrothed maybe?

"You're here." A brilliant statement, that. But it was all he could manage as he ran his gaze over the milky skin and strong jaw he hadn't seen in far too long.

She swallowed softly—he knew because he was watching her that closely. "S-s-so are y-y-y-y-you."

She still had her stutter then. And with the three words she'd just spoken, it seemed it had gotten worse. Had he been foolish to hope she'd one day grow out of the bumbling words that had caused her so much hardship as a child?

"Oof!" Something plowed into his shoulder from behind.

"Sorry, I didn't see you." A worker stumbled past him, crates stacked to the point he could barely see over the top of them.

"It's all right."

A gentle smile curved the corner of Victoria's mouth. "T-t-too b-big for your own g-g-good."

"Never." He nearly reached for her hand—an old habit, since he had no business touching her when half the town could see them. He offered his elbow at the last second. "Can you take a walk?"

She looked around the dock then toward her house before slipping her hand onto his arm. No diamond rings sparkled on any of her fingers. "F-f-f-for a b-bit."

"There's a new baker in town. I'm told she makes the best strawberry pies. Want a slice?"

"If it's n-not far. F-Father… we're l-l-leaving t-today."

Would he only get this one conversation with her? He led her off the pier toward Front Street. "When did you arrive?"

"Y-yesterday."

She should've sent word when she reached port. They could have gone fishing or taken a stroll along the beach like they had a decade ago. "Have you done any fishing in Milwaukee?"

She smiled the full, beautiful smile that always appeared in his dreams of her. "W-what do you th-think?"

"You should make time for it. People would be happier if they fished more often."

"Try t-telling that to M-M-M-M-M-Mother."

Mother. The name still made her stutter terribly, just like it had in grade school. "So if you're not spending your days fishing, what are you doing?"

She blushed. "L-L-Lillian has a s-string of s-suitors."

They turned from Front Street onto Center Street, needing to pass both the Donnelly and Sinclair houses before they reached the block with Tressa's bakery. He stayed silent, yet she gave no more information about her days in Milwaukee. There'd been a time, once, when details of her life would've poured from her mouth, her stutter lessening until it nearly vanished in a stream of words.

There'd been a time, once, when he'd taken her hand freely.

There'd been a time, once, when he'd kissed her.

"I wasn't asking about your younger sister." There'd been a time, once, when she'd trusted him with her innermost thoughts and worries. "I asked about you. How long is your list of suitors?"

She stopped walking, no matter that they stood directly in front of the Sinclair mansion, and looked up at him. "Oh, Elijah, I've n-never been good w-wife material. Y-you know th-th-that."

What a pile of tripe. "You're perfect just the way you are." *And you always have been.*

Bright splotches of red appeared high on her cheeks, and she looked away.

There'd been a time, once, when she'd held his gaze no matter how awkward his questions or how deep their conversation.

There'd been a time, once, when he'd hoped for a future with her.

Maybe a corner of his heart still clung to that stupid, stupid hope.

Instead, he should pray she'd find a good man, one who would love her stutter and her shyness right along with her hazel eyes and strong jaw. "Come, we'll never make it to the bakery if we keep stopping."

She pulled away from him and shook her head. "I shouldn't. M-M-M-Mother says I n-need to watch my f-figure."

Truly? Was this the newest addition to the list of things Mrs. Donnelly pestered her older daughter about? He swept his eyes down Victoria. "If anything, you could use a cookie or two."

"L-L-Lillian's waist is s-seventeen inches, and m-mine ... M-M-M-M-M-Mother s-says—"

"Victoria? What are you doing here?"

The front door to the Sinclair house had opened, and both Edward Donnelly and Byron Sinclair descended the steps.

Her father scowled furiously. "I thought you were at the dock seeing to your mother's china."

The embarrassed splotches of color that had appeared on her cheeks a few minutes ago drained to leave her skin completely white. "I ... M-M-M-M-M-Mr. C-C-C-C-C-Cummings and I w-w-w-were g-g-g-g-g-g-g-g-g-g-g..."

No, her stuttering hadn't gotten any better. In fact, he'd only heard her stutter this badly when the schoolteacher had insisted she give an oral report. He patted the top of her hand resting on his arm.

A mistake, since her father's glower grew darker and she took her hand back.

Sinclair stopped next to Elijah, his face no friendlier than Donnelly's—not that Elijah had expected otherwise.

"Victoria and I were headed to the bakery for pie, then I'll return her to the dock."

"You must be mistaken." Donnelly stepped closer, his large girth edging Sinclair out of the little circle they'd formed on the street. "Victoria isn't to have sweets."

Victoria looked down at her shoes.

"And you ought not to be frequenting the bakery considering who runs it." Sinclair shifted subtly, edging back into the group. His eyes remained disinterested, as though he wasn't attempting to divert income from a woman who desperately needed it.

Elijah's back teeth clamped together. "As a matter of fact, I—"

"Who runs the bakery?" Donnelly blundered.

"A widow who—"

"Do you not remember from last summer?" Now Sinclair spoke over him. And why wouldn't he? It wasn't as though the shipping baron had any regard for a mere fisherman's son.

Elijah glanced at Victoria, still standing with her head down, her shoulders hunched inward and her body positioned a step back from everybody else's. Trying to disappear—yet another thing that hadn't changed about her. His hand itched to reach out and take hers.

"Otis Danell's wife bought it and has gotten herself into a heap of debt," Sinclair answered. "She owes me money, and I intend to collect no matter how badly she balks."

Elijah tensed. Sinclair had enough funds to easily forgive any debt Mrs. Danell owed him, yet the thought had probably never crossed his greedy mind.

It was the biggest reason he'd left Eagle Harbor. He didn't have the heart to watch a man like Sinclair use his money to control the town.

"That's the way to do it, Byron." Of course, Donnelly would agree. "You can't forgive a man his debt simply because he's poorer than you. The poor have to learn responsibility just as the rich do."

They were sick men, the both of them. How did Victoria stomach spending so much time with them? He cast another glance at the girl who had regularly shared her lunch with him whenever the schoolyard bullies had stolen his. She was still trying to be invisible.

Unfortunately, Sinclair noticed her. "You'll have to forgive me. I'm being terribly rude." He stepped forward, his eyes no longer apathetic as he watched Victoria. "Victoria, dear, how are you? It's been an age since I've seen you."

"I-I'm w-w-well, and y-y-y-y-y-you?"

"Just fine, just fine. Any announcements to make? News to share?" Sinclair took her hand, kissed the back of it, and kept it for a moment, genuinely awaiting her answer.

Likely because her father owned the second largest house in town rather than a rambling cabin on the beach.

"Gilbert was just asking about you. He's recently finished his studies down in Ann Arbor."

Gilbert. Elijah's right hand tightened into a fist, a familiar action whenever Gilbert Sinclair was mentioned. Had the dandy truly asked about Victoria? In grade school it had seemed obvious the two would one day marry since no one else in town was as wealthy as they were. But then their families had moved their primary residences, the Sinclairs to Chicago and the Donnellys to Milwaukee, and the two older men only came back for business purposes in the summer. How long had it been since Gilbert and Victoria had seen each other? Did Gilbert harbor feelings for her?

Anyone but him, God. He'll never appreciate her, never love her for who she is. If Gilbert married Victoria, he'd only try to change her, try to make her more socially acceptable, and he'd likely end up destroying everything that was good and beautiful about her in the process.

"T-t-t-tell G-G-Gilbert—"

"Your boy was studying business, wasn't he?" Donnelly plowed through Victoria's attempted words.

"Engineering." Sinclair's jaw clamped together. "I encouraged him to go into business, but he can be rather stubborn."

Donnelly slapped a hand on Sinclair's shoulder. "A chip off the old block, I'd say."

Elijah would agree, but for entirely different reasons.

"Well, as charming as this meeting has been, we best be going." Donnelly extended his arm for his daughter in a way that cut Elijah from their circle. "Come along, Victoria."

But she didn't take her father's arm. Instead, she turned to him, a silent apology in her eyes. "G-g-g-g-g-g…" She swallowed and opened her mouth again. "G-g-g-g-g-g-g-g-g…"

"Goodbye, Victoria." He reached out and lifted one of her hands, now fisted with tension, and kissed it softly.

Donnelly humphed and took Victoria by the shoulder. "Let's see if your mother's china was loaded properly. She'll swoon if so much as a teacup breaks in transit." He settled her hand on his arm and turned her away.

Sinclair looked at Elijah for a second, his brow slightly raised. "You know better than to consort with Miss Donnelly. If she returns to Eagle Harbor, I best not see it happen again." He spun on his heel and walked away.

How had his father done it? How had he dealt with Sinclair and Donnelly whenever they were in Eagle Harbor and still managed to keep the respect of the townsfolk?

"You haven't time to dally with riffraff. I want to leave before noon." Donnelly's voice floated back to him over the quiet morning, the volume likely intentional. "I don't care whether you knew someone when you were younger. You're not the daughter of a fisherman or miner and shouldn't behave as such. And you remember what your mother said about eating sweets, don't you?"

Should he turn away and pretend he wasn't listening? Run up and wrench Victoria from her father's hold?

But he stayed and watched until they rounded the corner and disappeared, because what more could he do? Edward Donnelly was right. Victoria had been born the daughter of a shipping tycoon, and he the son of a fisherman.

Their worlds would never merge, no matter how badly he wanted them to.

Chapter Eleven

Mac curled his hand around the iron beam separating two of the lighthouse tower windows and stared through the rain-streaked glass. East of the harbor, a small sailboat tossed wildly in the waves, drifting closer and closer to the rock reef with each gust of wind.

"Tighten the sails." He slammed his hand against the iron. The craft shouldn't still be out there. It had plenty of time to make harbor before the worst of the storm hit, but instead had drifted listlessly in the water the entire time.

"Mac!"

Boots pounded on the staircase, and he glanced down through the grates to see Elijah bounding up the steps two at a time.

He lifted the trapdoor in the floor, and Elijah burst through the entrance and sprang onto the platform. "Rebekah..." He wheezed and sputtered for breath, turning to survey the thrashing lake below. "Is she still out there?"

Mac set the trapdoor back in place. "She was back before the wind even picked up."

Elijah stared at the beach. "You're certain?"

Mac pointed toward the sand, where a little dinghy had been turned upside-down. "Saw her with my own eyes."

He let out a breath. "The storm came out of nowhere. One

minute I was at the bakery apologizing to Mrs. Danell for Rebekah's behavior, and then I heard thunder. Thank God she's safe."

"Rebekah is, yes." Mac tapped the glass facing northeast. "But that sailboat isn't faring so well."

Elijah squinted through the window, though by now the driving rain and endless gray of water and sky nearly obliterated any glimpse of the single-masted vessel. "The wind's going to take her straight into that rock reef."

Mac turned away and rubbed at the ache starting at the back of his neck. Elijah might be able to watch, but he hadn't the heart, not with Hiram's death so fresh in his mind. "Those folks had plenty of time to make harbor, but they couldn't seem to turn downwind."

Elijah curled his fist helplessly around the same beam Mac had gripped just a few minutes ago. Minutes passed in silence as they stood staring at the floundering vessel, helpless to do anything but watch. "Was this what it was like for Rebekah and Isaac? For you?"

Maybe it was a good thing Elijah had been sailing the Atlantic when Hiram died. He'd be as crippled as the rest of them had he watched his pa perish. "Worse. I don't think I know the people in the boat, but I knew your pa."

Elijah slammed his hand into the iron again, and this time the window rattled. "I'm taking the dinghy and going for them."

Mac stared at his friend. Elijah couldn't be serious.

But Elijah stalked to the trapdoor and raised it.

Mac set his boot down on the iron, causing the door to drop back in place with a clank. "You'll end up like your pa. Your family can't handle another loss right now." *Neither can I.*

Elijah's eyes flashed as fierce as the lightning that rent the sky. "Maybe I will and maybe I won't, but I refuse to stand here and watch. Not when I know the grief of losing a loved one. Not when I might make a difference."

"No." Mac croaked the word through a blisteringly dry throat.

"How can you say that? You act as though Pa's death was unstoppable, but what if it wasn't? What if you and Rebekah had gone out in that dinghy instead of just watching? You don't know if you could've saved him because you didn't try. I won't let someone else's family stand over an empty grave, not when there's a chance I can help." Elijah bent and flung open the door before bolting down the stairs.

Mac stared at the opening in the floor. Did Elijah fault him and Rebekah and Isaac for not attempting to save Hiram? Doing so had seemed a certain death sentence on that fateful afternoon—just as it seemed a death sentence now.

But somehow, it seemed even more dangerous to let Elijah face that storm alone. He started down the stairs. "Wait, Elijah. Let me get Grover so I can go with you."

⌐.⌐.⌐.⌐.⌐

Mac wiped the rain from his eyes and dug his oars into the water, staring over his shoulder at Elijah in the front of the boat as he heaved the little dinghy through the wild waves. "You better not get us killed!"

"They do this all the time on the Atlantic," Elijah called above the rumble of thunder.

"Yeah, with trained men and life-saving equipment." Which was far different from stealing the Foley's dinghy and heading into a storm by themselves, especially when rowing a dinghy meant he had to face the stern of the boat rather than the bow. Something told him the life-savers on the Atlantic actually got to look where they were going when they rowed their surfboats.

But as foolhardy as Elijah's plan was, it seemed to be working. The dinghy was light enough to skim over some of the waves that would rock a larger vessel, and knowing the water like they did, they stuck near the shore, dodging the dangerous boulders that every mariner in Eagle Harbor had memorized.

"Are you getting tired? Do you want me to row?" Elijah eyed him through the flash of lightning that illuminated the sky.

Mac put the full weight of his back into the next row. The sailboat they headed toward was stuck upon the rock reef that ran a half mile out from land. It had to be taking on water, but with the way the waves thrashed to and fro and the rain beat down, he couldn't guess how much the vessel had sunk. This close, she looked to be some kind of personal watercraft, a yacht, perhaps. Anyone could up and decide to sail one of those, regardless of experience.

Had he seen this one before? The new sails being tattered by the wind and sleek wood of the hull looked vaguely familiar. He blinked more rain out of his eyes. Probably just the storm playing tricks on him.

"I don't see anyone on deck." Elijah stood at the bow of the boat and waved his hands wildly.

"Maybe they tried swimming for…" He ran his eyes over the vessel once again, the pristine, shiny wood of the gunwale being pounded by wind and waves, bright white sails now tattered nearly beyond recognition. "I think that's the new Ranulfson yacht."

"Since when do the Ranulfson's have a thirty-two foot sailboat?" Elijah called over the wind that seemed to be growing more thunderous by the moment.

"Arrived last month." A wave crashed into the side of the dinghy, soaking both of them and sloshing water onto the floor.

Elijah gripped the side of the dinghy, his face obviously pale despite the water droplets clinging to Mac's lashes. "Dear God, I hope they're all right."

"How close do you want to get?" Mac turned back toward the stern and heaved them closer to the rock reef and the precariously tilting vessel. At this point in the rescue, the life-saving service would throw life rings to those stranded on deck, wouldn't they? Or use some other equipment so they wouldn't have to leave their own boat?

"Closer. I still don't see anyone."

Mac looked over his shoulder again and eyed the mast, swaying in the wind while torn sails whipped violently about it. If they got any closer and the vessel went over—

"We have to try." Elijah leaned over the gunwale as though that would get him close enough to touch the sailboat.

Mac dug the oars into the water, fighting the current that wanted to pull them out to sea. The muscles in his back and arms were warm, but in a good, invigorating sort of way. He might truly be going daft, because were it not for the lives at risk on the yacht, he'd almost say this was fun. The bobbing of the waves, the way his muscles fought to control the oars despite the driving wind and tugging water…he should row in heavy seas more often.

"Stop here." Elijah called. "I'll be back."

"Elijah, you can't…"

But he could. Elijah tossed his hat and boots into the boat and dove overboard before Mac could stop him—not that Mac could have left the oars with the way the wind was fighting to drive the dingy into the sailboat.

How long Elijah stayed under, he couldn't guess. Perhaps it was ten seconds or twenty, but it felt like an hour before Elijah's dark blond hair bobbed above the surface of the water near where a ladder hung by the stern of the boat. He climbed aboard and then disappeared below deck.

Mac fought to hold the dinghy steady in the waves. Having his craft collide with the other vessel or one of the boulders would mean death for the lot of them. He stared at the deck of the yacht for what seemed another hour without Elijah appearing. The mast swayed violently, a boulder embedding itself farther into the hull with each little movement. If not for the rock reef holding her above the waves, the boat probably would have sunk before he and Elijah ever arrived. Though the inside had to be flooded by now, which brought up the question of what was taking so long.

Allow Elijah to find someone, Father. Don't let us be too late. He prayed half for the lives of those they might save—the Ranulfsons if it truly was their yacht—and half for Elijah. What would Elijah do if they came this far only to fail?

What would *he* do?

What would the town do if it lost more loved ones to the lake only a month after losing Hiram?

"Mac, row closer." Elijah's voice rose above the wail of the storm.

Mac looked up to find Elijah heading for the ladder. In his arms was a little girl with sunny blond curls.

⌐.⌐.⌐.⌐.⌐

"How long until the storm blows over, Ma?"

Tressa glanced over her shoulder at where Colin sat on a stool, staring out the window above the sink. She curled her bare toes against the floor planks worn soft by time and shoes. She'd given up on her boots a full hour ago, when she'd stepped in some kind of sticky, indiscernible mess and hadn't wanted to stop baking to clean them.

"I don't know." She whisked the muffin batter in her mixing bowl with quick, firm strokes. "I haven't control over the weather."

Or anything else in her life.

"If I'd known it was going to storm, I would've gone sailing with Leroy, Martin, and the Dowricks earlier and worked at the lighthouse now."

"I never said you had to work. You were more than welcome to go sailing."

Colin merely huffed. "I hate storms."

"If you're bored enough to sit there and complain, then you could help. I need eight cups of flour and—"

"Tressa Danell, just the woman I wanted to see."

Her whisk fell to the counter, and she turned to face Byron Sinclair, standing in the doorway between her kitchen and storefront. Somehow, he was still impeccably dressed despite the rainwater dripping from the brim of his hat onto the floor and a splotch of mud scuffing his left boot.

Had the storm been too loud for her to hear him come in? It must have, though that gave no indication as to why he was here during a storm in the first place. She doubted it was to buy cookies. "What can I help you with?"

"We never finished our conversation at the general store, if you recall. And this might be of interest to you." He waved a piece of paper at her.

She wiped her hands on her apron and stepped forward to take it. One glance at the contents of the promissory note, and her lungs struggled to draw breath. She reached to balance herself on the counter, knocking her batter-covered whisk to the floor in the process.

"What is it, Ma?" The stool scraping against floorboards filled the otherwise silent kitchen.

"G-go upstairs, Colin." She barely managed the words over her thick, sluggish tongue.

"Ma?"

"Just go."

Small feet pounded on the floor behind her, then stomped up the stairs.

She drew in a breath and met Mr. Sinclair's gaze. "This can't be correct."

No hint of emotion crossed his face.

That was something, she supposed, as a lesser man might allow his lips to curve in a twisted sort of glee.

"Which part? The one that says your husband owes me a total of a hundred and forty dollars for the boat he purchased and a gambling debt from last fall? Or the part that declares I can take labor in the form of compensation if the debt isn't paid in full by June first?"

Her heart stopped beating at his words. Just completely gave up and stopped. It must have, because her body was too cold to still be pumping blood, and her chest ached with a fierce heaviness.

"He never told me about the gambling debt."

"Didn't he?" Again, Mr. Sinclair spoke without the barest hint of compassion in his voice. "He was to pay me come spring, after he saved his winter wages."

"But the logging camp owner..." She wouldn't think of how the man had insisted Otis left no money behind while also saying he'd paid Otis for February's labor two days before his death. The man was likely lying, but how to prove different? He'd be gone by now anyway, scouting another patch of woods, purchasing it, and making plans for next season's camp.

She shoved the promissory note back at Mr. Sinclair. "Otis is dead, so doesn't that make this note void?"

"On the contrary. It makes you responsible to fulfill it." His lips did twist up then, the condescension on his face enough to make her wish…

What? That he would leave and never come back? That she had a secure home for Colin and herself? A way to earn a living? No debt? "I haven't the hundred and forty dollars to pay you."

"Which means you're soon to become the cook on one of my ships."

She didn't need to ask whether he meant it. "I can't leave Eagle Harbor, not with a son to care for and a bakery to run." Besides, she couldn't manage more than a half hour in a boat without heaving the contents of her stomach overboard. She may have been young when she'd come over from Cornwall, but she well remembered the hours of misery being at sea had caused her.

"I expected you'd say as much, though I'm afraid you'll find that promissory note legally binding. Nevertheless, Judge Matherson will be in town on Thursday. I assume you've received your court summons."

"What?"

"Your. Court. Summons." He spoke as though she were a child inept at understanding the simplest of words, then pulled another piece of paper out of his pocket. "Mine arrived on Thursday."

She reached to take it with shaky hands. It was indeed as he said. She and Mr. Sinclair were to appear before the circuit judge at ten o'clock on Thursday morning. "I-I didn't… that is, I haven't…"

"Have you picked up your mail at the general store?"

She shook her head bleakly. She never did, because she never had any. A woman only got mail if she had friends and family to correspond with, and she had no one, save Colin.

"Your summons is likely waiting for you then." He took the paper back from her and folded it crisply before slipping it back into the pocket of his suit coat. "I'm a reasonable man, Mrs. Danell, but I don't like being cheated. If I let you off without paying your husband's debt, how many other men will try to filch on their obligations to me? I can't be generous, you see. I fully intend for you to work off your husband's debt on one of my ships and will entreat Judge Matherson to that end. Considering room and board is provided on the ship, I pay my cooks twenty-five dollars a month."

Panic flooded her body. "But it will take me six months to earn that back!"

Mr. Sinclair reached for the promissory note, folded the paper neatly, and slipped it back into his pocket. "That's hardly my concern. My advice to you? Make arrangements for your bakery and your boy during your absence. I don't allow brats aboard my cargo ships."

"No." She shook her head. "I won't go without Colin."

He put his hat back on his head. "Perhaps you might consider sending him to the mine in your absence. There's always a need for drill boys, and Central Mine hires young."

She shook her head again, more adamantly this time. "My father died in that mine."

She wasn't sending her son into the bowels of the earth with grown men from all manners of living. She wasn't sending him down to a place where explosions and tunnel collapses would threaten his life. She wasn't sending him anywhere at all.

Mr. Sinclair disappeared through the doorway, but his absence didn't erase the images of the promissory note and court summons from her mind. With the boat and gambling debt owed to Sinclair, the tabs from Reed Herod's brothel and the Foley-Smith General

Store, and the payments she'd failed to make on the bakery, she owed nearly two hundred and fifty dollars. And what if some of Otis's gambling friends found a way to make her pay off the list of creditors at The Rusty Wagon?

She slumped beneath the weight of it all, her shoulders drooping and her knees turning weak. Tears burned hot behind her eyes, and she blinked them back once, twice before they filled her vision and slid down her cheeks.

What was the point in fighting anymore? For her bakery? For her son? For any of it? She was only going to fail.

Chapter Twelve

Thunder clapped loud overhead as Mac heaved the oars through the water. The storm seemed to be right atop them now, its lightning flashing ferociously and the thunder booming across the sky. Rain drove hard atop his wide-brimmed hat, which only prevented half the drops from clinging to his eyelashes and pelting his cheeks.

"How much longer?" Little Olivia Dowrick watched him from where she sat on the bottom of the boat by his feet. Though her arms were wrapped tightly around her body, her jaw chattered and gooseflesh pebbled her skin.

"We're almost there." Why hadn't they thought to bring blankets? Olivia would be frozen soon. He squinted into the rain and plunged his oars into the water again. He glanced over his shoulder to his left, where the lighthouse shone as bright as possible through the mass of gray rain.

"You need a hand with anything?" Elijah watched him from the bench near the bow where he sat with three Spritzer boys, his words mixing with the wails from the babe at the stern.

"I got it. How's Jake?"

Elijah craned his neck to peer behind Mac. "Looks like Jake might be waking up."

Mac glanced toward the stern he was already facing, where a half-conscious Jake Ranulfson sat propped up between Clifford Spritzer and Jessalyn Dowrick, who also clutched a crying Megan to her chest and had Claire seated on the floor gripping her skirt. They'd borrowed the sailboat to take Clifford's brothers out, but Jake Ranulfson had been the only one familiar with sailing. When the collision with the reef caused Jake to hit his head, everyone else had expected to drown in the storm.

When he'd left shore in the little dinghy, he hadn't reckoned he and Elijah would be bringing eleven people back. Good thing most of them were children who could sit on the floor and the Spritzers were all so thin. Even so, the boat was riding awfully low in the water.

"Here we are." Mac muttered, heaving the boat the last few feet to shore.

Sand slid along the bottom of the hull, and Elijah and Clifford jumped out to haul the dinghy farther onto the beach. The warehouse owner, Mr. Fletcher, appeared with his two oldest boys, one of whom plucked Olivia out of the dinghy while the other rushed to the back.

"If that isn't the craziest thing I've ever seen!" Mrs. Kainner appeared beside him, the feathers of her hat fighting valiantly to stay upright despite the downpour.

The children all scrambled from the boat, the young Spritzers seemly unfazed by their near-deaths. Mac set down the oars and stood gingerly, his back and arms aching from the effort of labor well spent and work well done.

"Mac, Elijah, are you well? Who needs to see the doc?" This from Mr. Foley, who'd also appeared beside the boat, dripping hat and all.

Mac looked around the beach, filled with an unseemly amount

of people given the lightning flashing overhead. Had half the town come out to watch him and Elijah?

"Here now, we've got to get you all to Doc Greely's." Mrs. Kainner rushed to take the babe from Jessalyn's arms.

"Mac?" Mr. Foley took a step nearer the boat.

"F-fine. I'm fine." He wasn't frozen with the cold rain like the others, not with the way his muscles burned from rowing. He stepped out of the dinghy and stretched while Mrs. Kainner and the Fletcher youths rushed everyone except him and Elijah across the street to Dr. Greely's office.

"That was amazing." Mr. Fletcher slapped him on the back, causing the chilly, wet fabric of his shirt to plaster against his skin. "I've never seen the likes of it. I can't believe you did it."

Mac stared after the motley group crossing the street. Even Jake Ranulfson was stumbling along on his own strength, a far cry from when Elijah had hauled the youth from the sailboat over his shoulders.

The rescue had been rather amazing, hadn't it? Though Elijah had done more than he, what with climbing onto the sailboat and all.

"Wasn't much choice about it from where I was standing." Elijah spoke as if the feat was a common occurrence, nothing more than doing a job.

But the rescue had been more than a job. It had been inspiring, empowering.

He'd do it again in a heartbeat.

One of the dockworker's hands landed on Mac's shoulders. "Never seen a man row through a storm quite like that. Anytime you want to haul a crate or two for us, you're more than welcome."

"Is it true?" A woman's choked voice rose above the crowd while thunder cracked overhead.

Mac looked to Elijah, who stood scanning the small group, then ran his own gaze around the cluster of people. Victoria stood several paces back from everyone, her hat drooping and her fancy silk dress surely being ruined by the downpour. But her gaze never wavered from Elijah's form. *Interesting.* But she hadn't been the one shouting.

"Someone tell me my boy didn't take that tiny boat out into the storm."

"He saved Jake Ranulfson, the Dowricks, and some of the Spritzers," Mr. Foley murmured.

Several of the townsfolk shuffled away from the dinghy to reveal Mabel Cummings standing at the back of the group. Her long, gray-blond hair fell loose and wet about her shoulders, and she clutched a flimsy shawl to her chest. But her eyes... her eyes weren't vacant and dull. No. They flashed with the same stormy gray as Elijah's.

"Ma?" Mac whispered. "You came down to the beach?" He took a step toward her, which prodded Elijah into action.

Elijah raced over the yards separating them and swung his mother up in an embrace. "You're out of the chair. You're outside!"

"Put me down." She pounded her fist on Elijah's shoulder as he spun her around. "I'm furious with you."

"I don't care." Elijah dropped her feet to the ground, a look of delight on his face, and then crushed her in another hug.

Mac moved forward, taking Mabel from Elijah's arms and wrapping her wet, frail form in his own embrace. "It's good to see you up and about, Ma."

She pushed weakly against his chest, tears filling her eyes and adding to the rain droplets already coursing down her face. "Oh, I should have known you would be in on the trouble. Why didn't you stop him?"

He looked at Elijah and grinned. "Because we saved nine lives. I reckon it was worth it."

"I don't." This from Isaac, who now stood to Mabel's left, his shoulders rigid and the muscle in his jaw clenching rhythmically.

"Well I do." Rebekah came up beside her twin brother and folded her arms over her chest. "And I would have gone with them."

"No!" All three Cummings shouted in unison.

Rebekah's eyes sparked. "I'm as good a sailor as Mac."

"It doesn't matter, because Elijah and Mac aren't ever doing that again," Isaac snapped.

"As though you have any say," Elijah retorted.

"Enough."

At Mabel's soft demand, quiet descended. Then Elijah turned and stalked across the street toward Doc Greely's.

Mac couldn't say he blamed him.

⌐.⌐.⌐.⌐.⌐

Are you certain you're all right? Tressa's arms shook as she clasped Jessalyn to her. "I can't believe you almost…" She swallowed back the sob welling in her throat.

"I'm fine. We all are, thanks to Elijah and Mac." Jessalyn rubbed little circles on her back, giving more comfort than she was receiving as they stood in the tiny sickroom inside Dr. Greely's office.

"I just can't believe… that is, when I think…" Her chin trembled and the words clogged in her throat.

"I don't remember giving you permission to disturb my patients, Mrs. Danell."

At the sharp words, Tressa pulled away from Jessalyn. "I had to come. As soon as I heard, I had to—"

"And now you have to go." Dr. Greely stepped into the room, his wide girth taking up too much space in the already cramped room. "I've medical business to attend, and you aren't a trained nurse."

"No," Tressa mumbled.

"Then good day." The foul stench of spirits wafted on the old man's breath, and he blinked his bloodshot eyes.

She turned back to Jessalyn, who mouthed the words, *I'm fine.*

Something told her that her friend would be better off with a doctor who wasn't perpetually drunk. He probably had to be pulled away from his seat at The Rusty Wagon to come tend his patients. "I'll go to your house and get dinner started, a warm fire going." She glanced at the girls, Megan sleeping on the tiny bed crammed into the corner while Claire and Olivia sat quietly on the other end of the mattress. "Do you want me to take them?"

"The children are my patients, Mrs. Danell, and I asked you to leave." Dr. Greely turned toward the bed, put some kind of strange device into his ears, and reached for Claire. "Hold still now. I don't want any wiggling."

"Mommy!" she called, tears streaking down the toddler's cheeks as she clambered back against the wall. "Man no touch!"

The noise caused Megan's eyes to flutter open, and she began to wail. Jessalyn sent Tressa a silent plea to leave and then hastened toward the bed.

Tressa stepped into the parlor and closed the bedroom door.

"Are they well?" Mac sprang up from where he'd been sitting on the tattered couch while Elijah stopped his pacing and turned toward her.

She pressed her lips together. Were they? They'd seemed fine, but evidently the doctor had yet to see them. "I... I don't know." A tear streaked down her face, then another. She wiped away the mortifying wetness.

"Hey, it's all right." Strong arms wrapped around her, pulling her to his chest. "Everyone got back safely. The doc just said Jake Ranulfson will heal fine."

"He already went home." Elijah's voice floated through the parlor, though she couldn't see him given the way her face was smashed against Mac's clothing.

"I know. I know." The embrace muffled her words into an indistinguishable slur, and yet she couldn't keep from babbling. "And you went out to save them. What if... what if..." Her arms came around his waist, and she squeezed tight. A most improper gesture, but she hardly cared as another bout of tears fell.

He held her, offering comfort while taking nothing for himself. She finally forced herself to push away. He'd likely hold her all day if she asked him to, and the idea was far too appealing.

"I'm sorry." Her voice warbled with the fading tears. "I shouldn't have lost control like that."

"It's all right." Compassion glinted in his eyes.

Compassion for her? Why? He'd been the one to risk his life today, not her.

"According to Colin, you've had a rather hard day."

Her face turned cold. Surely Colin hadn't told Mac about Mr. Sinclair's visit. She wiped the lingering moisture from her eyes and looked around the small parlor. "Where is he?"

"Went home with the Spritzers just before Doc Greely headed in to tend Jessalyn and her brood. I didn't think you'd mind."

"Home. Dinner. I nearly forgot. Oh, what was I thinking?" She rubbed her forehead and started for the door.

"Where are you going?" Mac's hand on her shoulder stopped

her, something that was becoming quite a habit of his.

"To Jessalyn's. I promised to begin dinner and get a fire started, and I can hardly do so by standing here caterwauling."

"You still haven't told me about Byron Sinclair's visit."

So Colin had told him. She turned away and wrenched the door open. She needed to have a talk about privacy with her large-mouthed son.

Darting out into the rain, she hunched her shoulders and raced across North Street towards Jessalyn's house. Lightning streaked in the distance, thunder rumbling close behind. But above the sound of raindrops hammering onto the drenched road, footsteps thudded behind her.

"Tressa, tell me." Mac followed her around the back of the Dowrick house, where she moved a rock along the wall to retrieve Jessalyn's spare key. Then he came up the back steps, waiting while she unlocked the door before he tromped inside after her.

"Mr. Oakton, being alone in a house with me is highly improper."

"Last I checked, so is running off in the middle of a conversation." He headed straight for the cook stove, grabbing kindling from the basket before squatting to open the firebox door.

The back of his shirt was damp but not soaked, as was the top of his head. He must have already changed into dry clothes and left his slicker at the doctor's to run after her.

Why had he bothered to come after her and get wet again?

He came because he cares. About you.

No, that couldn't be. She'd given him no reason to care what happened to her. But then, he had little reason to care about the sailboat he'd seen caught in the storm, yet he'd risked his life in a rescue.

She blinked away the tear that threatened to slip down her

cheek. She'd already shed far too many tears this afternoon, first over Otis's promissory note, then over Jessalyn's rescue. If she let one more fall, she just might start crying all over again.

"So." Mac stood, leaving the door to the stove open a crack to let the fire catch fully. "What's this business between you and Sinclair?"

She headed toward the icebox, a convenient place to go given it meant she turned her back to him. "Nothing."

Which was a lie, because leaving her child for six months while she worked on a ship was far from nothing.

And she would have to leave him, because Byron Sinclair would get his way. Men always did in matters such as this.

Why had she ever dreamed she could own a bakery or make a decent life for Colin?

"Tressa?"

She wrapped her hand around the icebox handle and pressed her eyes shut. "Just go away."

"What's he done to you?" Strong, sure footsteps clomped across the floorboards as he came up and trapped her between himself and the icebox. His gaze warmed her skin and made her hands shake as she pulled open the door. He wasn't going to leave until she told him.

Did she even want him to?

Oh, what was wrong with her?

"Colin said something about going to work as a drill boy."

She stared blindly at the nearly empty contents of the icebox. Had Colin eavesdropped on her conversation with Mr. Sinclair? She jerked out the remnants of a picked over chicken and turned. "I'd never let him do such a thing."

"Calm yourself." Wide hands covered hers on the platter that held the chicken, then wrested it from her grip and set it atop the counter.

"My father… died." Why did her jaw have to tremble when she spoke?

"I know."

"I can't send Colin."

"I never said you should."

"But what if I have to?"

He took her by the arm and tugged her to him, his body near enough that heat from it emanated into her. "What aren't you telling me?"

She stared at the tips of her muddy boots. "Mr. Sinclair… Otis… There's a promissory note from Otis to Mr. Sinclair."

His hand tensed on her arm. "What does it say?"

"That if Otis didn't pay Mr. Sinclair back by the beginning of June, he'd work on one of the Great Northern ships until the debt was paid—in full."

"And now that Otis is dead?"

She focused her gaze on Mac's chin. It was easier than meeting his eyes. "I'll get twenty-five dollars a month to cook aboard ship, and Mr. Sinclair says I can't take Colin with me."

He muttered something unintelligible, the muscle in his jaw working back and forth. "He can't force you to work for him."

If only Mac were right. "He's taking me to court in two days, and Judge Matherson will agree with him. There's no use pretending otherwise."

He settled her head against his shoulder, his large, solid shoulder still damp from chasing her through the rain. "We won't let Sinclair win."

But she could draw no solace from his words, not when they were so blatantly powerless, not when her heart was so empty. "He'll win, and then I'll have to leave Colin. And where am I to leave him? Jessalyn can't afford to take him, you're moving away, and…"

"Shhhhh." He stuck a finger against her lips. "Calm down."

"I just wanted a home for Colin. Was that so much to ask?"

He rubbed her arm, up and down. "Seems to me like you have a home already."

"I'm going to lose it."

"You don't know that." Up and down, up and down, his hand kept up the steady movement. "There's a Bible verse in Isaiah that talks about how God's ways are above our ways, His thoughts above our thoughts. He has a plan in all of this, even if you don't understand what it is."

She broke away and turned so she didn't have to face him, staring instead at the fire crackling inside the cook stove. "A plan? God doesn't care one whit about me."

No one did.

"He cares." The distant thunder should've drowned out Mac's voice, quiet as it was.

Yet she heard it, felt it, sensed it echoing somewhere inside the empty cavern that had replaced her heart. "If He cared so much, he wouldn't split up Colin and me."

"Do you know He cared enough that He died on the cross for you?"

She nodded bleakly. "I went to Sunday School at Central before Pa died."

He took a step toward her. "If He cared enough to die for you, then he cares about you and your son. Enough to prevent you from working for Reed Herod after your father's death. Enough to—"

"You think marriage to Otis was God's way of caring?" She spun to face him. "That being six months late on my mortgage for the bakery and being summoned to court shows God's caring? He has no plan for me, Mac. He forgot me long ago." Tears pricked the backs of her eyes, but she shoved them away, her blood coursing hot as she heaved in a giant breath.

⌐.⌐.⌐.⌐.⌐

Mac's hands dangled helplessly at his sides while Tressa glared at him. He'd seen her upset, flustered, happy, even sobbing earlier at the doctor's office, but he'd never seen her so angry. And at God, no less.

Though, if he faced an insurmountable debt along with the threat of losing his son, he'd be angry too.

He ran his fingers through his hair, his hands itching for a way to calm her. He'd wrap her in a hug if she wouldn't turn stiff and pull away again.

What, God? What am I supposed to do? How can I help her?

No clear answer cut through his thoughts, nor did a soft assurance whisper through his heart.

"Go back to the lighthouse, Mr. Oakton. I'm hardly in need of your assistance while I make soup." She busied herself lighting two lamps, then took a pot hanging from the rack on the wall and pumped water into it before setting it on the stove.

He grabbed the leftover chicken. He wasn't about to go away. Now if only he could make her problems go away, wrap her in his arms, take her home, and... and...

Was the answer as simple as that? A visit to the minister and he could take her home? Having a wife when he went down to Port Huron wouldn't hurt anything.

He carried the chicken to the stove and dumped it in the pot, ignoring the glare she sent him. Yes, that was it. He could be a father to Colin, teaching the boy everything Hiram had shown him. And he could teach Tressa too, not about fishing and throwing punches, but about God and His love.

He'd be a heap better husband than Otis Danell or Finley McCabe.

But her debt.

He could probably manage payments to Byron Sinclair, but what about the money she owed on the bakery? And there was that list of creditors at The Rusty Wagon, though as far as he knew, she hadn't agreed to pay any of them back. The problem was men of that ilk weren't apt to leave her alone until they had their money. How much did she owe when she added everything up?

Mac swallowed. He had money stashed in the bank, sure, but after he paid for his share of the boatyard in Port Huron, there wouldn't be much left. And it would be a couple months before he and Elijah pulled in a profit.

Could he afford to marry Tressa? There was only one way to find out. "How much do you owe everybody altogether?"

She dropped a handful of sliced carrots into the soup with a loud plop. "It's hardly your concern."

He winced. "Just tell me. Please."

She turned away and chopped the onion with a bit more force than necessary.

"Besides Sinclair, the bank, and the list at The Rusty Wagon, do you owe anyone else?"

"I already told you." She kept her back to him as she spoke. "None of this is your business."

It would be if they wed. "I'm only trying to help."

The crack of her knife against the cutting board resonated through the kitchen with hard, swift *thwacks*. "Otis had a personal tab at the general store, and then there's Reed Herod."

"The brothel owner?" The words exploded from his mouth.

That was worse than Sinclair. What if Herod demanded she work off her debt like Sinclair had? Or Herod took her before the judge? Could the court order a woman to earn money in such a way?

"Tell me it's a small amount." *Please, God, let it be a small amount.*

Her knife clattered against the cutting board. "It's not."

"Has he demanded payment?"

Even standing behind her in the dim light of the kitchen, he could see the flush creep up the back of her neck and into her cheeks. "I'm not giving him a penny. Not when he expects me to pay for... for..."

For Otis's women.

Humiliation hung thick in the air between them.

What kind of man treated his wife like that? Had Otis not found Tressa satisfying? Two minutes in her presence, and he wanted to carry her home and cherish her for the rest of her life.

He moved forward, the thunking of his boots against the floor and the soft crackle of the fire the only sounds in the room, and rested a hand on her shoulder.

She jerked away, putting two full steps between them. "You should go now. Jessalyn will be back soon, and as I said before, it's hardly appropriate for you to be here alone with me."

"I want to help."

"I don't need help with dinner. I need..."

He stood still. She had only to tell him what she needed, and he would see that she had it.

She needs money, you dolt! And you likely don't have enough.

"Time." Her words were soft against the rain still pinging the windows and ground outside. "I need time to think of what I should do about Sinclair. Now please, leave me alone."

A tight sensation wrapped around his chest. But at least he had the ability to give her what she wanted, even if every muscle of his body revolted against the idea.

"All right, Tressa, but I'll be back tomorrow." After he'd done a little digging to discover how much debt she had.

If only he could be sure he'd be coming back with a proposal.

Chapter Thirteen

Mac let himself out Jessalyn's back door and headed toward North Street and the general store. Reed Herod. Of all the people for Tressa to owe. He shouldn't be surprised by it, not with what he'd known about Otis and the rumors that always followed him. Tressa couldn't have been that surprised either. But the boldness of Herod to approach a bereaved widow and demand payment? Mac's hands tightened into fists. Herod had been in Eagle Harbor a couple days ago. Had the man gone back to Central?

Part of him hoped so, and the other part...

Well, right about now, knocking Herod flat seemed like the best idea he'd had all day.

Knocking Sinclair flat wouldn't hurt much either.

He raised his head to the sky, never mind that little droplets of water struck his cheeks and nose. "Do you want me to marry her, God? What if the debt's too much?"

What a day he'd had, rescuing a sailboat full of people only to turn around and try rescuing the woman he... he... he...

He didn't love her. He'd only been visiting her bakery for a week, and that was hardly enough time to fall in love with someone.

But the idea of loving her, of waking up by her side every

morning and sitting with her by the fire at night, of taking early walks on the beach and watching Colin grow from boy into man…

Maybe he wasn't schoolboy crazy about her the way Elijah was over Victoria Donnelly, but he could look at Tressa Danell and see a future with her.

Would she be able to see one with him?

He reached North Street and crossed it, then a burst of laughter sounded behind him. He looked back across the street, glaring at the saloon that had once been called The Golden Wagon. With its rusted door hinges, grimy windows, and dilapidated roof, folks had started calling it The Rusty Wagon instead. In spite of the dinginess, the place was fair to bursting, what with the storm having driven everyone indoors and all. And if a dockworker or mariner was going to kick up his feet, why not do so at the saloon?

He headed back across the street. Here he was wondering how much debt Tressa owed, when he could go inside and have a peek of the list of creditors himself. If Tressa owed under a hundred dollars between Herod and The Rusty Wagon list, he could probably afford to marry her.

A familiar shadow crossed in front of the window. The dirty panes of glass might blur the man, but they didn't hide the straight, proper way he stood, the arrogant tilt to his head.

Suddenly Mac didn't need to peek at that list nearly as much as he needed to have a talk with Sinclair. He barged through the door, sloshing mud from his boots as he strode straight toward where the man sat at a card table. "How dare you?"

The men at the table quieted, but Sinclair merely raised an eyebrow. "Been to see Danell's widow, have you? I suppose it makes sense to have Clive Oakton's son sniffing around Danell's leftovers. You're of the same ilk."

Heat rushed up the back of his neck and burned the tips of his ears. The men at the table burst into laughter, and more guffaws sounded from behind him. Had the entire saloon quieted to watch their exchange? He planted his hands on the table and leaned in until only a few inches separated him from Sinclair. "You have no right."

Sinclair plucked the lint from the arm of his coat. "She owes me money. I have every right, and I'd wager the others here agree with me."

"Here, here," a voice rang out from behind him.

"Otis done borrowed ten dollars from me last summer." This from a man seated at the table. "I wrote my name on the list on the wall there. When's she going to pay me back?"

"If her husband didn't pay, then I say the woman's responsible."

"How's Sinclair planning to get his money back? I want mine back too. Otis's wife hasn't even been in to take the list."

"Give the list to Oakton. He can take it to her."

"I want my money by the end of the month."

Mac glared at Sinclair as the cacophony of voices rose behind him. "I think we should take this conversation somewhere private."

Sinclair smiled, sharp and quick. "I think the conversation is already finished."

Mac clenched the rough wood of the table until his stubby nails gouged the surface. "You have enough money to forgive her debt."

The voices of saloon patrons continued behind him, intent on finding a way to wring every last penny from Tressa and not caring what she was left with in the end.

"Do you think that's how I built Great Northern Shipping?" The feral smile dropped from Sinclair's lips. "By giving away money and forgiving people's debts? That woman owes me one hundred and forty dollars, and I aim to collect, one way or another."

Did the man before him think of nothing besides adding money to his ever-expanding bank accounts? Mac swallowed. He might have had a swindler for a pa, but he couldn't imagine being born to Byron Sinclair. The man's heart pumped ice rather than blood. "You'll be separating a mother from her son."

Sinclair waved his hand absently in the air. "She can send him to work at Central and have the debt paid off quicker. Or perhaps she could do so herself on my ship if she visits the sailors at night. I've no rules about such things, and she's pretty enough to turn a penny or two."

Such a statement deserved only one response, and Mac didn't think about it in the least. He merely pulled back his fist and swung.

..*.*.*

Elijah gripped the stick in his hand, running it along the crack in the boulder he was sitting on. It dislodged a bit of dirt and a straggly weed that shouldn't have been growing on one of the lighthouse rocks given the lack of soil. The energy that had coursed through his blood during the water rescue had given way to fatigue, and with it came too many thoughts.

How many more shipwrecks would happen before he and Mac left? Most of Copper Country boasted a dangerous, rock-strewn coastline and vessels wrecked every year coming into Eagle Harbor.

The town needed a life-saving station, plain and simple. Life-saving stations had teams of trained men who swam and practiced rescues every day. They had boats designed specifically for rescues; storm suits to keep them warm and dry; breeches buoys, life rings, and life cars to transport the stranded to safety; and a Lyle gun powerful enough to shoot rope four hundred feet from a beach to a sinking vessel.

Yes, a life-saving station was what Eagle Harbor needed, but while the United States Life-Saving Service might have a good presence on the Atlantic, they'd mostly forgotten about the Great Lakes and had completely forgotten about Lake Superior. Though it was the largest of the five Great Lakes, it only had two stations.

Elijah heaved out a breath, staring out over the water which was now calm and glistened a soft blue beneath the evening sun. The storm had passed over an hour ago, leaving no remnant of violent seas and gusting wind in its wake. His eyes trailed instinctively over the path Edward Donnelly's schooner had taken as it sailed toward the horizon.

When he'd returned from the rescue, Victoria had been standing on the beach several steps away from everyone else, not speaking to anyone. She'd been concerned for him. The somber glint in her eyes had said as much, as had the unsure way she held her shoulders.

He'd expected her to stay for another day because of the storm. But no, Edward Donnelly had steered the schooner out of the harbor as soon as the wind calmed.

At least he'd been able to talk to Victoria for a few minutes this morning and knew how she was faring—or rather, how she wasn't faring. Did none of the dandies in Milwaukee see her for the treasure she was?

They probably heard her stutter, saw the insecure way she slid to the back of the room, and wanted nothing to do with her.

All the more reason for her to come back to Eagle Harbor.

And do what? Marry him?

He would laugh if the impossibility didn't hurt so much.

He dug the stick into another crevice in the rock, dislodging more dirt. With him headed to Port Huron and her back to Milwaukee, would he ever see her again?

If he even went to Port Huron. Ma was up and about now, but was she well enough that he could leave? And what would happen to Rebekah if he left? To Isaac?

"Mr. Cummings." Clifford Spritzer approached from the direction of Front Street, his long, gangly legs carrying him quickly up the rocky incline. "I've been looking for you."

"How are you feeling?" Elijah shifted over the slightest bit so Clifford could sit on a relatively smooth patch of stone.

Clifford plopped down beside him. "Fine, except Eagle Harbor needs a new doc. Greely's terrible."

He was, but getting a good doctor to set up shop in a forgotten town like Eagle Harbor wasn't exactly easy. Pa had tried asking a couple of the mine docs to work in Eagle Harbor instead, but the mines paid more than a doctor would earn on his own up here.

"Is that what you came to tell me? That we need a new doctor?"

Clifford looked out at the water. "I want you to teach me to sail."

Elijah surveyed the young man from his red hair to his clear green eyes to his lanky torso to his scuffed shoes that looked ready to fall apart. "Are you sure you didn't get whacked in the head along with Jake this afternoon?"

Clifford clutched Elijah's arm, the young man's jaw tense. "You don't know what it was like out there, with Jake knocked out and my brothers crying, not to mention the Dowrick girls. Then there was the look on Mrs. Dowrick's face. I tugged on the rigging. I swear I did. I tried to move the sails, tried to do what I saw Jake do earlier, but it wasn't... wasn't... well, nothing wanted to move right, and—"

"Calm down." Elijah rested a hand on Clifford's shoulder. "It's over and done. Everyone's safe."

"But I was so helpless." Clifford stared down at his hands before curling them into fists. "I'm never going to be that helpless on the water again. So I thought maybe you could take me fishing with you. I'm a quick enough study, I promise. I can learn to sail, and if I get good enough to be of help, maybe you could pay me a little. Ma could use the money."

"That's right admirable of you, Clifford. You live in a town accessible mainly by ship, so it's a good thing to learn to sail." Elijah looked out over the water. "I can teach you for a few weeks, I suppose, but I'm not staying in town long, and I can't promise to pay you much seeing how the *North Star* still needs to be repaired. Though I can teach you enough to get you a job as a mariner, even write a letter or two to a shipmaster for you if you're looking to sail full-time next year."

The young man's jaw worked back and forth, his shoulders hunched as though he carried the weight of the boulders that lined the shore atop his back. And he probably did, what with all the siblings he had at home and what had happened today. The boy was in a fix, for sure and for certain. He was old enough to work and give the money to his ma, but would his ma be able to manage without him?

Clifford gave a curt nod and pushed himself to his feet. "Reckon you want me on the beach tomorrow at dawn?"

"Take a day or two first." The youth was too hard on himself by half. "You don't need to go back on the water so soon."

"But I do, Mr. Cummings. I do."

Elijah sighed as Clifford tromped off toward town. Now if only Isaac would force himself to face the water as well, but his younger brother had shown nothing but fear toward the lake that surrounded them.

"Elijah." Mrs. Kainner's bright voice broke through the quiet of the evening. She brushed past Clifford, a smile on her face and a pair of shears in her hand.

So much for having a moment or two to himself this evening.

"I've been meaning to thank you," she called as she approached.

"Thank me?" He stood and swooped his hat from off the top of his head.

"For the roses. Mr. Fletcher said we could keep them as long as the beautification society pruned them." She gestured to her shears. "That's what I was coming here to do when I saw you."

Weren't roses supposed to be pruned when the snow was melting, before trees got their buds? He scratched the back of his neck and shrugged. "It didn't take more than a minute to talk to Fletcher."

"But he listened to you." Her bottom lip poked out and her eyes watered. "My Jack, he helped me plant those bushes, and they make these lighthouse grounds look so pretty."

Elijah fished in his pocket for a handkerchief. "Fletcher would've listened to you too."

She shook her head and dabbed at her eyes. "I hardly think so."

"You'll have to start talking to the members of the council yourself after I leave."

She sniffled and peered up at him. "You mean you're not staying? Considering the rose bushes, your ma, and the rescue this afternoon, I thought…"

His hands involuntarily clenched, crushing his hat brim. "I have a business agreement, Mrs. Kainner. I'll lose money if I don't go to Port Huron and buy that shipyard."

"Oh. It's that certain?"

"Yes." Or at least, it should be. But at the moment, the only thing that felt certain was his decision to stay in Eagle Harbor for the rest of the summer and send Mac on alone.

"I don't suppose you could speak with Mr. Fletcher about something else before you go?"

He held back the sigh welling in his chest. "Mrs. Kainner, you'll have to talk to him eventually."

She shifted awkwardly on her feet. "Perhaps, and I'm sure he'll talk, but he won't listen, not to a widow like me. But you…"

Her words trailed off, but her meaning rang clear. *Fletcher would listen to you. Fletcher would listen to Hiram Cummings's son.*

Did the entire town think he was his father?

"What do you want me to talk to Fletcher about this time?" He couldn't keep the wariness from his voice.

"The brothel, of course. Unless you already have?"

He frowned. "What brothel?" Eagle Harbor had a saloon, The Rusty Wagon, but not a brothel. It was one of the few towns in Copper Country without one, and his father had worked hard to keep it that way.

"Don't tell me you haven't heard? Everyone at the beautification society meeting last night was talking about it."

He could well imagine. It was a wonder the beautification society got any work done considering the amount of gossip spread at those meetings.

"Mr. Herod wants to add a brothel onto The Rusty Wagon." She surveyed his face closely.

"Mr. Herod doesn't own The Rusty Wagon."

"He's buying it from Neville Greer."

Elijah took a step back. Reed Herod had enough money to change The Rusty Wagon from a grimy saloon people endured to a fancy place people wanted to frequent. He could easily make it into an elaborate brothel like the one he owned at Central. "That had better be a rumor."

"That's what I thought the first time I heard it, but I was at the general store last night and overheard Mr. Foley complaining about it to Mr. Sinclair. Sinclair seemed right pleased by the notion though, and that's when I knew it was true."

Oh, Sinclair would be pleased indeed, seeing how his shipping company brought boatfuls of randy sailors into town.

"Do you think you can stop it?" Mrs. Kainner bit the side of her lip.

Of course he was going to stop it. What kind of man would stand by and allow such debauchery into the town he'd grown up in? Especially when he had a sister pretty enough for the brothel owner to notice?

"If you'll excuse me, Mrs. Kainner, I'd better pay a visit to Mr. Fletcher."

"Oh, I knew you would help." She reached out and patted his upper arm, beaming as she stared up at him. "Don't you see? The town needs you."

"Good day, Mrs. Kainner." He pulled his arm away, settled his hat back atop his head, and started down the rocky trail to the warehouse.

The brothel coming to Eagle Harbor could be stopped easily enough. The town council just needed to pass a resolution forbidding prostitution within the town limits. Herod could have his saloon—which he'd no doubt pretty up—but he couldn't have a brothel.

And as for the rest of what Mrs. Kainner had said, well, she simply didn't understand. He couldn't stay in Eagle Harbor, not when he had commitments to fulfill in Port Huron, not when he'd already made a down payment on a shipyard.

But if he hadn't made that down payment? If he wasn't committed to Mac and the shipyard?

An uncomfortable itch started between his shoulder blades. There would always be ships in need of rescuing. If he stayed, he could start a volunteer rescue team and create Eagle Harbor's own little life-saving service. He could see that the *North Star* was fixed, convince Isaac to fish with him, and make certain Rebekah set her trousers aside and settled into more womanly pursuits.

God had a plan. Mac kept telling him that. But what if God's plan for him wasn't a shipyard in Port Huron? What if God's plan meant he stayed in Eagle Harbor?

⌐.⌐.⌐.⌐.⌐

"You have to let me out." Mac gripped the bars of the jail cell and craned his neck to peer down the hall toward the sheriff, who was bathed in a swath of gold-tinted light from the setting sun.

"I don't have to do nothing, Oakton." Sheriff Jenkins tilted back in his chair, his stomach bulging over the waist of his trousers, and his feet propped up on his desk.

Blood still streaked Mac's knuckles from where he'd punched Sinclair over an hour ago. If only he'd been able to get another punch in before he'd been grabbed from behind. "It's getting dark. I have to get back to the lighthouse."

Sheriff Jenkins reached for the bottle of forty-rod whiskey on his desk and swigged it. "Should have thoughta that before you hauled off and punched Byron Sinclair while I was sitting at the bar."

Mac gritted his teeth. "If you were sitting at the bar, then you heard the things he said about Tressa Danell."

Jenkins yawned. "There ain't nothin' illegal about talking. Punching another man, now, we don't stand for that kind of behavior here in Eagle Harbor. Got to keep this town respectable."

Respectable? If every man who threw a punch spent time in a jail cell, the sheriff's office would have to take up an entire block of the town. He wasn't in jail because he'd thrown a punch—he could have punched anyone else in the saloon without landing himself in this cell—he was in jail because he'd punched the most powerful man in town. And like most people in Eagle Harbor, Jenkins didn't have the gumption to go against Sinclair.

Mac blew out a breath, long and hard, and glanced at the shaft of sunlight changing from gold to pink across the sheriff's desk. Being stuck behind bars was unfair, no way around it. But saying so wasn't going to get him out of this cell any sooner. Apologizing, on the other hand, might change a thing or two.

"I'm sorry for punching Sinclair." He forced the words over his leaden tongue.

"Good."

"So let me out."

"Nope." The sheriff leaned farther back in his chair.

Was it wrong to hope the chair collapsed under his weight and left him in a heap on the floor?

"Figure a night in that there cell might do you some good."

"You don't understand. I need to get to the lighthouse so Grover doesn't—" He clamped his teeth down on his tongue. Grover would despise him if he spread news of the lightkeeper's condition around town.

Sheriff Jenkins jerked his feet off the desk, his chair hitting the floor with a thud—and not collapsing, unfortunately. "Now listen here, Oakton, I've heard about enough from you."

"I've got duties at the lighthouse."

The sheriff lumbered to his feet. "You keep up that yammering, and I'll keep you in the cell an extra day for making yourself a nuisance. We got enough of them 'round here already. If you want out come morning, then settle in for the night."

"But morning will be too late." He could well imagine Grover forgetting to fill the lamp with kerosene. Then later tonight, groggy from getting no sleep after having to take Mac's watch, the lamp would go out. Grover and his shaking hands would refill the kerosene, would hold the match to the lamp wick, dropping it just before...

The door to the sheriff's office crashed open and boots raced across the floor, bringing in one of the mariners who'd been sitting in The Rusty Wagon with Sinclair. "There's a fire at the lighthouse. Come quick."

Chapter Fourteen

A fire. Oh, goodness! There'd been a fire. Tressa flew around her kitchen, packing every last baked good she had into the overlarge basket on her counter. The workers would need food. She didn't have a venison roast to bring, or even a handful of fish to cook over a fire, but bread and sweets should still be helpful.

"Hurry, Ma." Behind her, Colin bounced up and down on the balls of his feet.

"Just let me check…" She spun and cracked the oven door open. The cookies inside were just turning brown. Perfect.

Why had no one told her of the fire last night? Was Mac that angry over her sending him away yesterday?

It had taken Colin showing up at the lighthouse for chores this morning to learn what had happened. Oh, if only she would have known. She could have spent half the night baking.

Could have rushed over to the lighthouse to make sure Mac was all right.

"You're sure Mr. Cummings said no one was hurt?" She looked over her shoulder at Colin while she carefully relocated the hot cookies from the tray to the basket.

He pressed up onto the balls of his feet again, as though his little legs couldn't wait to race back down to the lighthouse. "I'm sure. Can I go without you? Mr. Cummings said there's plenty of work to be done."

"Sure, sure. I'll be right…"

The door to the back of the bakery slammed shut.

Behind you.

She packed the last of the cookies into an already stuffed basket and stepped into the morning sunshine. Colin had disappeared, likely running up Front Street toward the lighthouse. The streets in general were oddly quiet for this late in the morning. Had that many people gathered at the lighthouse to help?

Indeed they had. She saw the crowd on the lawn as soon as she turned onto North Street. But the lighthouse stood just as it had the day before. Its red brick tower jutted into the sky and the schoolhouse-like structure attached to it looked fine. Had the fire been a small one?

Small or large, she had to see Mac.

Colin and Mr. Cummings might claim he was fine, but it wasn't the same as seeing for herself. What if he'd been in the lighthouse when the fire started? Had he been the one to put it out? Maybe he'd been burned—

"Mrs. Danell." Mr. Cummings appeared before her, his smile wide as he took in the basket weighing down her arms. "Done some baking for us, have you?"

Her cheeks warmed and she nodded then glanced around the grounds. A group of men were headed toward the lighthouse with Rebekah Cummings among them, several carrying shovels.

"Here, let me take that for you." Mr. Cummings took her basket. "The food is set up over here." He led her around the side of the lighthouse, where a window had been shattered and dark trails of soot rose up the brick wall. Mr. Cummings then walked toward a table where a handful of women set out food. She surveyed the grounds again. Still no sign of Mac.

Was it too forward to ask where he was?

"Got more food for you, ladies." Mr. Cummings set the basket on the table.

"Oh, those muffins look scrumptious." Mrs. Fletcher moved closer to the sweets. "And you brought blueberry, my favorite."

Yes, the warehouse owner's wife was in the bakery at least twice a week for a blueberry muffin.

"The strawberry pie takes my fancy." Mrs. Kainner held out her hands for it. "And I know the bread will be good. My boarders simply love it. I don't know that they'll ever let me go back to baking it on my own."

"Thank you." Tressa smiled at the grandmotherly woman, but couldn't help glancing around once more in hopes of spotting—

"Tressa."

She turned.

Mac walked across the grass toward her, his shirt stained with soot while ashes smudged his cheek and forehead.

"Mac." She breathed his name without thought.

Behind her, one of the ladies let out a little squeal and a clap.

"Er—Mr. Oakton. You're..." *Alive. Safe. As handsome and tall and vital as you were yesterday afternoon.*

He stopped before her, his broad chest and towering form nearly eclipsing the lighthouse from her sight. She wanted to launch herself at him, to feel those strong arms wrap around her as they had in Dr. Greely's parlor and in Jessalyn's kitchen. Just to make sure he was alive, of course, and that her brain wasn't imagining such things. Oh yes, the desire to hug him was merely rational. It had nothing to do with her erratically thumping heart or the heat creeping up her neck and into her cheeks.

"You're well," she finally managed.

She expected him to grin and brush off her statement, perhaps make some comment about the strawberry pie she'd brought. But his gaze stayed serious, his eyes searching her face as intensely as she'd searched his.

"Yes, I'm well. And you?"

Her? "Oh, I'm… I'm fine." Why was he asking about her? She hadn't been through a fire.

"Are you?" His gaze stayed pinned to her despite the whispering sounds coming from the other side of the table.

She licked her lips. "Were you here when the lighthouse caught fire?"

"I told you, Erma!" Mrs. Kainner didn't even attempt to whisper.

Mr. Cummings started coughing and came forward, slapping Mac on the back. "Why don't you have a word with Mrs. Danell privately?"

"Oh, don't mind us." Mrs. Fletcher gave them a wide grin. "We're just busying ourselves with the food, is all."

"And having us married off before lunch," Tressa muttered.

The faint lines around Mac's eyes tensed. "What did you say?"

Her cheeks turned warm. "Nothing."

"Yes, yes," Mrs. Fletcher hurried around the table toward them. "Mac's been here since dawn. He needs a break. Why don't you two go over by the rocks there? That's a real pretty spot for a talk."

And fully in view of the women at the food table. Did they have nothing better to do than matchmaking?

He extended his elbow, but rather than take it, Tressa twisted her hands in her skirt. The last thing she needed was to have more rumors about her spreading around town. "That's quite all right M—Mr. Oakton. I need to get back to the bakery."

She would have stayed to help, had she been needed. But the

lighthouse grounds were already overrun with workers.

Mac took her forearm and settled her hand on his arm, clamping his hand down on hers so that pulling away would cause nothing short of a scene.

"I want a break before you go." He started off toward the rocky shoreline, tugging her along.

She glanced back over her shoulder at the smiling women they'd left behind. Mrs. Kainner actually grabbed her hanky and waved.

She jerked her head around and faced forward. "Where was the fire at? Did you put it out yourself?"

"It started in the kitchen. Grover put some coffee on but left a towel laying on the stove. By the time I got word and came, the fire was nearly out. The kitchen will need to be replaced, so we're cleaning out the rubble today. The Lighthouse Service has already been wired. Hopefully the inspector will come quickly."

"Oh." She peeked up at him, his jaw set and shoulders tense. "Did the fire happen while you were with me?"

"No, Tressa, not then."

She exhaled the mass of tension that had been knotting her chest. At least she hadn't been to blame, even inadvertently. "But you helped put the fire out? After you helped rescue Jessalyn and the others from a sinking sailboat? You're quite the hero."

And he was. From spending his money at the bakery to inviting her to town gatherings to paying Colin to do chores to rescuing families and putting out fires, the man was nothing short of heroic.

He took a small step closer—hopefully one of the ladies at the table didn't swoon. "Enough about me. Did you make any decisions last night? You seem more at peace today than you were yesterday."

"Yes." Though the peace had more to do with learning Mac

was safe than what she'd decided to do about her debt.

"So did you figure out a way to pay back Sinclair?"

"Ah…" She shifted from foot to foot. "Yes."

His hand tightened on hers. "How?"

"I'll work on one of his ships as he wishes."

His arm tensed beneath her hand. "No."

"It's the quickest, easiest way for me to pay him back."

"Judge Matherson might not rule for Sinclair. He could side with you."

She stared at the uneven boulders lining the shore. "When has old Judge Matherson ever sided with a woman?"

"So you go to court and fight for him to champion a woman for the first time. Don't give up. Think of what working for Sinclair will mean for Colin. For your bakery."

"That's where you come in, I hope. I was wondering if you could take Colin while I'm gone?"

He tugged his arm from her hand and turned to watch her.

"I know it's a long time," she rushed on before he could refuse. "And I know you'll be in Port Huron, but I'll be on a ship, so it's not as though I'll be near Eagle Harbor either. Colin adores you, and I would ask Jessalyn but—

"Stop." He held his hand up. "If you working for Sinclair is the only option, then yes, I'll take Colin. But I'm hoping and praying for a different way through your problems. One that involves the two of you staying together."

He might live in a world where dreams such as that came true, but she certainly didn't. "Don't get your hopes up."

"You never know. God might—"

"And don't speak to me of God." Her voice came out harsher than intended, but God allowing her and Colin to be separated was the last thing she wanted to dwell on, and He was the last place she would look for help.

"You can't mean—"

"Mrs. Danell." Leroy Spritzer rushed toward them, his dirty blond hair flopping into his eyes as he ran. "It's not true, is it? You can't be leaving."

She was, but seeing how Mac was the only person she'd spoken to about it, how did Leroy know? "Have you heard something around town?"

"From Colin." His eyes were wide and panicked. "I didn't know. I promise I didn't know. His pants fit him, and you were always giving us extra food. If you had money for clothes and food, I figured you had extra, that's all. I didn't know about the bank. I didn't know about Mr. Ranulfson. I didn't know you were going to get kicked out if I took it."

"What?" Her throat constricted, and she blinked. Her son's best friend couldn't be saying what she thought.

Mac rested a hand on Leroy's shoulder and kneeled down. A ten-year-old boy would be taller than most kneeling men, but Mac was so big, it only brought them face to face. "What are you saying, son? Why don't you start at the beginning, and try to be clear."

Leroy's eyes filled with tears. "I stole the money."

"More than once?"

The boy nodded through his tears. "I didn't know Colin would have to leave if I took it. I promise I didn't."

Mac glanced up at her, his gaze a strange combination of sad yet compassionate. She merely shook her head, the lump in her throat too thick for her to speak.

"Where is it now?" he asked.

Leroy burst into sobs then. "It's g-gone."

"All if it?"

Leroy nodded. "My pants were too small this winter, and Ellie and I had holes in our boots, but we didn't have money for new. And Colin said something about how his ma was careful to save up extra money. And his boots didn't have holes, and..." The boy fully broke down then, his words unintelligible beneath his sobbing.

Mac took Leroy in his arms, patting his back through the sobs, and glanced up at her. What was she supposed to say? Like the sheriff, she'd always assumed the thief to be a man Otis owed. Never would have guessed it was one of Colin's friends.

She shifted on her feet. She should probably say something. Do something. But what did one say to a little boy that had stolen her money so he could have warm feet?

"Am I going to jail?" Leroy looked up at her through his tears. "Do you reckon it's warm in jail during the winter? Or do they not run the wood stove during the day like Ma and just lay a fire at night? And if it's cold, will they let me wear my new boots? Or will I have to give them back?"

"You're not going to jail." She hadn't been sure what she'd do until the words came out. "I'm glad you were able to get boots for the winter." Though by the look of things, he'd never gotten pants that fit.

"You are?" Leroy wiped at his tears.

"Yes." She gave an emphatic nod. What other choice did she have, really? The money was gone, and given the mess Otis had left her in with Byron Sinclair, having that seventy dollars wouldn't have made much difference. She'd lose the bakery when she went to work on one of Sinclair's ships, whether she'd been paid up or not. And if someone was going to steal her money, she'd rather it be spent purchasing clothes for children than gambling and womanizing.

"But you can't do something like this again, do you understand? Mac's voice was hard, though his grip on Leroy's back looked gentle. "And we're going to have to tell your ma and the sheriff."

"Will he put me in jail?" Leroy blinked tears away and looked between them. "I thought Mrs. Danell said I didn't have to go."

"You don't have to go to jail, but you might have to help pay back some of the money you took." Mac's jaw was firm, his eyes serious, yet his face didn't fill with the rage that had so often consumed Otis's when he was upset, and the words that came from Mac's mouth were calm and measured rather than enraged shouts. "Maybe do work around town or at the bakery."

"Is Colin still going to have to move?" Leroy's jaw trembled.

Tressa bent to meet Leroy's gaze straight on. "Probably, yes, but it doesn't have much to do with the money you took" At least not anymore. "When Colin's pa died, he left us in a bad way, and we need to leave because of that."

"Maybe," Mac snapped. "That's not for sure yet."

"Mr. Oakton." A skinny man in a three-piece suit called from across the yard.

"Inspector Heathman." Mac straightened, his voice tinged with frustration as the man strode toward them. "I sent you a letter two months ago. It's taken you a rather long time to arrive."

The inspector stopped before them, a white pad of paper and pencil in hand. He scrawled something onto the paper before squinting up through his glasses at Mac. "I understand there was a fire last night and you weren't on the premises?"

Mac sighed. "No. It was Grover's watch. Now about that letter I sent."

"What letter? I don't recall receiving anything from you."

Tressa took Leroy by the shoulder and stepped away from the

men. "Let's go find Sheriff Jenkins and get this business over with."

Leroy nodded, his eyes rimmed with red. "Do you think he'll be angry?"

"I don't think he'll be happy, but I bet he'll be glad to find out who's been stealing, and I won't let him throw you in jail."

The boy nodded solemnly. "I'm sorry, Mrs. Danell. I never meant to cause you trouble."

No, he'd just wanted shoes. She sighed. If Byron Sinclair had a heart like Leroy's, then she wouldn't be in half the mess she was in.

~.~.~.~.~

Mac wiped his sweaty hands on his thighs and pushed open the door to the bakery, setting off the now-familiar jingle of the bell.

Do you want me to marry her, God? Is that your plan? He'd prayed countless times between yesterday and today.

"Tressa," he called into the bakery. It was unlike her not to appear the moment the bell tinkled. He moved behind the counter into the kitchen, which stood dark and cold.

"Tressa?" He tromped toward the stairs. Colin was still clearing rubble from the lighthouse, but Leroy had said Tressa headed back to the bakery after taking him to see the sheriff. She had to be here somewhere.

"Tressa?"

A thump sounded above him followed by the faint rap of footsteps. "Coming."

She hurried down the stairs, her head bent and cheeks pale, hair slipping from her updo. "I'm sorry, Mac. I must not have heard the bell. What can I help you with?" She paused when she reached the bottom step and looked up at him.

He should probably move back a pace or two so she could walk between him and the stairway railing into the kitchen. But staying in place meant he stood close enough to see the dark rim of brown on the outside of her irises, close enough to smell the traces of sugar and flour on her skin. He leaned closer, his nose grazing her hair as he whispered, "I came to see you."

A faint splotch of color appeared on her cheeks. "Shouldn't you be at the lighthouse?"

How was he supposed to work when he kept wondering whether or not he could afford to marry her? If she owed a small enough amount, then he'd get down on his knees here and now and ask her to be his wife.

Better yet, he'd invite her for a walk on the beach tonight and ask her then, or maybe take her for a picnic at that spot on the river he and Elijah had loved as boys. She wouldn't be able to refuse him surrounded by the green of the forest and the rushing of the river, the chorus of birds and the music of frogs.

Or so he hoped. He wiped his damp palms on his trousers. But at the thought of proposing, he was barely holding down the urge to grin like a lad getting his first shotgun. *Debt first, Mac old boy. Find out about her debt first.*

"Mac?" She blinked her large maple-syrup eyes at him as though waiting.

For what? Had she asked him something?

"The lighthouse?" she prodded.

Right. "We didn't finish our conversation from earlier."

"All I wanted to know was if you'd take Colin while I'm gone. Thank you for agreeing to do so, but that's all I needed."

"I, ah, stopped by The Rusty Wagon on my way here and got your list of creditors."

The color disappeared from her cheeks. "I told you I'm not paying them. Besides, I hardly think that list is any of your concern, Mr. Oakton."

Mr. Oakton, was it? "I needed to see it."

She turned away, though doing so didn't hide much of her face given how he'd cornered her.

"How much do you owe Herod?"

"Not a cent. I refuse to pay." Her hand balled into a fist at her side.

"Fine. Refuse to pay it, but I still want to know." Because he didn't believe for an instant that Herod would leave off without being paid, just like none of the men who'd written their names on the paper in his pocket would either.

"You've no reason to know any of this."

Why was she making things so difficult? "I have a reason, all right."

"Why?" Her head came up. "Do you wish to add your name to the people who want money from me? I know Otis owed you money. You're precisely the kind of man he looked for. Kind. Soft-hearted. Unable to say no."

"Confound it, Tressa." He slammed his hand on the stairway railing. "I don't want to add my name to anything. I just need to know how much debt you have so I know whether or not I can propose."

The air stilled around them. She didn't gasp, didn't move, didn't even appear to breathe. Instead she stared at him, her eyes wide; and if her face had been white before, it was doubly so now.

His own face turned cold. *You dolt. What are you thinking proposing that way?*

If that even counted as a proposal. He hadn't asked her a question so much as blurted his intent out of his bumbling, incompetent mouth.

"No," she whispered.

His throat grew suddenly tight. "No, you won't tell me how much? Or no, you won't marry me if I ask?"

She braced a hand on the wall. "Don't ask."

Don't ask? He took a step away, allowing her to move into the kitchen. She couldn't mean it, was probably upset that he'd asked by slamming his hand on a railing and demanding information rather than taking her somewhere nice like the river. "Forgive me, Tressa. I'm going about this all wrong. I only meant that were we to wed, I'd—"

"You'd assume my debt. No."

He blinked. "I have money already set aside. True, I need most of it to go into business with Elijah, but I can manage some payments to Sinclair."

"And Reed Herod? Can you pay him too? What about Mr. Ranulfson? Or the people on the piece of paper in your pocket?" She stormed to the sink on the far wall, where she began furiously pumping water.

"Outside of the list at the saloon, how much do you owe altogether?" He walked toward her.

"It doesn't matter because I won't let you pay. This is my responsibility, not yours." She stopped pumping and shaved soap into the basin inside the sink then tossed in some utensils coated in dried batter.

"No, it's not. It's Otis's. But he's gone now, and I won't stand by while you drown in your husband's wrongdoings. It's like watching that yacht stuck out on the rock reef all over again. I have to help."

"But I don't have to let you." She plunged her hands into the water and scrubbed so hard she'd likely sand away half of the wooden spoon she held. "It's too great a sacrifice for you to make. For anyone to make."

"Too great a sacrifice?" His voice echoed through the kitchen. Did she think she was worth nothing more than the broken shards of Grover's pottery they'd thrown down the outhouse pit? "You're willing to give up six months with your son to pay your late husband's debt though he dishonored you, never loved you, and gave you no choice about marrying him."

She kept her eyes downcast, her attention focused on the deuced dishes in the sink. "I plan to pay Sinclair back, yes, but I won't drag you with me. Now go. Please."

Frustration welled inside him. Did she truly expect him to stand by and do nothing? Why wouldn't she let him help?

"If it weren't for the money, would you say yes?" Why was he asking? It wasn't as though they could pretend a several hundred dollar debt didn't exist. Besides, he was offering her a marriage based on convenience, not love.

Or was he?

Light from the window above the sink slanted across her tightly hunched shoulders and set jaw, casting its yellow rays over the hair falling from her sloppy updo and the creamy skin on the back and side of her neck.

I'm almost in love with you.

I'm falling a little more in love with you each day.

I love you.

What was the truth? Which should he say?

Nothing. He'd already allowed his mouth to run off without his brain once in this conversation. More disaster was sure to follow if he let it happen a second time. "Tressa?"

"No, Mac." She set a whisk and spoon to dry on a towel and turned, her hands covered in suds. "I wouldn't say yes if all my debt was paid. I need you to care for Colin while I'm gone. That's all."

His heart ceased beating for three full seconds—which just might mean he loved her—at least a bit. "Am I not good enough somehow? Is it because of what my pa did?"

"It's nothing to do with you. I don't even know what your pa did, nor do I care."

"My old man created a mining scam." There was little point in hiding the story now that she'd refused him twice over. And the notion of her hearing all of it from the likes of Finley McCabe or worse set the unreachable spot between his shoulder blades to itching. "Said he'd discovered copper up on the eastern tip of the Keweenaw past Copper Harbor a bit, and talked like if everyone in town pooled their money, we could stake a claim and start up our own operation rather than letting the dandies in Boston own everything and make all the money.

"Most townsfolk found spare money one way or another. Some pulled funds out of the bank, others dug up chests of savings buried at the bases of forgotten trees in the forest." He could still remember it, young as he'd been. The hope in folk's eyes as they handed money to his pa, the excited whispers that followed them around town, the way everyone seemed to puff out their chests and carry an extra bounce in their steps. "Everyone thought... well, if they didn't think they'd get instantly rich, they at least thought the copper claim was a sound investment.

"And then he left. In the middle of the night. With all the money." With his words came the feeling of loss all over again. Of waking up in his bed only to find his pa nowhere inside their little clapboard house. Of thinking his pa had busied himself with something in town while he ate cold biscuits for breakfast. Of opening the door later that morning to find Sheriff Jenkins standing there with five more dollars he'd scrounged up to invest.

Of the suspicion that distorted the sheriff's face when he'd told him pa wasn't home.

"At the end of the day, I'm still the son of a thieving swindler." He glanced at Tressa, and the sympathy in her eyes was enough to make the little ten-year-old boy inside him start crying for his lost pa all over again. "It's not that I don't like my job at the lighthouse, but Grover's sick. Doc Greely thinks he might have something called shaking palsy, and if so, it's not an illness that'll get better. He can't stay on as head keeper, so the inspector offered me his job. But I can't stay in Eagle Harbor. Everyone remembers what my pa did. And when they look at me, they see only…"

"Someone else's wrongdoings."

~.~.~.~.~

He would have been Colin's age when his father left. Had he ever healed from the wounds of having his father disappear on him? Tressa's heart ached for the little boy that had lost so much more than money that day.

Should she wrap her arms around him, not for her own solace as she had yesterday, but to offer comfort this time?

She couldn't, not when she'd just turned down his offer of marriage twice.

Mac blinked, and the glaze of memories faded from his eyes. "I can wait for you. I think it'd be best to go to the minister and get hitched now so we can work out a way to handle your debt together, but I can wait."

Yes, he would probably think that. Because he was sweet and kind and good. Far too good for her.

She pressed her eyes shut. *Stop. Don't make me say no again.*

"I want you and Colin to move down to Port Huron with me, but if you want to work off your debt to Sinclair first…" His voice grew thick, his words slow. "That is, I guess I'm saying... I'd be honored should you choose to become my wife. And whether you decide that today or tomorrow, in six months or two years, the offer will stay open."

Her heart left the vicinity of her chest and thumped hard against her throat. She twisted her hands in the folds of her dress until the fabric was sure to permanently wrinkle and fought to even out her breathing. Why was he doing this? Didn't he understand it was easier to let debt be the reason she refused him?

He clearly didn't, and he wouldn't understand her other reasons for not marrying again, reasons that pertained to marriage itself. Like how everything she ever owned would belong to him, and she couldn't stop him if...

"Tressa?" He shifted his towering form awkwardly from foot to foot, his eyes latched onto hers.

"No."

"That's it? Just no? You won't even tell me why? You say it's not because of my father, but that's the true reason, isn't it?" He ran a hand through his hair and stared up at the ceiling. "And here I thought you, of all people, would understand a son shouldn't be judged by his father's deeds."

"It has nothing to do with your past." She reached out to touch his hand for the briefest of moments. "You're a wonderful man. Too wonderful, because you're willing to make such large sacrifices for me. I'm not worth a one of them. And even if I was valuable enough to wait six months for, I still couldn't... I couldn't..." She blinked away the threatening tears, remembering all too well the first time Otis had come home with the scent of a woman's cheap perfume on his shirt. She'd refused to let him touch her that night, but in the end he hadn't given her much choice.

"Tressa..." Pain laced Mac's voice.

She didn't want to hurt him. Save Colin, there had never been another person she'd wished so badly not to hurt. But the man expected something from her that she simply couldn't give. "You'd be a great husband, I'm sure of it. But as for me… I don't think you understand. There were women… other women… nights that…"

He took another step closer, but she was already pressed as tightly against the counter as possible. "I'd never be unfaithful. A vow of marriage is a vow before God, not something to be broken."

A vow of marriage also meant she belonged to her husband. That he would have control of her property, of her life.

Of her body.

Bile rose in her throat. "That's why I can't marry again. Because marriage is forever."

His forehead puckered into a jumble of tiny lines. "What if I told you I loved you? Would that make a difference?"

Did he have to be so wonderful? He was too nice by half, too compassionate, too giving.

Too completely and utterly perfect.

She could see herself going into his arms, taking his hand and walking to the church, standing before the minister with him as they took their vows. She took a step toward him—a small, unplanned step—then looked away. "Don't waste your efforts loving me. There's a good woman out there somewhere for you. One who doesn't have a ten-year-old boy to chain you down. One who doesn't cringe when she hears the word marriage or have her stomach churn at the thought of the marriage bed. You go to Port Huron and you find her, marry her."

He closed the space remaining between them with another step and took her by the shoulders. "I can't just snap my fingers and forget you." His breath puffed warm against her cheek, swirling the wisps of hair that had fallen. "Even if I could, I wouldn't want to."

"You should." She moved back until she felt the counter against her hip again. "You tried telling me about God's plan yesterday and this morning. Well, maybe His plan for you is somebody else. It would be easier for both of us if you just forgot… forgot…" She pressed her eyes shut. She wasn't going to cry over him. She wasn't!

A hand landed on her shoulder, soft and gentle. "You say God doesn't care about you, that His plan is for me to forget you and find someone else to marry. While I might not be able to look into your future and know God's plan, I can tell you what His plan isn't." His voice was low and gentle, beseeching even. "It isn't being separated from your son so you can work on a steamship, it isn't spending the rest of your life alone and unloved, and it isn't carrying the burden of Otis's debt by yourself.

"God's love, Tressa, it burns hot and bright for you. It's not like the lighthouse lamp, subject to man's control and man's errors. It doesn't go empty and need to be filled. It's constant, forever, like the sun. It burns all on its own, and nothing can stop it. It doesn't matter how dark and cold the night is, because it always rises again in the morning."

Tears blurred her eyes in earnest, and she glanced at the window above the sink, where rays of afternoon sunlight filtered onto the counter. Was God's love truly that constant? And if so, where had the sun been after her father died? Where had it been during her dark years of marriage to Otis?

Where was it now?

She looked up to find Mac's tawny eyes on her. Could she take his hand and share her problems with him? Could they face her difficulties together with God's support?

No.

Not when a decade of marriage to Otis haunted her, and the man before her deserved so much better than a debt-ridden failure for a wife.

Chapter Fifteen

She'd said no.

Not once, not twice, not thrice, but four times.

He'd proposed on accident. He'd proposed in earnest. He'd proposed and offered to wait for her. He'd proposed and told her he loved her.

No. No. No. No.

She'd looked at him with clear eyes, raised her chin, and said the word as though she were telling Colin he couldn't have his tenth muffin of the morning.

But they weren't discussing muffins or pies. They hadn't even been discussing her debt at the end. They'd been discussing the rest of their lives.

And she'd still said no.

Mac stared at the narrow river, the clear water frothing and churning as it raced down the hillside toward the big lake. He cast his line and stripped it back in, causing the fly on the top of the water to zigzag in a familiar pattern before he recast.

Did Tressa truly feel so little for him?

He loved her. He'd realized it sometime in between the second and third time she'd said no. Sometime around the moment she'd told him she wasn't worth waiting six months for. Wasn't worth the cost of her husband's debt.

She was a good mother. She'd faced numerous struggles and tragedies without complaint. She was generous enough to bring food to the lighthouse today when she could have sold her pies and muffins and bread for profit.

How could he do anything but fall in love with her?

Was he that hard to love in return?

He rolled his shoulders, aching from the tension coiled inside them, and recast his line before stripping it back in. His shoulders only grew more knotted.

He scowled at the familiar trees and the old tree house peeking through the leaves on the opposite bank.

He cast again, the white mayfly lure doing little to attract the fish that lurked in the water. How long had he been here? One hour? Two? The sun's western rays were slowly turning the forest from green to gold. Another half hour and he'd need to head back and light the lamp. And since Grover had now been officially relieved of his lightkeeper duties, he was the only one to tend the light all night.

Which was fine. He'd choose staying up all night for the next week over hearing Tressa refuse him again, over seeing the pale tinge to her face and determined lift to her jaw as she turned him away.

Because no matter how much he loved her, she wasn't going to accept his suit. And his moving to Port Huron next week would end the possibility of any future together.

Except he'd likely have Colin with him. If only he'd known Tressa was going to refuse him before he'd agreed to take the boy. How was he supposed to look at Colin, with the same coppery hair and brown eyes as his mother, and not long for Tressa?

One day Tressa would return for Colin. Then what? Was he

supposed to let the boy go? After being his father for six months?

And where, for that matter, would Tressa go? Ranulfson would certainly take back her bakery while she was gone. Did that mean she'd move on to another town or city? One where she knew no one? One where she was all alone?

Apparently she'd rather do that than marry him.

He recast the silken fishing line, too hard this time. The lure pinged off a rock on the far bank of the river before plunging into the water. He drew the line in and made ready to cast once again.

"Better let some of that tension out of your shoulders if you want to catch anything."

He jolted as he threw, causing his line to snag and tangle in the tree above.

Elijah appeared through the brush. "Angling is supposed to be relaxing. Try to enjoy yourself rather than treating it as a battle."

Easy for Elijah to say. His heart wasn't currently locked in a battle with his head. "The only time fly fishing becomes a chore is when your friend causes your line to get tangled."

Elijah surveyed the hopelessly knotted line. "Best cut it."

"That's my favorite fly."

"But not the fish's favorite, apparently."

Mac scowled and stared up at the little mayfly snared on one of the lower branches. The tree was too scrawny for him to climb but too high for him to retrieve the fly from the ground. He reached for the knife attached to his belt then cut the line as high up as he could.

"But as I said earlier, your lack of fish might have more to do with how tense your casts are rather than your lure."

Mac growled in the back of his throat.

Elijah gave a short laugh. "What do you think you are, a bear?"

"No. I think you're a nuisance." He stalked to his box of fishing tackle and studied the lures. Maybe a stonefly would work better. Or should he go with a wooly bear? He grabbed the little black stonefly and tied it onto his line, then glanced over his shoulder at Elijah. "Did you want something, or were you just rambling through the woods and happened upon me?"

"You disappeared from the lighthouse." Elijah nudged a rock embedded along the bank with the toe of his boot. "Everyone was wondering where you were."

"I had business to tend."

"The kind of business that involves taking the job as head lightkeeper? Rumor says Grover won't be able to stay on."

"More like the kind that involves proposing to a woman and being turned down," he muttered.

Elijah's foot stilled on the rock. "You proposed? To Mrs. Danell?"

"No. To Mrs. Kainner." He angled himself away from his friend and cast the line.

"How did you go from barely kissing the woman Saturday to proposing four days later?"

Mac shrugged lazily, or at least he tried to make the shrug lazy. It might have come off jerky instead—like the movement of his fly atop the stream as he stripped off line. "She needs a husband, and having a wife in Port Huron certainly wouldn't hurt anything. So I asked."

Elijah might be standing behind him, but the intensity of his calm, gray-eyed gaze probed his back. The man was too much like his father. With all that quiet patience wrapped up in genuine concern, a person couldn't help but confess their innards to either man.

"I might love her too."

"Did you tell her that?"

"Yes, and she still doesn't want me." He flung his fishing line over the water as though it were a stick of lit dynamite. The hook clattered onto the rocks on the opposite bank and sank between two stones. He tried to jerk the line free, but it stuck tight, the fly likely wedged behind the rocks.

He tugged again, then a third time.

"Easy, Mac. You're going to—"

The line snapped.

"Break the line."

He whirled on Elijah. "Satisfied now? Done telling me how to fish and interrogating me about Tressa? You can head on back to town and tell everyone that the son of the town swindler isn't good enough to marry the widow of the town scoundrel."

Elijah held his hands up. "I didn't come for any of that. I needed to talk to you."

Fishing pole still in hand, Mac crossed his arms. "Then why am I the one who's done all the talking?"

Elijah sat on one of the boulders. "First, I'm sorry for what I said yesterday about Pa being alive if you would have tried to rescue him. That was a cruel thing to say, and we don't know what would have happened. Those verses you quoted to me the morning after I got here keep running through my mind. God has a plan." Elijah's voice grew quieter and tighter with each word. "At the moment, I don't have more than a general idea of what it is, but if God wanted Pa to still be alive…"

"Elijah." Mac looked down at his hands, large and calloused from half a life spent working with his hands in one form or another. "Going out and attempting a rescue was Rebekah's idea, not mine. You're the one who's been on the Atlantic for two years. You're the one who's seen life-savers and life-saving stations. I've heard stories, sure, but I'd never seen anything of the like until I went along on that rescue yesterday."

Elijah rubbed the back of his neck and squinted up at him. "You're a good brother, Mac. I could never have asked for a better one."

He blew out a breath. If only Tressa thought he'd be a good husband.

"That's why I hope you understand when I tell you I can't go to Port Huron." Elijah's voice turned tight again.

Mac walked toward Elijah, still slumped on the rock near the riverbank, and laid a hand on his shoulder. "We already talked about this and it's fine. I don't mind waiting for you to come after things are situated with your family."

"I don't mean I can't go now." Elijah swooped his hat off his head and crushed it in his hand. "I mean I can't go at all. Ever."

A coldness started somewhere inside Mac's chest and spiraled outward, coating his arms and fingers, legs and feet in an icy crust. "What do you mean you're not going ever? You have to go. We signed an agreement. We put money down."

Elijah dug the toe of his shoe into the dirt. "You can have my part of the down payment and run the shipyard as your own. Look for a business partner once you're in Port Huron or an apprentice you could train and then let him buy into the company."

"Confound it, Elijah. I don't want to go by myself. You're supposed to come. We had a deal."

"I can't. My family—"

"They're my family too!" He threw up his hands, never mind that the tip of his fly rod scraped against the trunk of a nearby sapling. "I understand you staying for another month or two, but to give up on the shipyard entirely? This was our dream. It's why you sailed the Atlantic for two years and saved your money. Why I've saved every cent I've earned since I was twelve. We were going to leave Eagle Harbor together and start a business. Boat building, making fishing poles, commercial fishing, we didn't care what it was so long as we were together. And now we're a week away from starting, and you're backing out?" He shouted the last words loudly enough to be heard clear in Eagle Harbor.

"You have to come." An unfamiliar burning sensation crept into his eyes.

Elijah raised his gaze to Mac's, and he didn't need to speak for Mac to see he'd lost. Again. Just like he'd lost his ma before he was old enough to talk. Just like he'd lost his pa when he was ten and his adoptive father a month ago.

Just like he'd lost the woman he loved earlier this afternoon.

Now he was losing his brother to a town that wanted nothing to do with Clive Oakton's son.

Crack!

He looked down to find his hands fisted tightly around his fishing rod, which was now snapped in two. Rather like his friendship with Elijah. He clenched his jaw and flung it into the river. "Go."

"Mac, listen. It's more than just my family. I want to start a life-saving team. A volunteer one."

He needed to talk about this about as badly as Reed Herod needed to hire another girl for his brothel up in Central. "I said go."

Elijah stood. "You don't have to leave town either. You could stay, keep the lighthouse, be my second man for the water rescues."

Mac laughed, the sound overly loud against the quiet evening. Of course Elijah would say such a thing. He was Hiram Cummings's son and beloved by the town. Mac might have lived with the Cummingses for over a decade, but he'd never be one of them, not really. "You know I can't stay."

Elijah took a step toward him, his eyes sincere and concerned, his face so like Hiram's that Mac could hardly stand to look at him. "Maybe this whole shipyard idea wasn't ever God's plan for either of us, and this is God's way of keeping us here."

"And be stuck somewhere that hates me for something I didn't do?" He'd be in the exact same place he'd been a month ago, a year ago, two years ago, a decade ago.

"A town that hates you? Stop grumbling about your father and look around. Half the town showed up to help at the lighthouse today, and don't go telling me that's because of Grover. The grumpy old coot has done nothing but make enemies since his wife died. And I must have missed all the people on the beach that hated you after we rescued that family. Oh, and all the people that hated you at the meal on the beach last week. You were positively scorned away from the dancing and food."

"Enough." Mac raised his hand to stop Elijah. "You don't understand. You see everything through the lens of being Hiram Cummings's son. I don't have that privilege."

"Who my pa is has nothing to do with this." Elijah tightened his hands into fists and stared at the river, as though he might just scoop up the ruined fly rod and snap it into more pieces. "Those people at the lighthouse weren't taking orders from me today; they were taking orders from you. And when you disappeared, people noticed. People wondered where you were. People wanted you back."

"Do you know how many times my mind has run over what happened all those years ago?" Mac kicked at a rock. "I wonder if I missed something I should have seen to keep everyone from losing their money. Others have to believe I missed something too. Why didn't I see it? Why didn't I look harder?"

"You were ten. You were a lad and not a well-kept one at that.

Maybe a handful of folks still think about that lost money from time to time, but you've redeemed yourself in almost everyone's eyes but your own. You don't have to leave Eagle Harbor and start new, you just have to forgive yourself."

Mac blinked and tilted his head back to stare at the sky, its golden hue barely visible between the thick green leaves above. Was Elijah right? Was his own guilt the true problem?

Had the truth been right in front of him all this time?

If he thought back, he could count on one hand the people who were unkind to him. Finley McCabe, Grover, Byron Sinclair. Sheriff Jenkins never brought up what his father had done, and he'd been the lawman when his pa had skipped town. Mr. Ranulfson, Mr. Fletcher, and Mr. Foley would all bend over backwards for him these days. As for everyone else in the town, well, they had shown up at the lighthouse, hadn't they? And at the beach after the rescue.

He moved away and plopped onto the rock Elijah had vacated. "Could you head back and see if Inspector Heathman can light the lamp for me? I need some time to think." Some time buried deep in the woods with nothing but him and God and nature. He probably needed longer than the four hours he'd have, but he wasn't about to miss a watch, not when he might well be asking the inspector to instate him as the head lightkeeper so that he could stay in Eagle Harbor.

⌐.⌐.⌐.⌐.⌐

"I told him no." Tressa took a skirt down from where it hung on the peg in her bedroom.

"You did the right thing."

She turned to face Jessalyn, her friend's face somber despite her sunny blond hair and bright blue eyes. "Do you think so? Mac saved your life yesterday. Maybe... maybe I was too hard on him. Maybe I should have taken time to consider..."

"You said he only wanted to marry you if he knew he could afford your debt, right?"

"It's too big of a sacrifice." She laid her skirt in the trunk she'd drug out, bumping the lid with her shoulder, and causing it to fall shut with a thump. The two older girls playing in the corner glanced up at the noise, but Megan let out a soft cry where she lay sleeping on the bed.

"Hush now, sweetie." Jessalyn went to Megan's side and rubbed soothing little circles on her back.

Tressa swallowed. She'd miss the trio of flaxen-haired little angels when she left, everything from the feel of Megan's warm small body nestled against her chest to Olivia and Claire's happy banter and sweet smiles.

"I think you're wrong." Jessalyn placed a soft kiss on Megan's head and straightened. "I don't think Mac is making too big a sacrifice. It's that he's not making a big enough one."

Her gaze shot to her friend. "What do you mean?"

"If the man truly loved you, he'd offer for you regardless of how much debt you owed."

Tears blurred her eyes. "He said he loved me." And she'd told him that love wasn't enough. Oh, what if she'd just made the biggest mistake of her life? They'd only known each other a week, true, but marriage to Mac would be nothing like marriage to Otis. What if she'd already given up the one chance she had for a happy future?

"He didn't mean it." Jessalyn's lips pressed into a firm line. "Not if he asked you a bunch of questions about money first. If you ever remarry, it needs to be a man who'll sacrifice everything he has for you without complaint. Anyone else will walk out on you eventually."

Rather than Jessalyn's eyes growing misty with old memories, they turned hard and cold.

Tressa wiped a tear from her eye and turned back to the clothes hanging on the wall. Was she worthy of the kind of love Jessalyn spoke about?

"Ma, what are you doing?" Colin peeked his head into the bedroom.

Tressa's hands tightened on the shirtwaist she'd just grabbed. "Are you back from working at the lighthouse already?"

He stepped into the room, his eyes moving from the trunk to Jessalyn to the trunk and finally back to her. "It's past dinnertime. Besides, they sent everyone home a while back, but I fished a bit with Leroy and Martin. Why are you packing?"

"We have to move." She forced out the words her son had heard far too many times during his short life.

"No we don't. We're gonna get that money you owe Mr. Ranulfson back by the beginning of August. Just you watch."

She shook her head. "It's not because of Mr. Ranulfson. It's because of something your pa did before he died. Something I can't undo without leaving."

"You mean, you're not going to lose the building, but we're still leaving anyway?" He glanced around the room another time. Something must have convinced him they were truly leaving, because he spun on his heel and bolted into the hall. "No!"

"Colin!"

The door to his room slammed so hard the walls rattled.

She darted after him, twisting his doorknob only to find something stopping the door from swinging open. "Let me in."

"I'm not letting you in, and I'm not leaving neither. If you want to leave, I'll stay here with Leroy and Martin."

"Colin, stop."

"You told me we could stay. You told me it would be different this time, that we wouldn't need to move unless we got kicked out of our home."

She rested her forehead on the door.

"You're just like Pa—promising things but never doing them."

The words sliced like a pastry cutter through pie dough. She slid to the ground and leaned her back against the door. "You know how your pa had a habit of borrowing money? Well, he borrowed some from Mr. Sinclair, and I might have to work on one of his ships until it's paid back. I go before a judge tomorrow to find out for sure, but I already know what he'll say."

The door swung open, causing her to nearly topple backwards.

"You're leaving me too?" Tears streaked his cheeks, stemming from eyes red and swollen.

She raised up onto her knees and held out her arms for him.

"Oh, my sweet, sweet boy." She stroked her hand up and down his back. How much taller would he get while she was away? Would he grow more freckles or lose a few? Would Mac remember to cut his hair every couple months, or would it fall long and shaggy like it was now? "I don't want to leave you, not for a minute. But I'm not going to have a choice."

His arms wrapped tight around her neck. "How long?"

She swallowed the sob welling in her throat. "Six months, but the good news is you can go down to Port Huron with Mr. Oakton. He's happy to take you in."

"Mr. Oakton?" Colin pulled away and rubbed his eyes. "He wants me?"

"Of course he does."

He threw his arms back around her neck. "I'd rather be with

you."

"I know, but you'll have fun with Mr. Oakton too. And as soon as I'm done working for Mr. Sinclair, I'll come to Port Huron to get you. We'll start over again somewhere else."

"We won't be coming back here?" He sniffled against her throat.

"I can't make payments on the bakery while I'm working for Mr. Sinclair. We'll have nowhere here to come back to."

"I'll miss Leroy and Martin."

She patted his back. "We'll find a new town to settle in, one where nobody knows your pa and nobody wants money from us. You'll make friends there."

"Maybe we can stay in Port Huron." He shifted away from her. "Mr. Oakton will be there, right?"

Tightness squeezed her chest.

I'd be honored should you choose to become my wife. And whether you decide that today or tomorrow, in six months or two years, the offer will stay open.

But that didn't change the fact that he deserved someone far better than her.

She pressed her eyes shut against her threatening tears. "No. I don't think we can stay in Port Huron either."

⌐.⌐.⌐.⌐.⌐

Mac settled the moneybag onto the floor beside him, looked around the nearly empty schoolhouse, and scrubbed a hand over his face. Byron Sinclair and a dandy in a three-piece suit sat at a table near the front of the room on the left while Tressa sat at her own table on the right.

She didn't turn to look at him as he crammed his long legs

beneath one of the larger desks at the back of the room. Did she know he was here?

Though she probably didn't care much one way or the other after refusing him yesterday afternoon.

He yawned and rubbed at his still-bleary eyes, not that he'd expected to be wide-awake for a ten o'clock court appointment when he hadn't gone to bed until four that morning. At least Inspector Heathman had been understanding about his staying in the woods until midnight. And by the time his watch ended at four, well, he'd need a right long nap at some point this afternoon.

The court clerk entered the room from the little door at the front of the schoolhouse, pushed his glasses up on his nose, and sat down at one of the desks that had been dragged to the front of the room.

The bailiff came into the schoolhouse next and stood to the side of the teacher's desk, raised on a little wooden platform for the judge. "All rise for the honorable—"

The back schoolroom doors burst open and a group of men sauntered inside, the stench of stale whiskey souring the air behind them. Neville Greer, owner of The Rusty Wagon, sat in the desk in front of Mac while the others filled seats around Neville like a swarm of hornets—ones that reeked rather than stung. Then Reed Herod entered and a sickening sensation swept through Mac's stomach.

He glanced at Tressa, still staring straight ahead as though the bailiff was the only other person in the room.

The bailiff glared at the dozen or so men clustered around Mac and cleared his throat. "As I was saying, all rise for the honorable Judge Matherson."

Mac and Herod stood, as did Sinclair, his lawyer, and Tressa. The others looked around and swatted each other on their shoulders before lumbering to their feet.

Judge Matherson strode through the door at the front of the schoolroom, his steps brisk despite his graying hair and wrinkled skin. He seated himself on the makeshift judge's bench without ceremony before banging his gavel once, then twice. "I call this court to order."

He looked over the top of his spectacles toward Sinclair. "I see here that you have a promissory note signed by the defendant's husband for the amount of a hundred and fifty-four dollars and thirty-six cents."

Sinclair's lawyer scrambled back to his feet. "We do."

"Let me have a look at it."

The wiry lawyer riffled through his papers and handed a single half sheet to the bailiff, who in turn approached the judge.

"That note has nothing to do with me." Tressa sprang to her feet. "I didn't sign it, nor did I know it was being signed. And while I regret my husband's passing and I'm sorry to Mr. Sinclair for his loss of funds, I don't feel as though I should be responsible for the debt when I had no part in it from the first."

The judge peered over his spectacles at her. "Mrs. Danell, I'm not sure what tomfoolery you're used to in a courtroom, but I expect order. Now sit down. I never granted you permission to speak."

Permission to speak? Mac shifted in his chair, his blood turning hot. Without a lawyer, would the judge bother to ask her any questions? What if he just pounded his gavel and proclaimed she had to work for Sinclair?

The sound of wooden chair legs scraping against plank flooring filled the room as Tressa sat down, her face white. Was she nervous? If she hadn't refused him yesterday, he could be sitting beside her right now, his hand clasping hers.

Or better yet, protesting to the judge on her behalf.

And he was the biggest dunce to ever walk Copper Country. She'd refused him four times, yet here he was, his heart pounding against his chest, his hands damp with sweat, and every inch of his body still wanting to protect her.

"This promissory note is dated last November, is that correct, Mr. Sinclair?" Judge Matherson scratched the side of his head, causing a tuft of feathery gray hair to stick up.

"Yes, Your Honor."

"And if Mrs. Danell cannot pay you the full amount of one hundred and fifty-four dollars and thirty-six cents, you'd like her to work on one of your ships in her husband's stead?"

"Your Honor." The lawyer stood from his chair. "Mr. Sinclair feels that with a debt as large as this, Mrs.—"

The gavel pounded on the bench. "I wasn't speaking to you, Mr….?"

The lawyer cleared his throat. "Lewiston. Mr. Lewiston."

"Mr. Lewiston." The judge peered over the top of his glasses in a way that proclaimed the lawyer little better than an ant. "I was speaking to Mr. Sinclair. I only need to speak to you if you were present when Mr. Otis Danell signed this promissory note. Were you present?"

"No, Your Honor."

"Very well then." The judged moved his gaze to Tressa. "Mrs. Danell, do you have the money to pay Mr. Sinclair?"

"No, Your Honor."

"She does." Mac scrambled from his desk, his knees banging against the bottom and sending a shock of pain through his leg that caused him to nearly drop his money bag.

The judged looked at him, as did every other person in the schoolhouse—except Tressa.

"That is…" He cleared his throat and raised his voice. "I'd like to pay Mr. Sinclair in Mrs. Danell's stead."

"No!" Tressa bolted from her chair. "Judge Matherson, you can't let him."

The judge rubbed his temple and pressed his eyes shut for a moment. "And you are?"

"Oakton. Mac Oakton." He strode toward the front of the schoolhouse, only stopping when he reached the table where Tressa sat. She stared straight ahead, as though the blank, dusty chalkboard had a riveting dime novel written on it.

"And your relationship to Mrs. Danell?"

I would've been her husband, if she'd had me. "I, ah…" He shifted on feet that felt too big for his body then plunked the moneybag down on the table. "My relation to Mrs. Danell doesn't matter. What matters is I've got money and I'm willing to pay Sinclair on her behalf."

Sinclair smirked. "Isn't this interesting? The son of the town's previous swindler coming to the defense of the most recent swindler."

"Tressa never swindled anyone," he gritted.

"Judge Matherson, pay no heed to Mr. Oakton, I beg you. He's not responsible for Otis's debt." Tressa gripped the edge of her table until her knuckles turned pale. "I don't have enough to pay Mr. Sinclair today, but I do have five dollars." She laid a bill on the table in front of her. "And if needed, I'm willing to send him five dollars every month until my husband's debt is paid. But I can't work on his ship, not when I have a little boy to care for. And though I'm planning to leave Eagle Harbor sometime in the next few weeks, I'm more than willing to mail Mr. Sinclair payments once I get settled elsewhere."

Tressa's words swirled through the courthouse, but all Mac

could do was stare, his tongue fumbling for some response. She couldn't be leaving.

"She can't leave!" Someone shouted from the back of the courtroom.

"Exactly," he muttered.

"She owes me money too."

Or maybe not. Mac turned and glared at the ruddy, overweight man seated beside Neville Greer.

"And me." Reed Herod shoved his way out of the row of desks and stormed down the aisle, waving a piece of paper in his hand. "I've got proof right here."

"Me too."

"We wrote our names on a list down at The Rusty Wagon, but she hasn't said nothin' about paying us back."

The gavel rang through the courtroom, though half the men at the back kept nattering.

"Mr. Judge, sir." Neville Greer led a few of the men to the front of the schoolhouse. "Tressa Danell owes everybody here money."

Mac tightened his hand around the fabric of his moneybag. Even if the judge didn't force Tressa pay these men, they'd make her life in Eagle Harbor hard until they got what they felt they were owed.

If she decided to stay, that was.

He glanced at the judge, who was scratching behind his ear and scowling. "I'll pay it all."

"I said no." Tressa stood with her hands still gripping the table, her hair tied back in a severe bun and her skin snowy white against the faded black of her mourning dress.

He wasn't going to give her a choice, and he doubted the men would either. She might be a determined woman and a hard worker, but Sinclair wasn't going to accept payments of five dollars a month when he could be paid in full now.

No one would.

Judge Matherson banged his gavel again, silencing the yammering. "I want order in my court. Now sit down, the lot of you." He banged his gavel again, and the men shuffled back to the desks. Mac moved to sit in the chair beside Tressa, which earned him glares from both her and the judge.

Oh well. The entire town of Eagle Harbor could glare if they wanted, but he wasn't about to leave Tressa alone right now. He reached under the table, to where her frigid hands were clasped together in her lap, and settled his own hand atop them.

Across the aisle, Sinclair and his lawyer also sat, and even Reed Herod stalked back to a desk.

"Do any of you have proof of debt from Mrs. Danell herself?" The judge's voice rang authoritatively over the makeshift courtroom. "I'm not asking about her late husband, mind you. I'm asking about Mrs. Danell. Did she borrow money from any of you? Do you have her signature on a bond or promissory note? If so, please hand proof of such to the bailiff."

Silence filled the schoolroom until the hitch in Tressa's breathing became the only distinguishable sound.

"I am a circuit court judge, not a justice of the peace." Judge Matherson smoothed the folds of robe that lay on his chest and surveyed the room. "I have no involvement with trivial debts and hear only cases involving sums greater than a hundred dollars. Furthermore, Michigan state law does not hold a spouse accountable for personal debts accrued by a deceased partner during a marriage. Thus I hereby proclaim Mrs. Tressa Danell free of any debt."

The schoolhouse exploded around them, Sinclair, Herod, and the lawyer all jumping to their feet, demanding explanations, waving pieces of paper frantically in the air.

Mac tightened his hand atop of Tressa's where they still rested on her lap and grinned.

Chapter Sixteen

Tressa ducked her head as she hurried away from the school. She didn't owe a dime, not to anyone. She'd assumed that the moment Judge Matherson looked at her worn, patched mourning dress, he'd agree with Sinclair.

He'd sided with her instead. *Thank you, Father.*

And there she was praying again. It was probably the third time since Mac had given his little speech about God's love and the sun yesterday afternoon.

Which brought her to yet another point. Mac Oakton had tried to pay Otis's debt. All of it.

Where had he gotten the money?

"Tressa, wait." At the sound of Mac's voice, she paused for the briefest of moments, more an involuntary action than anything.

It took only a second for him to catch up with her.

"What were you thinking?" She thrust a hand toward the money bag, stamped with First Bank of Copper Country in square black letters.

"You already know." He reached into the bag and pulled out a stack of ten-dollar bills. "Here take this."

"For what?"

"Anything you need. A new dress. New shoes. Supplies for your bakery. A dinner that consists of more than leftover ham bones and a few wild greens."

Her heart thrummed so hard it might well burst through her ribs. "You need that money for your shipyard."

"Not anymore. You're looking at Eagle Harbor's new head lightkeeper." He grinned in a way that made the bright sun's rays look dim.

She shook her head as a cold sense of dread filled her. When she'd told Mac marrying her was too great a sacrifice, she'd never intended for him to make another sacrifice in its stead. He had to know that. "Don't give up your dream because of me. You worked hard for that money. You take it and do what you want with it."

"I am." He nudged the stack of bills toward her.

"No." She shoved her hands behind her back and clasped them tightly together so he had nowhere to put his money. "Paying my debt is never what you intended to do with your savings."

His eyes held hers, the soft, tawny brown of them so warm she could almost wrap herself in his gaze the way she would enfold herself in a quilt on a cold winter evening. He dropped the money back in his sack and reached out to tuck a strand of hair behind her ear, his finger lingering for one beat, then another before he dropped it. "Plans change. Elijah isn't going to Port Huron anymore, and I decided yesterday I wasn't going either. Now I've got a job that will keep me firmly rooted in Eagle Harbor for as long as I wish.

"But at the moment, I'm more concerned about you. You can't mean to leave." His words, gruff enough to be coated with crushed mine rock, drew her gaze up to his.

"I have to. For the very same reason you were going to leave Eagle Harbor." For the very same reason she'd given Colin yesterday. They'd do better in a town where no one knew her late husband had been a swindler. She was better off taking the money she'd saved to pay back Mr. Ranulfson over the past two weeks and using it to start somewhere else than trying to pay back her debt by the beginning of August.

"Don't tell me you're leaving because of what folks think about Otis." He took a step closer and rubbed his forehead, nearly knocking his hat from his head. "What I said yesterday about people blaming me for what my pa did was wrong. You saw how many townsfolk showed up to help at the lighthouse. They wouldn't do that for a man they wanted to run out of town."

She shook her head. "Don't make things seem better than they are. I heard what Mr. Sinclair said back there about you being the son of the town swindler."

"No doubt about it. Sinclair lost big when my pa left. And Finley McCabe will always dislike me as well. But that's two men. Two bitter, unforgiving, greedy men. Not everyone in town is like that. I did some thinking yesterday, and what I said about needing to leave, it was more because I was unwilling to forgive myself." He blew out a breath, and his gaze travelled to the ground before coming back up to meet hers again. "Because sometimes I think I should've been smart enough to figure out what my pa was about. Surely there was some sign he intended to steal all that money, and I missed it."

"No." How could he let himself carry around all that guilt? She reached out and laid a hand on his arm. "You're no more responsible for your father's actions than Colin is for that tree falling on Otis."

His gaze dipped to the ground again. "I think other folk have an easier time seeing that than I do myself."

"Even if you had known what your pa was up to, I doubt you could have stopped him." Though, she could imagine a shorter, scrawnier version of Mac crossing his arms over his chest and attempting to demand an explanation from his father. And who knew what his father would have done. Whipped him? Taken him into the woods and abandoned him? Even if his father had taken Mac along when he'd skipped town, Mac would have turned out poorer for it. She might not know every detail about his childhood, but being raised by the Cummings family had been best for the hurting little boy.

Just like spending time with Mac did her hurting little Colin so much good.

"I'd hoped you'd understand." The words rumbled from his chest. "So will you stay?"

She stared at where her hand rested on his sleeve, at the tiny pores in the blue fabric of his shirt, until her vision began to blur. He wanted her to stay. Here. In Eagle Harbor. With him.

And she could see herself doing it. Even now she could see herself stepping closer to him, pressing a kiss to his cheek, taking his hand, heading to the church…

And then what? Going home to the marriage bed? Mac had given her one kiss, the briefest, gentlest brush of lips on lips, and she'd pulled away as though it had scalded.

Because she wasn't ready to be married again.

And even if she was ready, Mac needed to wed someone with a better reputation than her. Perhaps she didn't have a mountain of debt to saddle him with anymore, but she still carried her mortgage on the bakery and the stench of Otis's deeds. Mac should look for a wife whose reputation would remove any reminders of his father's actions, not draw them to the surface. He deserved to marry the most wonderful woman in America, and she was as far from being that woman as a crow was from being an eagle.

And the thought of staying in town and watching him fall in

love with another woman made her stomach roil as though she'd just gulped some of the strong spirits Otis had been so fond of.

Then there was Colin to think about. It would still be best to take him somewhere that no one knew his pa. Yes, he'd miss the Spritzer boys, but once he settled elsewhere, he'd make new friends.

She took a step away from Mac. "I still have to leave. I'm sorry."

And she was. In more ways than she could list. "Now if you'll excuse me, I need to get back to the bakery." She turned and left him standing on the street, and he, being the gentleman that he was, let her go.

Because unlike Otis, Mac had never once forced her to do anything. Not even talk to him.

It was just as well. More talking meant being near him longer, meant smelling the sunshine and soap on his clothes and the deeper, muskier tinge that emanated from his skin. Meant looking into those soft eyes so full of love—

No. His eyes weren't full of love. He only thought he loved her. One day he'd meet another woman, a good woman. One who hadn't been married to a swindling ogre for eleven years. One that would make him laugh and smile rather than pour problems into his lap.

One that would make him realize he'd never truly loved Otis Danell's destitute widow.

She hastened her steps along the road, brushing past a trio of Cousin Jacks as she hurried toward the bakery. She needed to finish up the bread she'd…

Wait. There would be no more bread and muffins. No more Mac stepping in through the back door to discover her kitchen floor splattered with dough and flour and strawberries. No more trips to Jessalyn's after a long day or spare food to send home with the Spritzer boys.

Jessalyn's. How had she forgotten Colin? He was probably pestering Jessalyn with his worries every five seconds.

She turned back for Third Street and headed north, increasing her pace until she reached the top of Jessalyn's steps. She knocked before letting herself inside.

Jessalyn's head came up from where she sat at her sewing machine, pumping her feet as the needle moved up and down in rapid succession.

Claire and Megan both sat on the floor beside her, the babe stuffing the head of a wooden sheep into her mouth while the toddler had a toy horse hitched to a miniature wagon.

"What's wrong, Ma?" Colin stood from where he and Olivia spun tops near the couch.

She looked around the room once more, the children playing on the floor, the dying hum of Jessalyn's sewing machine, the little motes of dust spinning in the light from the window. "Everything's fine. Just fine."

At least it was inside Jessalyn's small parlor. Everything was far from fine in her heart.

Colin took her hand, staring up at her with buttery brown eyes the same shade as her own. "Are you going to have to go away?"

"No." She rested her hand atop his mop of floppy hair. "Not to work on Mr. Sinclair's ships."

"Then why are you crying?" He squeezed her hand.

"I'm not." Her eyes were just a little teary. Or maybe a lot teary.

"If you're not going away to work, how are you going to pay Mr. Sinclair all that money?"

Tressa sank to her knees and wrapped her arms around Colin so tightly his little heartbeat thumped against her own. Perhaps Mac hadn't paid Otis's debt to Byron Sinclair, but if needed, he would have sacrificed a lot to give her six months with her son.

"Ma, you're squishing me."

"Sorry." She released him and stood only to find Jessalyn beside the couch, one hand propped on her hip.

"What happened?"

"Yeah. How are you gonna pay Mr. Sinclair back all that money Pa owed?"

Her throat tightened. "I don't have to pay anything."

"Yippee!" Colin bounced on the balls of his feet. "Mr. Oakton and me prayed that ol' judge would be nice to you!"

"That's just wonderful, isn't it, Colin?" Jessalyn's eyes narrowed on her. "Now do you mind watching the girls for a few minutes while your mother and I slice bread for lunch?"

"Yes, ma'am." Colin plopped himself back onto the floor by the tops while Jessalyn moved weightlessly into the kitchen.

Tressa followed on feet that felt strapped down with copper ingots.

"What happened at court?" Jessalyn whirled on her the second she stepped through the doorway.

She slid into a chair at the table and buried her face in her hands. "Mac Oakton."

"Mac Oakton, the man who proposed yesterday?"

Heat crept into her cheeks. Why had she told Jessalyn what happened between her and Mac?

"Oh, for heaven's sake." Jessalyn stomped her foot on the floor, probably in an attempt to demonstrate her frustration, but she was too small and blond and pretty for the display to be effective. "Talk to me or I'll go find out from him myself."

She dropped her hands and stared at the checkered tablecloth instead. "You remember how Mac is supposed to leave for Port Huron next week? Well, he decided not to go. He took the money he'd saved to buy that shipyard, came to the school, and offered to pay my debt instead, and not just my debt to Mr. Sinclair. Others that came as well, Neville Greer and some of the men that made that list over at The Rusty Wagon. They wanted the judge to make me pay Otis's gambling debts to them as well."

"That's ridiculous. Since when does a bereaved widow have to pay her husband's gambling debts? Was Reed Herod there too?"

She nodded. "He wanted that sixty-some dollars he says Otis ran up over the winter."

"And Mac paid him?"

"No. The judge didn't make me—or Mac—pay anyone. I thought for sure he'd give Mr. Sinclair whatever he asked for, but he said the debt was Otis's, not mine. And since I hadn't signed the promissory note, I don't have to work on his ship either. But still…"

Jessalyn gave a curt nod of her head. "It's about time that old coot did something that made sense."

The image of Mac striding down the aisle, moneybag in hand, filled her mind. "Mac planned on giving up his every last cent to clear my name." She crossed her arms on the table and slumped her head on them. "What am I going to do?"

Jessalyn plunked down into the chair beside her. "You're going to marry him, that's what."

Her head shot up. "I can't. Certainly you of all people understand."

Now it was Jessalyn's turn to stare at the tablecloth. "I learned something last night after I left the bakery."

The apologetic tone in Jessalyn's voice made her pause. "What?"

"You know how you told me Mac wasn't at the lighthouse when the fire started? Rumor is he wasn't there because he was in jail."

"Jail?" Her stomach churned sickeningly. "That has to be a mistake. Mac would never do anything to land himself in a jail cell."

"Evidently he stormed into The Rusty Wagon and punched Byron Sinclair in the face." Jessalyn raised her eyes from the table. "Because of you."

The sickening sensation worsened.

"They supposedly had a nice little argument about you. Probably all things Sinclair needed to hear, but unlike the rest of us, Mac had the courage to tell him."

No. She pressed her eyes shut. Mac wouldn't have ended up in jail because of her, would he? But she could picture it all too easily, Mac yanking Mr. Sinclair away from whatever card game he played and speaking his mind about her court hearing. Mr. Sinclair offering his cat-like smile and saying something intended to rile Mac up, and Mac tightening his fist. "But the sheriff must not have kept him long. Mac said he helped put out the fire."

"He let Mac out as soon as they got news of the fire. Listen, Tressa." Jessalyn squeezed her hands together atop the table. "I know I told you to be careful about getting hitched yesterday when Mac said he'd marry you only if he could afford your debt. But if he's willing to confront the most powerful man in town for you, if he's willing to take his own savings and spend it for you after you turned him down, then he loves you something fierce. Heaven knows I don't think very highly of men in general and husbands in particular, but if I had a man who was willing to pay three hundred dollars or better to save me, I'd snap him up in a heartbeat."

The ticking of the wall clock filled the kitchen. There were reasons she should leave Eagle Harbor, myriads of them. Even more, there were reasons she never wanted to marry again.

But suddenly, she couldn't remember a one of them.

⁓.⁓.⁓.⁓.⁓

"Tressa, why didn't you tell us?"

Tressa paused as she came around the corner of her bakery and spotted Mrs. Kainner and Mrs. Ranulfson standing outside the door. "Tell you what?"

Mrs. Kainner pressed a hand to her bosom. "That wretched man was taking you to court? We would have been there to support you."

"I'm glad Judge Matherson had some sense about him." The ostrich feathers on Mrs. Ranulfson's hat quivered with her indignation. Never mind that the woman hadn't stepped into Tressa's bakery once since she'd fallen behind in the payments owed to her husband's bank. "Making a widow with a child pay for gambling debts. Who'd ever heard of such a thing?"

Tressa stared at the women with their straight postures and tidy hats. Did they really care so much about her court case?

"Mrs. Danell?" Mrs. Kainner blinked expectantly. "Were you going to let us in? I want some muffins, and Betty here is in need of a pie—strawberry, I believe."

"Right. I made a pie this morning." She'd pondered baking a second but put the idea off due to her court hearing. She pushed the key into the lock and opened the door, holding it open for the women.

Mrs. Ranulfson breezed past her, the ostrich feathers that stuck up from her hat nearly brushing the top of the doorway. "Ernest just raved about the piece of pie he had at the lighthouse yesterday."

Ernest? Was that Mr. Ranulfson's Christian name? And even though she'd owed the bank money, Mr. Ranulfson had been in at least once a week for a pie. Perhaps he ate it at work and had never told his wife?

"What kind of muffins do you have today?" Mrs. Kainner strode over to the shelf where the muffins were displayed. "I thought my boarders might enjoy trying something besides your bread."

"These muffins here look positively delightful. You'll want this kind, Eleanor." Mrs. Ranulfson turned toward Tressa. "What do you use for the topping? Some sort of streusel?"

"Brown sugar, nuts, butter, and flour." She scampered behind her counter and took out a paper sack. "Mrs. Kainner, how many would you like?"

"I'll take a dozen and a half."

"Ah, I only have a dozen." Which the woman would know if she'd bother to count. Tressa put the first two into the sack, careful to stack them so the topping didn't rub off. "I can make six more and have Colin run them over in an hour or so."

"That sounds delightful, thank you. Can I pay for all of them now?" Mrs. Kainner dug through her reticule and laid three dollar bills on the counter.

"It comes to one dollar and eighty cents." Tressa nudged one of the bills back across the counter.

Mrs. Kainner bit the side of her lip, her blue eyes holding a bit of sparkle. "I know the muffins are ten cents apiece, but I'd like to give you the extra dollar just the same. What, with all you've been through lately, losing your husband, being robbed, and having Byron Sinclair come after you, I imagine you can use the extra."

Tressa's jaw opened. How did Mrs. Kainner know about the

robbery?

"Oh, there now, don't look so shocked." Mrs. Kainner reached for her hand, still lingering on the extra dollar, and patted it. "It's the least I can do after everything. Do you think you could have another dozen and a half muffins for me tomorrow afternoon, along with the usual bread?"

Tressa cleared the lump out of her throat before answering, "Certainly."

Although maybe she shouldn't agree since she was supposed to be packing up and talking to Mr. Ranulfson about letting the bank take the bakery back.

"I'll take the strawberry pie." Mrs. Ranulfson set the pie on the counter beside the muffins. "And a half dozen of those cinnamon and sugar covered cookies."

"They're Colin's favorites." And Mac's, but she wasn't thinking about the tender-hearted lout of a man who'd tried to pay her debt earlier. No. Certainly not. She swallowed yet another lump threatening to form in her throat, put the last of the muffins into the sack, and headed over to the cookies.

Mrs. Kainner took the bag and peered inside, then back up at Tressa. "I've been meaning to ask you if you're free Tuesday night. I probably should have asked before, but it seemed to always slip my mind."

Her hand stilled on the cookie. "Tuesday?"

"It's no trouble if you are." Mrs. Ranulfson interjected. "We just wanted to invite you to the Eagle Harbor Beautification Society meeting."

Weren't they the ones responsible for the atrocious looking rose bushes by the pier?

"Yes, we'd love to have you," Mrs. Kainner added.

"The meetings don't last more than a couple hours, really."

Mrs. Ranulfson took a cookie and stuck it into the sack Tressa was supposed to be filling. "We bring snacks and visit and discuss ways to beautify the town."

"Maybe you could bring muffins?" Mrs. Kainner's nose was still stuck in the top of the bag.

"Or a pie." One of Mrs. Ranulfson's eyebrows rose.

The bell above the door jangled and a young man with a hat pulled low over his brow tromped inside and headed straight for the counter. "I need a couple loaves of bread."

Tressa took a second look. His voice was distinctly feminine.

"I say, Rebekah." Mrs. Ranulfson slid two dollars across the counter and picked up her pie before turning to the younger woman. "You must give your mother apoplexy every time she sees you dressed like that. Where's your skirt?"

Rebekah looked away from Mrs. Ranulfson, and Tressa didn't need to see her eyes—still covered by the hat brim—to imagine the way she rolled them. "Have you ever tried sailing in a skirt? And I don't mean sitting around and reading while your husband and sons man the sails. I mean working the rigging yourself."

Mrs. Ranulfson stiffened. "Yes, well, for that to happen we'd need to have a sailboat that wasn't dashed to pieces."

"Rebekah, we were just inviting Tressa here to the beautification society meeting on Tuesday." Mrs. Kainner smiled a little too brightly. "Maybe you'd like to come as well?"

The woman mumbled something about rather gutting a hundred fish, then she moved to the counter with a clipped, efficient gait and slapped two bills down. "About that bread."

She handed Rebekah two loaves. "Keep your money. I heard tell that Otis borrowed from your pa and never repaid anything. I'd like to settle the score."

Rebekah pushed her hat up and watched her with eyes the color of springtime grass. With her creamy skin, pert little nose, and delicate jaw, she was beautiful enough to be pictured in one of those advertisements for female complaint elixirs that always appeared in periodicals. Even her too-big shirt and britches couldn't hide her comeliness. "Heard you saw Sinclair in court today. I count anyone who stands up to that scoundrel a friend.

"And as for that other bit of business." Rebekah squirmed uncomfortably. "I may have been wrong about... ah, what I'm trying to say is..." She nudged the money farther across the counter. "I know my pa lent that money to your man, not you, and if you knew my pa, he probably didn't expect to see a penny of it back. So take my money. I've had your bread before; it's worth it."

Tressa sucked air into her lungs and couldn't quite remember how to release it. Rebekah hadn't been into the bakery since her pa died, and now she suddenly appeared and wanted to spend money? Wanted to forgive Otis's debt? And Mrs. Ranulfson had apparently decided to start patronizing the bakery again too—at the same time as Rebekah. Maybe the changes were due to her standing up to Byron Sinclair, but another answer came to mind too, and with it flashed the image of a towering man standing to his feet and proclaiming to the entire court that he would pay her debt.

Had Mac convinced Rebekah and Mrs. Ranulfson to be nice to her so she'd stay in Eagle Harbor? Yet even if he had, both women appeared sincere and not like they'd been forced to come inside the bakery.

She slipped the bills into her money box. "Thank you."

The bell jingled again and in walked Ruby Spritzer, her graying brown hair pulled back in a sloppy bun and stains marring the worn fabric of her dress. Two small children trailed behind her, each gripping one side of her skirt, their faces dirty and clothes three sizes too small.

Did Mac have something to do with this as well? Had he gone on some kind of campaign to flood her bakery with customers?

"Hi, Ruby." Rebekah smiled at the other woman and then squatted down until she was eye level with the little ones. "Hi, Janey. Hi, Joe. You come to town with your ma today?"

Two dirty little heads nodded up and down.

"Well, it just happens I stopped by the general store before coming here." Rebekah pulled two pieces of penny candy from her pocket.

The girl—Janey, was it?—tugged on her mother's skirt. "Can we, Mama? Can we?"

Two splotches of color appeared high on Ruby's cheeks. "I suppose."

The children let go of their mother's skirt, reached for the candy, and stuffed it into their mouths.

"Thank you, Mith Cummingth," Joe slurred around his sweet.

"Yez, thank you."

Ruby used the distraction to step to the counter and bend her head near Tressa's. "I ain't here to buy nothing, just to give you this." She set a bill and some change onto the counter.

The crisp ten dollar note looked awfully similar to the stack of those Mac had tried handing her on the street earlier. Tressa slid the money back toward the older woman. "I can't take money from you."

Ruby adjusted the threadbare shawl around her shoulders. "Now don't be stubborn. I know what my Leroy did, and the baked goods you sent home with my boys this month alone are worth twice what I've got here."

"No." Tressa ducked her head and leaned over the counter, bringing her lips as close to Ruby's ear as possible so as not to embarrass her, though the woman's situation was hardly a secret in a town like Eagle Harbor. "I forgave Leroy. I'm glad you used the money to buy coats or boots or whatever else you needed. And as for the food, it's not worth anything. I only give you the items that don't sell. It's either feed you or the birds, and I'd much rather help my son's friends than the animals."

"I want you to take the money anyway. Every last bit of it."

She sighed and glanced down at the money. The bill had to have come from Mac, but the change was likely from wherever Ruby hid money so her husband didn't find it.

The bakery had fallen silent, and the heat of multiple gazes weighed on them both. She couldn't keep the money, but there were better ways of getting Ruby to take it back—ones that involved sending extra bread home with Leroy rather than declaring the woman too poor to pay for food in front of a couple town gossips. "All right."

Ruby stood a little taller as Tressa put the funds into her moneybox. Then the older woman covered Tressa's hands with her own thin ones. "You're a good woman, Tressa Danell. You just remember that."

"Well, Mrs. Danell, it appears as though your bakery is quite crowded."

Tressa jerked her head up as Mr. Ranulfson's fancy shoes tapped out a rhythm on the floor. He sent his wife a smile—or as close to a smile as Mr. Ranulfson could probably manage. It didn't have anything on the way Mac Oakton could grin.

"You make excellent pie, Mrs. Danell I'm glad to see Betty's bought one." Mr. Ranulfson looked around the bakery.

"Yes, well…" She shifted on her feet and reached for her moneybox. He likely wanted the money due on her mortgage, and with the rush of customers today, she just might be able to pay enough of her debt to make him happy.

Except she didn't owe him another payment until the first of July, which was still a week away. She scrunched her forehead. So why was he here?

"If I might have a word with you?" He looked around the bakery once more, filled entirely with women and children. "A private word."

She twisted her hands together in the front of her dress. Was she in some sort of trouble? If she legitimately owed anyone in this town, it was him. He could probably take her to court, but he'd promised she had until the beginning of August to catch up. Then again, it hadn't been in writing...

And why was she worried about such a thing when she'd already decided to give the bakery up?

"Mrs. Danell?" He arched an eyebrow.

"Right. Yes. Ah... how about we step into the kitchen?"

His fancy shoes clacked against the floor again as he followed her behind the counter and into the back room.

"If this is about the money I owe, I think I can—"

"You might want to look at these papers first." He handed her a folder.

She opened the thick yellow leaflet to find a paper she'd seen only once before, about a year ago, lying on top. "The deed to my bakery? Does this mean you're taking it from me?"

Why did it feel as though her heart had dropped to her knees? She'd already intended to give the bakery back.

The edges of his lips curved into the same almost-smile he'd given his wife in the storefront. "No, Mrs. Danell. It means the bakery is yours."

"It can't be. I owe you money, and Otis and I signed a seven-year mortgage."

He riffled through the papers until he came to one that listed the payments she'd made. "Someone came into my bank this afternoon and paid off your loan." He tapped the big number at the end of the paper. "The bakery is yours."

She looked up at him, a different type of panic igniting in her chest. "No."

"Yes."

"You can't take Mac's money," she choked. "You have to give it back."

"You expect me to refuse money on a property that's behind in payments? Perhaps you don't understand how a bank functions. You have proven to be a risk, Mrs. Danell. This money was guaranteed."

"He... he... he's spent years saving that money. He isn't thinking clearly. He doesn't know what he's doing." Except something told her he knew precisely what he was doing, just like he'd known precisely what he was doing when he'd offered to pay her debt to Sinclair.

Mr. Ranulfson's forehead pinched between his eyebrows. "Mr. Oakton opened his first account at my bank when he was fifteen. I'm very aware of the manner in which he's saved his money and how long it's taken him to do so. Now I suggest you keep these papers somewhere safe, as they prove you're the sole owner of this property." He turned and walked toward the storefront.

"Is this legal? Don't you need my signature to make this official?"

He paused in the doorway. "I have your signature on the original mortgage, which specifies what happens in the event you pay off your property early."

"But—"

"If you have further questions, talk to Mr. Oakton directly. All

I'm doing is delivering business papers."

She stared at the deed to her property, her hands shaking.

"Is Mrs. Danell back there?" Finley McCabe's warbled voice called. "Got some business to settle up with her."

"Yes, I was wondering if she had anymore pies for sale," said a female voice she didn't recognize.

Tressa stared at the typed words until the black and white began to blur.

Mac hadn't gone on a campaign to convince her she needed to stay in Eagle Harbor. Oh, no. He'd plucked her dreams down from the heavens and handed them to her instead.

Chapter Seventeen

The lake lay calm under the slanting sun, creating a pattern of twinkling diamonds atop the water. From his position on the grass below the lighthouse, Mac picked up a rock and tossed it into the lake. The pebble hit with a plunk, sending out little ripples as it sank to the murky bottom.

"Heard you bought a bakery." Elijah's words carried on the wind behind him.

Mac kept staring out over the water, where an eagle swooped and snatched a fish from the rocks on the opposite side of the harbor. He'd figured Elijah would come around soon enough.

"Heard you took the head lightkeeper job too." Elijah plopped down beside him on the lawn. "Seems you'll be pretty busy staying up all night to tend the light then heading to the bakery to open nice and early."

Couldn't the man just stare at the water without complicating the silence of the afternoon?

"Also heard Sinclair took Tressa to court this morning."

He kicked at a lone stick lying in the grass. Evidently expecting Elijah to leave him alone was asking a bit much. But then, if Elijah had just dumped his life's savings into a shop for some woman... "She didn't expect things to turn out in her favor."

"So neither of you told anyone about the court date?" Elijah's voice tightened.

"Sinclair told people. Reed Herod was there, along with Neville Greer and some of The Rusty Wagon patrons."

"Oh, so it was you and Mrs. Danell against two rich, greedy men and a bunch of drunkards. Glad I could be there to support my friend and his woman."

"I didn't need support. And she's not my woman."

Elijah swiped his hat off his head and rubbed a hand back and forth over his hair. "Did you take the lightkeeper post because you wanted to stay in Eagle Harbor, or because you wanted to pay Tressa's debt? Or because I backed out of our deal?"

The breeze off the lake suddenly turned thick and heavy. Elijah's penetrating gray gaze rested on him until he had to tamp down the urge to squirm like a schoolboy who'd hidden a frog in the teacher's desk.

He kicked at the stick in the grass again. "With everything happening as it did, I realized staying was God's plan for me. I suppose it's the same as you knowing that starting a life-saving team was God's plan for you when we went out and saved Jessalyn."

A grin spread across Elijah's face. He reached over and slapped Mac on the back, then kept his hand in place. "So why haven't you taken Tressa to the minister yet?"

"I told you yesterday. She said no. Four times. She added a few more no's after the court case too."

Elijah's brow furrowed into a scowl. "Paying her debt didn't change her mind?"

If only it had. "Says she's still leaving town."

"So you bought her the bakery with the hope she'd stay?"

Was that why he'd done it? One would think that giving up his savings would win him the woman he loved, but Tressa had fought him hard in that schoolhouse and harder on the street afterwards.

And she'd probably be here in a matter of minutes, fighting with him about the bakery.

At least now she could sell it and start over somewhere else if she so chose. He wouldn't be made to feel badly about providing for her and Colin.

If she stayed, it needed to be her choice. And if she let him woo her, that needed to be her choice. And if she one day stood hand in hand with him before the minister, well, that needed to be her choice too. She'd already been forced into one marriage she didn't want.

But did he have the strength to watch her sell the bakery? To carry her trunks down to the pier and stand on the dock as her ship left harbor?

God, be gentle on my heart. It can only take so much.

He looked over at Elijah. "I feel like I owe you an apology."

"For not telling me about the court date? Apology accepted."

"No, you dunderhead, for all the years I teased you about Victoria." He hadn't even begun to understand the way it felt to love a woman he couldn't have.

Elijah stared out over the lake, suddenly as riveted by the waves as Mac had been a few minutes ago. "I wish I could tell you loving someone that way is easy. Wish I could promise things will end well."

For him and Tressa, or for Elijah and Victoria? He wasn't sure he wanted the answer either way.

Didn't the Song of Solomon say something about many waters not quenching love nor great floods drowning it?

Then again, Song of Solomon also said something about Solomon's woman having teeth like sheep and hair like a goat. Or maybe it was teeth like a goat and hair like sheep.

Tressa's teeth weren't exactly goat-like, but her stubbornness sure was.

And he was mighty near to drowning in his love for her.

Which was a deuced thing seeing how that very love also kept him from traipsing down to the bakery and kissing her until her thoughts turned mushy enough she accepted his proposal.

He'd not force her. Not even a little.

"Mac," a familiar feminine voice called.

He could listen to that faintly lilting voice say his name for the next century.

If only he could tell her such a thing without having her grow quiet and distant.

He turned to find Tressa walking up the rocky hill toward him, but rather than striding with a determined gait and squared shoulders, her steps were slow and unsure, her shoulders slumped.

"I think I need to get back to... somewhere." Elijah grabbed him by the shoulder and pulled his head down. "And if you end up in front of the minister tonight, you'd better tell me. Before it happens."

They both stood, Elijah tipping his hat to Tressa as he passed.

Tressa's eyes followed Elijah down the hill for a moment, then she held out a single cookie. "I brought this for you." Her knuckles clenched tight around the cookie, which was probably what had caused most of the cinnamon and sugar coating to fall off. He took the offered treat, but the part she'd been holding half crumbled away.

"Thank you." He took a bite—or rather, he tried to take a bite. A large chunk disintegrated the second his lips touched it and fell to the ground in a heap of golden crumbles.

"You paid for my bakery." Her maple syrup-eyes clouded with

moisture. "How can I ever repay you?"

He stopped chewing, swallowed the lump in his mouth, and thrust the cookie back toward her. "If this cookie is supposed to be the first installment in your pay-Mac-back-every-penny plan, then you can keep it."

"You should never have done it." She ignored the cookie, her whispered words disappearing against the sound of lapping waves and circling gulls. "It's too much. I don't deserve…"

He tossed the handful of remaining crumbs over the rocks and into the lake below, then drew her stiff form against his chest. "What don't you deserve? To have your debt paid? Does anybody?" He stroked a hand up her back and then down again. "God paid a bigger debt for you than what I did today, and that's truly something you can never repay."

She tried to push away from him. "But…"

He anchored his arm around her shoulders and pressed a finger to her lips. "God has a plan, Tressa. And right now, that plan is for me to stay in Eagle Harbor and be the head lightkeeper. I don't rightly understand why that's what God wants, but it became clear to me yesterday. I thought you were about to lose your son for six months, and God had given me the money to stop it, so that's what I was going to do. Turns out I wasn't supposed to pay Sinclair, I was supposed to pay the bank instead."

She moved her lips to speak, but he only pressed his finger down harder. "You don't owe me a dime. I did it so you could be free, not so you would be beholden to me. I've got a notion that you want to stay in Eagle Harbor, that you secretly like it here and will get along just fine as soon as this fuss over Otis settles. But if you want to leave, then sell the place and use the money to start new somewhere else. You've got choices now."

He stared down into her eyes, their rich brown depths clouded with confusion, and he sighed. She didn't understand, and he wasn't sure she ever would. Maybe she was too proud to take his gift, maybe she felt too unworthy, maybe it was a combination of both.

And while he was hardly an expert on marriage, he'd only frustrate himself if he married a woman who refused to let him do things for her, to give her gifts, to love her freely.

She'd taken a step toward him by coming here today, but it was just that, one tiny little step.

Marriage might as well be clear on the Canadian shore of Lake Superior.

~.~.~.~.~

The afternoon sunshine was warm, but as Mac took his arm from her shoulder and stepped back, coldness engulfed her.

Tressa searched his face. Was he going to mention anything about marriage being in God's plan for them? He'd been talking like it was God's plan yesterday, so why didn't he say something now, when the idea of loving him didn't quite terrify her anymore?

She stood silently, waiting for the words to fall from his lips, but he only tightened his jaw.

He'd said he'd wait six months for her, but what if he hadn't meant it? What if he'd already changed his mind?

Yes, he'd probably done that very thing. Surely he realized by now that she wasn't worth waiting six months for.

Wasn't worth marrying at all.

And wasn't worth a bakery either.

She cleared her throat and searched for something, anything to end the terrible silence pulsing around them. Waves washed softly onto the rocks and a fish jumped in the harbor.

He remained quiet, his eyes so large and sad she could barely hold his gaze.

"Did you give everyone in town ten dollars and tell them to spend it at my bakery?"

He shrugged. "I tried to give you the money. When you wouldn't take it, well, a man's got to do what a man's got to do."

"That's the most ridiculous thing I've ever heard. You can't expect to keep my bakery afloat by giving away your savings so people do business with me." Except it suddenly didn't seem so ridiculous, not when the thought of it made her want to cry.

"I won't have to." Mac scratched behind his ear, knocking his hat askew. "Once I started pulling out those bills and giving them to people, well, only Finley McCabe and Ruby Spritzer took any money. Even Jessalyn said no. And Ruby only took it because I insisted. Everyone else went of their own accord."

She looked at the ground. "Some of the ones I hadn't seen since Otis died said they'd be back tomorrow."

"And they probably will. You're a good baker, and you didn't have any trouble at all bringing in money before you got robbed and news came out about Otis's debts, did you?"

She shook her head.

"See there?" A muscle clenched and unclenched at the side of his jaw. "You're free, Tressa. Go where you like, do what you wish. Though I think you'll find the bakery turning a bigger profit from now on should you choose to stay in town."

Yes, she was free to do as she wished, perhaps for the first time in her life. And all because of the man in front of her. Her throat closed. Jessalyn was right. He was the most wonderful, supportive, trustworthy person she'd ever met.

He'd told her God's love wasn't like the lighthouse lamp that could blow out, but like the sun. And Mac's love, while not as perfect as God's, wasn't the type to fade or die either. Why hadn't she understood that yesterday, before he'd given up his life savings and dream of a shipyard for her? "I'm sorry."

"For what? Me paying your mortgage?" His lips pursed together into a tight little circle. "I want you to choose what's best for you and Colin without a load of debt and Otis's poor choices hanging over you."

"No, for not believing you." She tucked a wayward strand of hair behind her ear and blinked away the moisture gathering in her eyes. "You told me you loved me yesterday, you've shown me I can trust you since the moment you first walked into my bakery, and I still didn't believe you. Not until today. Not until it was too late."

"Too late for what?" Mac's voice rumbled low and deep in his chest, a chest she suddenly wanted to rest her head against and keep there until the sun went down.

She looked out over the water instead. "For you to keep your money."

"I don't care about the money."

"Of course you care about the money. You saved for years."

He pressed his eyes shut and ran a thumb over his forehead before opening them again. "I care about you more, but I suppose it's my fault you don't believe me. I asked how much debt you owed before I proposed yesterday. When I went to your bakery, I was only willing to marry you if I could afford both your debt and the shipyard. It wasn't until after..." His voice trailed off, and he shook his head slightly. "That's why I bought the bakery, Tressa. Because you're more important."

His words swirled through her head. He believed she was more important than the shipyard, and he wasn't merely spouting trite words to please her. No. He'd proven every one of those words at court this morning and again at the bank. Her mouth opened and then closed as she searched for something, anything to say.

"I know you're still working through things that happened when you were married to Otis." Mac jammed the toe of his boot into the soft ground. "But if you decide to stay in town, and after you get those things settled, when you think you might be ready to marry again, well, I'd be honored for you to consider me."

Above her the red brick lighthouse tower jutted toward the sky and the sun burned bright over the water. She'd wondered where God's goodness was, and here it stood before her, as tall and broad and solid as an oak tree. Yes, she could love this man. Yes, she could make a life with this man. And yes, she could still be making a life with him thirty years from now.

She licked her suddenly dry lips. "What if I don't want to wait? What if I want to go to the minister tonight?"

"Tonight?" He closed the space between them with one long-legged step. "I'll marry you in a heartbeat." His arms wrapped around her waist so tightly they pushed the breath from her lungs. Then they crashed to the ground, her in a fit of shrieks and him in a chorus of laughter. Somehow she ended up on top of him with his long body stretched out on the stubbly grass beneath her.

"Mac! Let me go!" She pounded on his shoulder, but he only squeezed her tighter, forcing her body down against his. She glanced around to see if they were attracting attention, but they were alone, hidden behind the lighthouse from anyone coming up the path. "This is highly inappropriate."

He snorted. "You don't seem too upset by it, Mrs. Giggles."

Another giggle broke from her chest. She should be upset—though for reasons different than he guessed—but she wasn't.

"Mac." She pressed against his shoulders, raising herself up to look him in the face. "You should know that there's some things... I mean, that is... Otis, he was never very... ah, kind in husbandly things and I might... or rather, I might not... um, crave the marriage bed overmuch."

He rested a hand on her cheek. "I know he hurt you. I don't expect that to go away in a day's time. Just promise to talk to me if something bothers you rather than get all quiet and tell me that you're not worth loving."

She swallowed and pressed her lips together, burying her nose in the hollow between his neck and shoulder, and reveled in the embrace of a man who comforted her rather than repulsed her. In a man who loved her. In a man she could trust to do as he said. "I probably won't be perfect at it, at least not at first."

"It just so happens I can be a very forgiving man, especially when a strawberry pie is offered along with the apology."

She smiled against his throat. "I don't know. Will I end up with strawberry filling slathered on my face and neck again?"

He nudged her head away from his shoulder. "I'm afraid that's rather the point, my future Mrs. Oakton. If I get strawberry mush on your neck after we're married, then I get to clean it off." His lips pressed against her neck, just below the curve of her jaw.

A gentle shiver traveled through her, and he kissed her neck again. "That just might be worth getting strawberries on my neck for."

"I thought so." He grinned and rolled her off him, keeping hold of her hand while he jumped to his feet and tugged her up. "Tressa Danell, I love you, and I'm honored to make you my wife."

His lips touched hers, soft and gentle. She wrapped her arms about his neck and shifted closer, tasting the sweetness of his snickerdoodle breath and the warmth that was Mac Oakton before she pulled away.

"I love you too, Mac."

A faint smile curled the edges of his mouth. "I know, but it sure took you long enough to admit it. Now come, we have a minister to visit, and you have a strawberry pie to make."

She laughed again, the sound filling her chest and bursting onto her face while her neck and lips still tingled pleasantly from the kisses he'd placed on them. His large hand engulfed hers, and he pulled her down the hill at a brisk pace, but not before she glanced over her shoulder at the sun, still high in the sky and burning hot and bright.

As hot and bright as her future with Mac. It was going to be good sharing her life with this man. And it was going to be a life full of strawberry pies and sunshine.

She would make sure of it.

~.~.~.~.~

A Note from Naomi...

Whew! Aren't you glad Mac and Tressa found a way to start a new life together? I don't know about you, but I kind of want to follow them down to the church and witness their wedding ceremony. I'm convinced there will be lots of strawberry pies and sunshine in their future.

Have you ever struggled with believing God is being good to you, especially when everything in your life seems to be going wrong? (Yeah, me too. Probably more times than I want to think about.) I'm so glad Tressa finally realizes God's love for her is constant and forever, "like the sun" as Mac puts it. And I'm equally glad she comes to see how dependable and trustworthy Mac is.

But even though Mac and Tressa are settling into the

lighthouse, they have a town full of friends with their own trials to overcome—and these friends just might happen to fall in love along the way.

Elijah is determined no more people should lose their lives on the dangerous waters of Lake Superior, but saving others requires putting his own life at risk, and his family doesn't like watching him head out into violent storms like the one that killed his father.

But at least one thing is going right for Elijah. Victoria Donnelly, the woman he's been pining for since grade school, finally returns to Eagle Harbor. Elijah is elated…

Until he learns she's only there to marry one of Byron Sinclair's sons.

Elijah might know how to save drowning sailors, but can he to save the woman he loves from the biggest mistake of her life?

And what is Elijah supposed to do about his family? They might need rescuing even more than shipwrecked sailors. Will his mother overcome her grief of losing his father and support his lifesaving missions? Is Rebekah going to continue her hoydenish ways or go back to acting like a proper woman? And when will Isaac get back on a boat and start fishing again?

If you're wondering what comes next for the family that raised Mac and the town where he grew up, pick up your copy of *Love's Every Whisper* and start reading. (There's love, feuding, a shipwreck rescue or two, and maybe even a couple Bible verses about making peace with your enemies.)

Love's Every Whisper is available now on Amazon.

P.S. Want a head start on Elijah and Victoria's story? Grab a blanket and turn the page for the first chapter.

P.P. S. If you're wondering why I told you to grab a blanket, you'll figure it out in about two seconds.

Love's Every Whisper
Chapter One

Eagle Harbor, Michigan: May, 1883

The wind whipped off the lake, thrashing the skeletal tree limbs back and forth like a bear tearing through the woods.

Victoria Donnelly stepped onto an ice-encrusted rock and steadied herself. Hard white snowflakes spewed from the sky, pelting her face despite the wide brim of the masculine hat she'd donned. "E-e-e-elijah. Elijah Cummings!"

She held her lantern out and surveyed the beach; but with the driving snow, gray sky, and foaming waves of Lake Superior, she couldn't see more than ten feet in front of her. A sickening wave rose in her stomach, similar to the one that crashed into the rocks and sent icy spray to splatter the bottom of her cloak. Was the *Beaumont* out there?

Please, God, let them have sought shelter somewhere. Let Father and Gilbert be safe.

She turned away from the lake, though she couldn't block out the ever-present roar of it, and scanned the rocky beach once more.

"E-elijah!"

Oh, if Mother heard how loud and unladylike she yelled, she'd get lectured for an hour, and probably another lecture for stuttering along with a comeuppance for being out here in the first place.

She headed toward a large boulder jutting above the others.

Maybe if she climbed atop it, she could see the light from Elijah's lantern—if she could glimpse anything besides the blinding snow and angry, froth-tipped waves, that was.

She stepped onto a wet rock and teetered for a moment before hurrying onto a dry one. How did Elijah search these beaches during storms without falling and breaking his neck?

"Elijah!" she called once more, then set her lantern atop the high boulder and searched for a nook to grab.

"Are you trying to get yourself killed?"

She jolted at the familiar voice behind her, and the heel of her boot slid out from under her. She tried to catch the boulder, but her hand gripped only air.

A strong arm wrapped around her ribs and she fell back into a solid wall of man. What a way to reintroduce herself to a friend she hadn't seen in three years.

"You shouldn't be out here," he muttered against her ear.

"B-but Father." She struggled to her feet and turned. No wonder she hadn't been able to find Elijah, snow clung to every inch of him, from his large hat to his woolen coat to the sturdy boots encasing his feet. "And Gilbert. The *Beaumont*. I th-think they're caught in the storm, and I knew you c-could help."

He released her and held his lantern up to survey the roaring lake. The mere thought of the ferocious waves crashing into the beach made her stomach roil. How did Elijah go out on rescues during storms like this?

"Have any other ships made it into harbor?"

"One about an hour ago. Said they almost m-missed the light."

"Glad they're safe." He glanced over his shoulder toward the lighthouse, or rather, where the lighthouse should be. Swirling white and gray smothered the orange glow.

Would Gilbert's ship be able to see the beam from the light in time to turn toward the harbor?

A sudden burst of wind ripped across the beach, and she shivered against its chilling force. Elijah reached for her hand, encased in its soft-kidskin glove, and held it up. "These aren't going to keep you warm." He jutted his chin toward the dainty little boots Mother had purchased for her in Milwaukee. "Neither are those."

She pulled her hand away from him. "I w-wasn't planning to be out long. I just wanted to t-t-tell you about Father."

Elijah's gaze moved back to the wide, open waters of Lake Superior. "I know the storm came up quick, but it's unlikely he's still out in it. If anything, he would have sheltered up in Copper Harbor."

She looked helplessly out to the lake and raised her hands to her sides before letting them fall again. Moisture gathered in her eyes, but she blinked it away. "Th-their steamer was due in three hours ago, b-b-before the storm even started. Please, Elijah. You h-have to help."

⸱⸜⸱⸜⸱⸜⸱⸜

Victoria's words ran like icy Lake Superior water through Elijah's veins. *Not someone else I know. Please, God. Not even Gilbert Sinclair.* This town wouldn't be able to handle another death at the hands of the lake.

Or maybe he was the one who couldn't handle another.

He pushed away the choking guilt that swelled whenever he thought of his father's empty grave sitting in the town cemetery. "You're certain the steamer left on time?"

She swallowed, the strained muscles of her creamy throat barely visible in the blowing snow. "Y-yes. F-father and Gilbert telegraphed Mother from Marquette last night. They meant to leave on the *Beaumont* this morning."

He nearly cursed. If Gilbert Sinclair's fancy new steamer had left Marquette by noon, it should have arrived before the storm. Had something else gone wrong? And what exactly did she think he could do about it? It was one thing to rescue men from a ship he knew was floundering. Taking his crew into dangerous waters to search for a vessel that could be miles away was quite another.

Victoria stared up at him, wisps of dark brown hair escaping from beneath her wide-brimmed hat. At least she'd had the sense to wear a good one of those, and a warm fur cloak, but her fingers and toes had to be nigh frozen. "Your father and fiancé probably harbored somewhere along the coast and are waiting out the storm."

Victoria's chin came up and her lips firmed into a straight line. "Gilbert's n-n-not my f-fiancé."

Yet. Though this was no time to start arguing about his choice of words.

Just then, the bell clanged, not the constant ringing that warned ships of fog, but three short chimes, a pause, and then another chime: the signal call to the life-savers.

"Maybe that's for the *Beaumont*. Come on." He grabbed her lantern off the ridiculous boulder she'd been trying to climb, snuffed it, took her other hand in his, and started crossing the slippery rocks.

How long had it been since he'd held her hand? A decade maybe?

The bell clanged again. Confound it. In the three years he'd been making these rescues, he'd never once gotten distracted. Now he couldn't keep his concentration for ten seconds.

"D-do you think F-f-father will be all right?" Worried shadows haunted the soft skin beneath her hazel eyes, the same hazel eyes that stared back at him from his dreams every night.

Double confound it. If only he had a moment to stop and take her in his arms, whisper that everything would be fine, hold her until she stopped trembling.

But she wasn't his to hold, never had been and never would be. And he could hardly promise everything would be fine in a storm like this. "I don't know, but your father and Gilbert, they're good sailors who know these waters. They've got a better chance than most."

He should drop her hand. Continuing to hold it was doing ridiculous things to his heart, despite the barrier of her thin, inadequate gloves. But he couldn't quite manage to let it go. "Quickly now."

They scrambled over the last of the rocks and climbed onto the lighthouse lawn. Above, the usually strong beam of the tower's light quickly diffused into the swirling snow. He raced with Victoria over the lawn toward Front Street and the sandy beach that rimmed the harbor.

"There." He pointed toward the shadow of a lifeboat pulled up alongside the surfboat his crew prepared to launch. "Maybe your father's already ashore."

She heaved in a breath and her grip tightened on his hand. "It's not the *Beaumont's*. Gil's dinghies are shorter than that."

She was familiar enough with Gilbert's ships to recognize his dinghies in a snowstorm?

Something tightened inside his chest. He'd known it was coming, that someday the woman he'd loved for as long as he could remember would marry another. He'd prayed every night it wouldn't be Gilbert Sinclair, but evidently God wasn't interested in answering that particular request.

"Do you still have that knack for nursing? Can you help those sailors to the doc's?" He pointed toward the snow-shrouded shadows staggering around the unfamiliar lifeboat on the beach. "Take them to the new doc, Harrington. Not Dr. Greely." Greely was probably slumped over on his bar stool at the moment.

"Of course."

The fog bell chimed again, though he was probably the only rescuer not at the surfboat. He dropped her hand and bent his head against the wind, starting forward.

She caught his arm and pulled him back. "Promise you'll do whatever you can for Father and Gilbert."

He put his hand to her wind-burnished cheek, never mind that he had no business doing such a thing.

A tear spilled onto her skin, freezing into a perfect drop before it reached his glove. "Please."

"I'll look for them as we head out, but if I don't spot the *Beaumont...*"

She dropped her head, staring at some unseen speck on the storm-ravaged grass. "I understand."

"Victoria..." But he didn't have any words of comfort for her, not with the wind whipping at them, the bell calling to him, the roaring waves carrying off half their words. So he crushed her against his side for one brief, sweet moment.

Then he let her go, just like he'd been letting her go for the past fifteen years.

He raced down the other side of the rocky incline to the sand below, where the surfboat rested on the ground. It was an appallingly small craft to take into a storm like this. But the twenty-six foot long boat was the exact size and shape as those used by the United States Life-Saving Service. He'd seen to that when he built it.

Shadows of men in oilskin coats and hats milled about the boat, likely checking the lifelines and oars and making sure woolen blankets were secured beneath the seats as he'd taught them.

Mac Oakton straightened from where he'd been hunched over the stern. Even with high waves pummeling the harbor beach, the man towered over the scene.

"Thanks for getting the men ready," he called to the man his family had unofficially adopted as one of their own.

Mac dipped his head and tightened the rope knotted to one of the life rings. "Spot anything from shore?"

"Not in this mess. Your wife all right back at the lighthouse?" The wind blew a burst of snow into his face.

"I left her at the light, snug as could be."

"You're sure?" Elijah wiped the snow from his eyes. Perhaps Mac had been going out on rescues with him since he started his volunteer team, but still, if something happened to the light while Mac was gone...

He glanced toward the orange glow muted by the blizzard.

"Don't worry, Elijah." Mac landed a bear-like hand on his shoulder. "It's not the first time I've left Tressa alone."

No, it certainly wasn't. Tressa had been tending the light ever since she and Mac married three years ago. So why the sense of foreboding that churned in the pit of his stomach?

"Where's the wreck?" Elijah headed to his own position and checked his ropes.

"About a mile to the east."

"East. Doesn't that just rankle? It's like the storm knew I was patrolling to the west." He glanced at the shrouded forms farther down the beach, the unmistakable silhouette of Victoria's fancy fur cloak among them. She'd see to the sailors that had rowed to shore right good, had always had a hand for things like that.

"The schooner was trying to make harbor when the wind caught her and threw her onto a sandbar." Mac hooked the life ring onto the side of the boat. "Twelve man crew on her, eight made it to a dingy and came for help, but she's got four left aboard, and we know one of them."

"We do?"

"Clifford Spritzer. The captain said he offered to stay behind and wait for us."

Clifford was aboard that ship? Something heavy fisted in his gut. He glanced down the beach toward where the Spritzer house sat just off to the right, but couldn't see anything in the snow. He'd been the one to teach Cliff to sail, the one to write Cliff a letter of recommendation to a shipmaster he knew two years ago.

What if something happened to Clifford in the storm?

"Elijah, you with us?" Mac's sharp voice carried through the storm.

Elijah tore his eyes away from the beach and checked his oar. Clifford wasn't the only one left aboard a ship that would be battered and sunk within hours at the rate the waves were rolling in. He didn't have time to get distracted. He drew the collar of his jacket up around his neck and ran his hands quickly along the blankets stowed beneath the seat. *Please, God, keep us safe. Let us reach those men in time.*

A sense of peace flooded him. The storm spat snow, the waves ravaged the coast, and the lake looked ready to shred anything that dared sail atop it. Yet somehow this was right. The rest of Eagle Harbor might sit huddled in their homes, but he belonged in the midst of this, heading out to rescue sailors so nobody else would have to stand over an empty grave.

One man. One person willing to help three years ago, and Pa might still be alive.

If only he would have been in Eagle Harbor to make that rescue.

"Stations men," he growled through the wind. The other figures hurried into their positions, and Elijah grabbed the portside gunwale near the stern. "Hope you're ready to get wet."

Across from him, Mac let out a howl, the crazy man. His best friend actually liked sailing in messes such as this.

"One." Elijah's voice boomed against the storm. The men heaved the boat inward then swung it out. "Two." Again the boat swung in and out, six men working together in unity to—

Wait. There weren't six men lined up, three on each side of the boat. There were... there were...

"Rebekah!" His nails dug through his gloves into the gunwale.

The slender form near the bow jumped, then turned to look at him. "Please, Elijah. Let me go. It's wild out there today. You know I can help."

He pointed toward town. "Go home."

"I didn't know she was here." Mac squashed his hat lower on his head. "She must have been hiding behind a rock."

And likely waited until he'd called the men to their stations to approach the surfboat.

"I'm a good sailor, and you can use the help." Rebekah didn't leave her position near the bow.

The five others looked between them. Each held the gunwale, ready to launch into the surf with a moment's notice. "You think this is helping? Men are on that lake in a sinking ship, and you're wasting our time arguing."

"Only because you're stubborn. If you let me go, then you'll see—"

"You're *not* going!" Ma would throttle him if he let Rebekah in the boat, not that he was too keen on the idea himself.

Rebekah dropped her hold on the gunwale. "Just this once?"

"No. And don't let me see you out here during a storm again." He pinned his gaze on the lake. "One!"

The boat heaved in then out, a fluid movement cultivated from hours of the team practicing on the beach.

"Two... three." They ran into the surf, six men, one purpose. The water churned at their boots and thrashed against their legs. Spray hit their faces and snow shrouded their vision. At the bow, Jesse and Emmett heaved themselves aboard, followed by Simon and Floyd in the middle.

Elijah launched himself out of the water at the same instant as Mac. "Fall in."

All six of them plunged their eighteen foot oars into the water and rowed.

In the three years since he'd started his volunteer life-saving team, he'd saved thirty-three people.

Tonight, he had every intention of making that number thirty-seven.

Order your copy of Love's Every Whisper *on Amazon.*

Thank You

Thank you for reading *Love's Unfading Light*. I sincerely hope you enjoyed Mac and Tressa's story.

Want to be notified when the next Eagle Harbor Novel is releasing? Sign up for my author newsletter. Subscribers also get a free copy of *Love's Violet Sunrise*, a prequel novella to the Eagle Harbor Series. Sign Up Here: http://geni.us/AqsHv

Also, if you enjoyed reading *Love's Unfading Light*, please take a moment to tell others about the novel. You can do this by posting an honest review on Amazon or GoodReads. I read every one of my reviews, and reviews help readers like yourself decide whether to purchase a novel. Please note that to leave a review on Amazon, you need to go directly to Amazon's website. Your e-reader may ask you to rank stars at the end of this novel. The star ranking that you give does not show up on Amazon as a review. You could also consider mentioning *Love's Unfading Light* to your friends on Facebook, Twitter, or Pinterest.

Other Novels by Naomi Rawlings

Texas Promise Series
Book 1—*Tomorrow's First Light* (Sam and Ellie)
Book 2—*Tomorrow's Shining Dream* (Daniel and Charlotte:
     releasing 2020)
Book 3—*Tomorrow's Constant Hope* (Wes and Keely:
     releasing 2020)
Book 4—*Tomorrow's Steadfast Prayer* (Harrison and Alejandra)
Book 5—*Tomorrow's Lasting Joy* (Cain and Anna Mae)

Eagle Harbor Series
Book 1—*Love's Unfading Light* (Mac and Tressa)
Book 2—*Love's Every Whisper* (Elijah and Victoria)
Book 3—*Love's Sure Dawn* (Gilbert and Rebekah)
Book 4—*Love's Eternal Breath* (Seth and Lindy)
Book 5—*Love's Winter Hope* (Thomas and Jessalyn)
Book 6—*Love's Bright Tomorrow* (Isaac and Aileen)
Short Story—*Love's Beginning*
Prequel Novella—*Love's Violet Sunrise* (Hiram and Mabel)

Acknowledgments

Thank you first and foremost to my Lord and Savior Jesus Christ for giving me both the ability and opportunity to write novels for His glory.

As with any novel, the author might come up with a story idea and sit at her computer to type the initial words, but it takes an entire army of people to bring you the book you have today. I'd especially like to thank Melissa Jagears, both my critique partner and editor for *Love's Unfading Light*. I'd also like to thank Roseanna White for being the second editor on this novel, Bruce Johanson at the Ontonagon Township Historical Society for double-checking the novel's historical accuracy, particularly in regard to the lighthouse details, and my agent Natasha Kern for encouraging me to keep working on the Eagle Harbor Series.

Author's Note

If you ever travel the long, winding road up to the tip of Michigan's Keweenaw Peninsula, you truly will find a little town called Eagle Harbor, complete with a lighthouse still in use today. In the winter, you'll find the road slick with ice and the scenery covered in snow. In the summer, you'll find the trees green, the wildlife plentiful, and the scenery breathtaking. You'll also pass several of the former copper mining sites of Central and Delaware, both of which were operational back in 1880 and used the natural port at Eagle Harbor to ship supplies and copper to and from this remote area commonly called Copper Country.

I hope you enjoyed reading a novel set in Eagle Harbor. I personally live just a couple hours away, also in Copper Country along the southern shore of Lake Superior, and since I moved to the area six years ago, I've quite simply fallen in love. I hope my appreciation for the wild beauty of this region and my respect for the formidable lake to our north comes through as I write the Eagle Harbor Series.

About the Author

Naomi Rawlings is the author of nine historical Christian novels, including the Amazon bestselling Eagle Harbor Series. While she'd love to claim she spends her days huddled in front of her computer vigorously typing, in reality she spends her time homeschooling, cleaning, picking up, and pretending like her house isn't in a constant state of chaos. She lives with her husband and three children in Michigan's rugged Upper Peninsula, along the southern shore of Lake Superior where they get two hundred inches of snow every year, and where people still grow their own vegetables and cut down their own firewood—just like in the historical novels she writes.

For more information about Naomi, please her at www.naomirawlings.com or find her on Facebook at www.facebook.com/author.naomirawlings. If you'd like a free Eagle Harbor novella (Mabel and Hiram's story), sign up for her author newsletter at http://geni.us/35Yn.

Made in the USA
Middletown, DE
07 August 2020